Born of Oak

and Silver

By Marie McKean

Book One of
The Caradoc Chronicles

For You—

Who has always given me wings to fly.

Acknowledgements

To my family, my amazing husband and patient children – thank you for putting up with me all of those innumerable times when I simply had to "just finish this paragraph" before I could give you any attention. I know, I fell off the radar there for a while. Hopefully the next time around I'll be able to find the proper balance.

To my husband John, thank you for helping me to see what you have always seen all along.

To my amazing friends who saw my desire to write a book as more than just another of my temporary whims, thank you for indulging me, being my unfailing sounding boards, as well as my continual read and re-readers while I worked through this.

And, to my father, who took me on a fateful trip to Mississippi that started it all, thank you.

"*It cannot be seen, cannot be felt,*
Cannot be heard, cannot be smelt,
It lies behind stars and under hills,
And empty holes it fills,
It comes first and follows after,
Ends life, kills laughter.'
— J.R.R. Tolkien

Chapter One

Today has been just another hot and stickily humid day in a seemingly endless string of many. Neither night nor day has offered any relief from the oppressive heat. Even the nonchalant insects seem to be overly burdened by the tyrannical sun. Not that there is anything noteworthy about this during the summer months. In Mississippi, it has always been this way.

The sun has just begun to set, splaying a soft pink glow between the darkening thunderclouds in the distance. The air is thick with an imminent promise of heavy rain. Sparrows exude an unspoken urgency as they quickly skim and dart in the skies, looking to make a quick meal out of the mosquitoes that hover unconcernedly amid the southern dusk. Thunder rumbles threateningly somewhere along the horizon, and a welcomed breeze that was not there a moment ago, suddenly picks up.

One look at the sky would tell you that it is not worth going out - this storm is sure to be a bad one. However, it is moments like these, when no one else can be found, that I choose to seek my refuge.

I close my eyes and permit myself a rare moment to breathe deeply, taking multiple thorough draws from the no longer stagnant air. Finally, I begin to feel that it is peaceful here. I remain motionless, allowing the hard earned solace to seep into my tired and over-wearied bones.

When I open my eyes, the solemn angels that silently guard their keep are painted in a deep sorbet of colors, highlighting the planes of their cold and chiseled faces. In this light, these pale stone markers of the dead serve only as softly warmer reminders of what once was.

It might seem odd to most that I find my time spent in this place to be rejuvenating. Usually, this is not where most living people readily choose to go. Rather, the opportunity to visit is forced upon them either by fate or a sense of obligation. To them, this place represents only the bad – death, loss, sorrow, unfulfilled dreams, and pain . . . all justifiably true. Though for me, if only for a moment, it is only when I am here that these same emotions are not so chokingly poignant.

You see, this is the only place where I am permitted a momentary courtesy from heaven – the briefest awareness that everything is, and will be right. Although the impression never seems to last, no matter how fleeting, it is a worthwhile gift nonetheless.

The air has continued to grow heavier. No longer are there any signs of the sparrows or the pesky mosquitoes. They've vanished as the thunder has grown increasingly louder, heralding the way of the storm. *It won't be long now,* I think anxiously as I glance up at the sky.

Right on cue, the sky loses its hold on the weighty burden it carries inside. A torrent of rain is released, a merciful break to the summer's seemingly incessant heat.

I wear only jeans and a t-shirt with some non-discrepant lace-ups on my feet. A jacket initially sounds like a welcome idea to the unmistakably chilly rain on my unaccustomed, sun darkened skin, but I remain seated on my cement bench beneath an ancient magnolia tree.

Relishing in this generous change in the weather, I close my eyes and tilt my face upward. My dark hair quickly begins to trickle with water, the rivulets leisurely running down my body. There is nothing quite like a summer rain. I soak up its vitality and newness. I cannot help but hope that maybe this time the rain will manage to cleanse my dirty and stained soul. Perhaps then I will finally be offered the absolution I have so long desired.

Thunder rumbles a reprimand, God's reminder of my folly.

Instantly, I am brought back to the painful reality of the hell I have been forced to live. Peace, yet again, is merely an imagined and forced perception. Just as quickly as my mood was heightened by the prospect of final release, the rain casts everything in a dank shade of gray.

The water continues to drip down my back, and bitterly I shiver at its sting. As I breathe in the rain, feel the contrast between its cool moisture and my hot, living breath, I accept that I can only remain oblivious to the obvious for so long. At last, I find the courage to stare at the headstone that lies before me.

A desolate hunk of rock carved in the shape of a tree stump looms in the shadows before me. It is moss covered, weather-worn, and neglected. Only a few indifferent words were given to remember its charge:

Daine C. Dalton
August 15, 1840 – November 22, 1915

Daine Dalton lived a good amount of time – seventy-five years. Seventy-five years, and this is all that is left of him a hundred years later – a rapidly deteriorating rock, decaying alone in the shade of an ancient magnolia tree. It is depressing.

I have often wondered if I were to dig up his grave, would I find anything that resembled a man remaining? After this much time, surely not. Besides, I do not think that he would appreciate it much if I did.

One would think that after visiting this place for what seems an eternity, never witnessing a renewal, and unfailingly bearing witness to the perpetual demise of the new, that I would be more convinced of the grave's terminal nature. I am sorry to say that I am not.

There was once a time when I hoped for as much. When I believed that eternal rest was granted irrevocably in death, and when I was confident that mortality was brief, but definite. No. All of that no longer applies, and the finality of the grave has been lost to me.

Daine Dalton's gravestone states that he has been dead for a hundred years - yet, here I am, still living, breathing, bleeding, feeling, and . . . unending.

I am Daine Caradoc Dalton.

This is my grave.

I remember my beginning and everything that existed until what was to be my end. And death, yes, I remember death. The deep cold that settled, leaving me paralyzed in a terrifying haze as consciousness detachedly slipped away . . .

After, there was no heaven or hell. Only a waking, in which I discovered myself lying naked upon my recently filled grave in my thirty-four year old form. Since then, I have not aged a day. I have tried to end this life, but death refuses to take me.

And so, here I remain - a man who both bleeds and breathes, but yet is unable to die. Tirelessly visiting the spot that is supposed to indicate his final resting place, but finding only disguised anguish instead.

Chapter Two

The sun had just begun to rise over the town of Strasbourg; however, most of its inhabitants were already awake and beginning their preparations for the day's work ahead. It has been said that the name of Strasbourg means "the town on the crossroads", a definition that has come to perfectly detail the dynamics of this city. Being located on the French and German border, with the Rhine River moving steadily through year round, a constant flow of people from innumerable places always came and went. In that, it is so much like the River, always changing but still remaining ever so much the same.

It was here that I was born, at the tail end of a modernizing world.

We lived on a small bit property just outside Strasbourg proper. It wasn't a large place, but was just enough that we were able to have two cows, some chickens, a reasonable garden, and an old three room cottage with a barn. The barn served not only to shelter the animals, but also as my father's woodshop. A majority of the property was heavily wooded, and in the middle of those trees ran a stream that meandered its way leisurely toward the Rhine.

By all accounts it wasn't a lot, but my parents were intensely proud of it.

They'd settled here just after they were married. For a time they were genuinely happy, blossoming as much as individuals as they were a married couple. But, their contentment was not to last. My mother was unable to bear live children.

One mild mid-November morning, my mother ventured out into their property in hopes that the sun might lessen her sadness. Thinking herself alone, it took her quite by surprise when an old and silvered man stepped out of the very trees she was about to walk into, and began to hobble his way toward her.

He seemed familiar, but the fact that she couldn't place him made her uneasy. However, he could not sense her apprehension, and upon seeing her look toward him, gave her a fully-toothed smile and a low bow of his head.

His entire being beamed with vitality, something completely at odds with his aged physique. His white beard hung to the middle of his chest, though it was well trimmed and neat. His hair too was white, but only a few straggling pieces strayed from a thickly knitted green woolen cap he wore on top of his head. Although his skin was pale, it was not a shade that conflicted with his frosted hair to give him an appearance of

7

being sickly. Instead, his cheeks glowed healthy and rosy, adding all the more to his air of vigor.

As he drew closer, she could see that his hands were knobbed and wrinkled; but Carine was sure they'd be as dexterous as any young man she'd ever met if put to work. He was thin, but maintained robustness. He was not bent over, but carried himself upright with great self-possession and awareness. His mouth was ever smiling, and a surprisingly delicate nose came to a sharp point on his weathered face. And his eyes - his sparkling green eyes gleamed with clarity, wisdom, and knowledge.

On top of it all, he was impeccably dressed. Carine liked him immediately.

"Bonjour, Mademoiselle," he spoke. "An absolutely wonderful day we are having, is it not? I just could not resist the opportunity of an unexpected sun-warmed winter stroll . . . the sun," he voiced on an exhale while opening his arms wide and lifting his face up toward it, "is good for the bones *and* the soul, you know." Remarking thus, he lowered his face from the sky, and seemed to radiate its warmth and kindness back to her.

Taken aback by this stranger's echoing of her own sentiments, she quickly, but warmly replied, "Yes, it most definitely is, Monsieur. I myself couldn't resist the opportunity to bask in its warmth and break up the winter's gloom either. Though, I must confess, I don't think I have ever before appreciated it as much as I have today. Although winter has barely even begun, it seems as though it has already been here for quite some time." With that, she finally offered the still sunny old man a small smile in return.

"Ah, yes, the winter has a way of making us quickly remember how much we love the warmth – though we are quick to forget it when the summer's heat is about to smother us, and we whole heartedly believe the winter's cold cannot return soon enough. Vicious cycle, if you ask me," and he waggled his bushy white eyebrows at her while voicing this in a voice of mocked authority.

Carine couldn't help herself; she allowed a small chuckle to escape her lips.

Encouraged, the man preceded, "Bram Macardle, Mademoiselle," he said removing his knitted cap, revealing a bountiful crop of shock white hair and giving Carine a slight bow, "at your service. I apologize for not having come to introduce myself earlier, but I've been out of country for quite some time. I am your neighbor, just there," he turned briefly and gestured behind him, "beyond those trees."

Carine dipped low in a curtsy, "Monsieur Macardle, it is a pleasure to meet you. I am Carine Dalton." She extended her hand to him, and Macardle placed a formal kiss on the back of her palm before he released it. "I had wondered if there was anyone else who lived in any of the adjacent properties," Carine explained, "and it makes me very happy to know that someone indeed does. Come, let me introduce you to my husband."

"Yes, it is always reassuring to know that one is not entirely alone in this vast world of ours. For the foreseeable future, it is here that I shall remain. There are others who live within a reasonable proximity, though," he paused and stroked absently at his white beard, "though, I think that I may be the nearest one. Should you or your husband need anything, consider me at your services. Here, let me help you with your things."

Bending, he picked up the rug that Carine had been sitting on, folded it ably and tucked it under his arm. He offered her his other.

Taking it, they began walking in the direction of the Dalton's house and barn.

"I must confess, I am sorry to hear that you are married. I was just about to begin wooing you before I learned that you belonged to another."

Carine looked over his wrinkled face, his long white beard, his kind eyes, and again rewarded them both with a rare laugh.

"Yes, I am sure I would have undoubtedly and completely succumbed to your irresistible charms. I consider myself to be *very* fortunate for having mentioned my espousal before you began to entice me beyond resistance." She smiled fully, chuckling, and giving him a humor filled quirked eyebrow. Her long auburn hair blew lightly in the warm breeze behind her.

All the while Macardle gently patted her hand that was tucked under his arm and chortled himself. "My dear, had I been even a year younger, I do not think I'd have had the ability to abstain from pursuing you, married or not. As it is, I am utterly satisfied at the opportunity of passing a portion of this blissfully warm afternoon with such a vivacious and beautiful young woman such as yourself on my arm."

She humored him, delighting in his candor. Their conversation flowed smoothly as if they had long been friends.

"You said that you had been out of country, where did you happen to go?" Carine asked.

"In other words, you can hear by my most atrocious accent that I am not from here. For that, I am sorry. It is always extremely thick when I get back among my own, and for a time, it makes my French almost impossible to speak - let along understand. I've been in Ireland - Dublin specifically. I've some family, and occasionally some business matters to attend to there," Macardle told her.

"Oh, your accent isn't *that* bad . . . As long as I try not to focus on anything else but your voice," Carine jibed, "I am able to understand almost every other word that I think you might be saying."

"Och, lass, ye'll be woundin' my pride if yer not careful. I happen to take a great sense of accomplishment in my grasp of your blasted language. It only took me twenty-five years to be able to speak it! And even then, it was all thanks to an ornery, hard-headed, and persistent teacher that I ever learned. It was my wife who taught me. She was stubborn, fiery, devilish, and held my soul in her very hands." His mouth was left with a bit of a smirk, and though they continued to walk, Carine knew that Macardle's mind was happily adrift in frequently repeated memories.

She allowed him to amble there, focusing instead on her own thoughts of her husband. They were once again strangers, sharing a room but neither of them knowing the other well enough to know what exactly the other wanted or needed.

"Anne had my heart that very first moment that I saw her." Bram resumed. "She had loved her family, and had wanted nothing more than to remain in Strasbourg. And so, I did my best to expand what business I could to here. However, for all my efforts, it was necessary to occasionally return to Ireland and maintain my partnership in the family enterprise."

Bram turned to look into Carine's considerate face, "Despite the fact that my wife has been dead for these many and long years, I cannot bear to leave this place. For every time that I do, I feel as though I am leaving her as well."

Carine understood his pain all too well, and allowed him to see as much.

He paused, seemingly grateful for the small courtesy. Looking forward, his old hand gestured toward the barn, "Ah, this must be where your husband is. The smell of freshly cut wood is a scent I have always found intoxicating. Had I not had a family venture to continue, I suspect I would have gone into carpentry myself."

With that, Carine nodded appreciatively as Macardle opened the door to Robert's woodshop.

Bram continued to visit the couple everyday thereafter. Carine's guess that Bram had dexterous and capable hands had been entirely right. It wasn't but a few moments after meeting Robert that Bram was working beside him, even lending a master's touch in ways that left Robert astonished at the old man's ingenuity and artistry.

Weeks later after enjoying the constant companionship of one another's company, Robert slipped off after dinner to find a book he was sure Bram would enjoy. It was here that Bram pulled Carine hastily to his side.

Making one quick glance toward the door that Robert had just disappeared into, Bram just as quickly turned his face toward hers. His green eyes sparked wildly with flecks of gold that caught in the firelight. Using a tone she'd not yet heard him speak, he told her, "I've something for you to take to ensure a strong pregnancy. I'll bring it to you on the marrow."

And just like that, the old man was instantly to be found once again sitting in the chair that Robert had left him in. His attention was completely focused on the approaching Robert who was in the midst of presenting his latest sure to be loved book to his friend.

Carine disappeared into the couple's bedroom shortly after the curious confrontation with Bram, leaving the men deeply in discussion and warmed through with brandy. She rubbed her arm, it was bruised where he'd brought her to attention. She'd known that Bram was stronger than he appeared, but he was even more so than she'd anticipated.

That night she dreamed of walking through a meadow on an uncharacteristically warm winter's day. Tightly, she clasped the hand of her child in her own, as they enjoyed the warmth together.

She awoke late the next morning. The lowing of a cow had woken her. Robert lay beside her, still sleeping off his evening nightcap. Quietly she stirred from bed, shutting their bedroom door behind her. Still in her night clothes, she crouched before the fire and lightly blew on the ashes, hoping that some were still warm enough to catch. They began to glow red with her breath, and kindling soon coaxed them into a flame that turned to a steady fire.

She dusted off her hands and turned to her pile of clothes that she had placed on the table, having every intention of then dressing herself completely. However, the presence of a small melon sized leather pouch on the table diverted her attention entirely. She picked it up, noting its light weight and but nonetheless dense packing.

A note had been folded and placed under the bundle. She held it to the growing firelight to read it. A strange feeling balled in the pit of her stomach as she read brief message –

Use these leaves to brew a strong tea.

Drink in the morning, and again in the afternoon.

Do so daily for one month.

Should you need more, ask.

-B. Macardle

When had Bram left this? He'd mentioned bringing something by the following day, but she had not expected it to be waiting on her table when she woke. She took a quick look around the room, and felt relieved to find that Bram was not in the room with her.

She placed the pouch and note back on the table, and while hurriedly dressing, wondered over when they had been left for her.

Robert awoke soon after, a lazy smile gracing his face.

"Good morning, Ma Belle. Did you sleep well?"

Carine smiled warmly and nodded, accepting his kiss upon her cheek.

"I haven't felt the desire to not get out of bed so strongly since I was a rangy youth," he said, turning Carine away from the stove and kissing her again. "I'll be out at the shop, I've got some great ideas for a few armoires that I need to commit to paper before I forget. Would you mind bringing breakfast out to the barn for me?"

"Of course," Carine managed to babble.

"Thank you, Mignon. And, if it's not too much trouble, would you bring an extra plate for Bram? I never know just when he'll show up in the morning, I only know that he will."

"Yes, that is no trouble at all. I'll bring out the plates and some coffee. As for now, go, you're distracting me from cooking these eggs."

Robert smiled back. He feigned a swagger as he crossed the room to the door. He stood in the doorway, looking back to give Carine an appreciative nod, before he closed the door behind him and walked out to his barn.

Carine gave an amused snort. He hadn't been this way in months. Instantly, she thought of Bram's pouch, and wondered if perchance the old man had given Robert something as well. She wouldn't be at all surprised if he had.

After taking both plates to the barn and feeling a huge sense of relief that Bram was not yet there for her to face, she stopped at the well before returning to the house. She was entirely settled on her decision. She put the kettle on to boil, and filled the tea steeper carefully with the dried leaves from Bram's pouch. They looked like any other tea leaves and had no unique aroma. But regardless of the tea's lack of uniqueness, she was willing to try anything that might help them. Anxiously, she watched her tea cup as she waited for her first cup of Bram's tea to brew.

It was surprisingly pleasant.

She enjoyed her second cup that afternoon just as much she had the first.

That night had been filled with the love-making of two people who'd been desperate for the touch of the other. Their routine continued this way for a month.

The day after she ran out of tea leaves, she noted that she was a week late on her courses. There was no doubt that she was once again pregnant.

Nine months later and two weeks earlier than was expected, I, Daine Caradoc Dalton, was born.

Chapter Three

My childhood was much like any other's during that time. Though, my mother coddled me incessantly and could only be made to part with me when either my father demanded or Bram requested it - which was frequently. My parents suspected that my presence eased Bram's yearning for his own grandchildren, and suffered no qualms about my accompanying him wherever and whenever he sought my company.

Initially, he would take me on short walks around my parent's property. But as I was able to walk on my own, he'd allow me to lead as we wandered aimlessly to fleeting strikes of fancy. The one exception to my carefree exploration was that he would never allow me to visit what we generally referred to as my mother's stream. If ever I ventured too close, Bram made sure that something absolutely extraordinary could be found immediately elsewhere.

When I asked why we couldn't go to the river, he was always quick to respond that it was too dangerous and was better left alone. I learned quickly that Bram was immovable once resolved upon something. And so it was that I learned to content myself with the walks he preferred to take in the countryside, learning key plants and animals native to our countryside that he would point out as we went.

As I got older, we began to venture farther away from home. It was then that Bram began instructing me in increasing detail. He'd tell me of why plants in a certain area might be dying, why animals were traveling the way they were, how to use a green forked stick to do some 'water witchin'', and even how to feel if it was going to rain. But, I couldn't content myself with only learning forever.

One day when I was just about five, I'd had enough of learning, and wanted to do something I'd been dreaming of for about as long as I could remember.

"Bram, how come we can't go fishin'?" I asked indignantly, my own dark wavy hair that was so much like my father's, flouncing to the side as I cocked my head at him. My hazel eyes implored him for mercy, as I regarded him with the same haughty uplifted eyebrow my own mother used.

Bram looked up at me from the plant cuttings he was collecting, his green eyes filled with genuine curiosity as quoted me with upturned white bushy brows, "fishin'?"

I knew that he was correcting me for improper grammar, but I was undeterred and retained my challenging attitude even while he kindly asked, "Why do you want to go 'fishin'' so badly, Daine?" His face was etched by the lines of a loving grandparent.

"Well, Bram," I replied authoritatively - if he was going to correct me on the proper way to say what I wanted to do, I was going to tell him exactly why it needed to be done my way, "It's what boys are supposed to do!" I told him exasperatedly.

"Papa's always working, and since you don't really have to work, you can take me. So, like I already asked you, how come we can't go fishin'?"

Bram couldn't help but chuckle at me as I stood looking down at him with my arms crossed over my chest, my hip cocked, and my eyes clearly stating that my logic absolutely necessitated that we go immediately.

"Daine, you are absolutely right. It is what boys do during the summer. But, I have another idea for you – a *better* idea. What would you think about going to school? Most of the other boys that you know will not have the opportunity to go. It would make you . . . *special*." He allowed the word to hang between us, letting the idea of being privileged above other children lure me in.

I silently toyed with the idea in my mind, getting a feel for it before I replied undeterred, "Hmmm . . . I don't know,

Bram. It's summer now, and I *really* want to go fishin'. William Thiery goes with his brother everyday, he says. He says they get lots of fish, and then, they eat them. I love fish, Bram. I've just *got* to catch some too! I want to catch the biggest fish ever! And," I schemed, whispering conspiratorially, "maybe, we could keep him in one of Mama's bowls on the table!"

Bram regarded me, his knobby hand thoughtfully brushing the length of his white beard. I could tell he was truly considering all the points of my finely crafted argument.

When I almost couldn't stand the silence a moment longer, Bram finally voiced his conclusions, "I don't know about putting a fish in a bowl on your mother's table, she probably wouldn't like that one bit," his eyes twinkled up at me, and I grinned at the idea.

"But, you are pretty convincing, Daine. So, how about I make you a deal? If we can talk to your parents about you going to school, then I will take you fishing."

Bram used one of his gnarled index fingers to beckon me closer. I knelt down beside him in the tall grass, the tall oak trees above shading us from the sun. As bent my head close to his, he looked readily around to make sure no one was near to overhear us. Whispering in an equally conspiring tone, he spoke next to my ear, "I know of a place where this really huge monster of a fish has been hanging out." His eyes were large and bright as he drew away to look directly into mine. "William Thiery will never catch anything like this fish in his entire life," he unnecessarily elaborated.

I leaned back, my eyes gleaming with promise and visions of glory.

"So, what do you think?" Bram inquired. "Do you think we can go and ask your parents about school?"

I was too caught up on the idea of catching his massive fish - that was no doubt at least as big as I was - that I could only manage an enormous grin and a wild nod of my head.

That evening Bram presented his plan of my receiving an education to my parents over dinner. However, Bram's idea of school was not exactly what I'd had in mind as I'd mulled over the suggestion that afternoon. I'd assumed going to school meant frequenting a structure of sorts that was widely recognized to be a school, with other children, and with a teacher whom I did not yet know. As Bram expounded his idea to my parents, my conclusion that school might not be as bad as I originally thought it would be - vanished.

Bram informed my parents that he wanted to be my private tutor. If permitted, he would teach me to read and write in French, Latin, Greek, and English; complete complex mathematical equations; and even, proficiently perform scientific experiments.

At first my parents were disbelieving that the old man genuinely desired to do such a thing. But, as Bram sincerely continued to tell them of his plans for me if they agreed, I could see the approval becoming ever more evident in their eyes with every word he spoke.

And so it was, with little to no convincing needed, my parents readily agreed to Bram's proposition. He was to be my teacher, and I, his only student.

In two weeks, the day after my fifth birthday, Bram would come to collect me from our home. And then everyday thereafter, I was to gain my formal education day by slow and difficult day in the confines of his home, until the evening when he'd finally return me home in time for supper.

As I lay in bed that night, I was secretly outraged that my parents had not even asked me what I wanted. They didn't even know that the only reason I'd agreed, was because Bram promised to take me fishing. Why couldn't I just be a boy and fish whenever I wanted to?!

The more I thought about it, the more I was convinced that after my parents saw the giant of a fish Bram was going to help me to catch, they were going to forget all about this whole school mess and decide that I should take up fishing permanently. With that in mind, I lulled myself to sleep on thoughts of a magnificent battle between boy and fish. In the end, I, bruised but still standing, stood victorious. And the fish that was no smaller than one of mother's cows, my unprecedented prize of triumph.

Bram arrived at our house early the next morning. I was just beginning my chores when he'd arrived. Upon entering the house, he informed my mother that he needed me immediately, and that my tasks would have to wait until I returned.

Seeing the pole in the old man's hand, my mother gave him her quirked eyebrow and with a smile began to interrogate. "Really, must you have him now? He's only just begun his chores, and I do not think that I can part with him until he is done." She loved to tease him by adding a haughty lift to her already upturned nose.

"Oh yes, Madame Dalton," he bowed his head low, "it is absolutely imperative, and will be a matter of life and death if he does not come with me now." Speaking so that only she could hear, he jovially added while looking at her with his head still bowed, "At least, for him it is."

My mother and friend stood silently while they exchanged knowing glances with one another. I looked on hopefully, and prayed to the god's of fishing that Bram could somehow convince my mother to let me go with him now.

"I don't know, Monsieur Macardle," she feigned a serious tone that I could not then tell was forged, "Daine has not finished his chores, and how will I ever teach him responsibility if you are always taking him away? I think it would be best if he were to stay until he has finished."

Hearing that, my hopes deflated entirely. If Bram couldn't convince my mother, then surely no one could. I looked down at the floor that I had been trying to sweep, and despite my best efforts, my bottom lip stuck out and began to quiver.

My despair was such that I almost didn't hear my mother when she spoke to Bram. I looked up at them from under the mass of hair that had fallen forward to cover my disappointment. It was her hazel eyes, so full of love and amusement, that drew me in.

"Ah, my Good Sir will not always be this way. You'd best take him now, Bram, before I'm able to reconsider. And," she added for good measure, speaking loudly and excitedly, "make sure, he catches me a really big fish!"

My face broke into the largest smile it could manage. I dropped my broom and ran out of the door, pausing only for a moment to turn and shout, "Com'on, Bram!"

The old man laughed as he quickly left the house in order to happily herd me to a pond that was on the edge of his property.

The pond was large, and over it hung the boughs of many leafy trees. The water rippled as fish mouthed the surface, eating their breakfast of various insects.

"Okay Daine," Bram whispered, "I want you to whisper from now on. Do you see that little eddy over there where the stream flows into the pond?"

I nodded my head.

"Just to side of that is where the fish I told you of has been lazing about. Now, if we walk quietly around that way, and set our line just between that eddy and the stream, I bet we'll have him."

We quietly walked around the pond. My little heart thumped with anticipation and excitement. We stopped on the bank not far from the eddy, and I watched completely engrossed as Bram deftly tied something to the hook that looked like a mayfly. "This is called a 'fly', Daine. You use it to hide your hook. The fish see something they think looks like breakfast, bite down, and much to their surprise find themselves with a hook instead. You ready?"

I again wordlessly nodded my head, my apple round cheeks were beginning to hurt from smiling as big as I had been for so long.

"Alright then, here's what we need to do," Bram whispered again as he came around behind me with the pole in his hand. Carefully, he placed the pole in my hand and adjusted my grip. When I had it, he placed his capable old hands over my own. "You need to cast the line into the water. Don't worry if you don't know how to do it. I'm going to help you."

With a few quick flicks of his and my own wrists, he easily zipped the hook to exactly where he'd said it had needed to go.

I waited, eyeing the water with large excited hazel eyes. Watery plops could be heard from where the other fish continued to chomp the surface of the pond. Instinctively, I doubted Bram's judgment. There were fish biting the water everywhere except for where we'd thrown our hook.

Bram continued to hold my hands. Together, we began to slightly jerk the fishing rod a few times, causing the fly in the water to twitch too.

The seconds seemed hours to my all too excited mind. Still leaning over me, Bram began to speak something that was barely over a whisper. I felt a thrill reverberate through my entire body as his words began. Just as quickly as he started, he was just as soon finished, and the echoing feeling vanished.

Suddenly, the rod lurched down in my hands as a fish pulled and darted in a wild attempt to release itself from our line.

I let out a whoop of surprise and joy. "Bram, did we get it?!" I exclaimed, reveling in the feel of the bowing pole and the strength of the fish it held.

Affectionately the old man replied, "We caught something, but I don't know if it's him. Let's bring it up and see."

Together we began to walk backward over the rocks and bramble. The line jerked recklessly as the fish fought to free itself. As we backed away, it was pulled out of the water and onto the muddy, pond's edge. It flopped determinedly against the hard ground, its gills working desperately in an attempt to bring water into its lungs.

I stood there dumbfounded as I looked down on the biggest fish that I had ever seen.

Bram was right, it was a monster. It was so big, that it would have been impossible for me to bring it out of the water by myself.

Bram clapped me on the back, "Excellent job, Son!" and then he walked to the fish. Placing a hand under its white belly and another toward its tail, he lifted it up and brought it over to me so that I could see it face to face.

I was absolutely terrified. I'd never fished a day in my life before, but yet here I was staring at the biggest fish I'd ever seen, complete with two matching rows of razor sharp teeth moving up and down in its gasping mouth. I just knew its un-blinking eyes were staring all of the hatred it could muster at me.

"Would you like to touch it, Lad?" Bram asked me gently.

I think he knew that I was afraid. But of course, I just stood there staring at my fish in stupefied wonderment. I barely managed to shake my head in a no.

Bram chortled and cheerfully laid the fish down on a bed of grass away from the pond. I followed him in silent awe. "Daine, I'll be right back. I need to go and get a basket from the house so we can carry that thing back for your mother."

He wasn't gone long, but in his absence I finally managed to compose my flood of emotions into something I could actually express – fishing was fun!

"Bram!" I shouted as I saw him walking toward me with a large wicker basket in hand, "that was the greatest thing ever!

And look at this fish! William Thiery is going to piss himself when he hears about it!"

Bram laughed as he walked to me and crouched down to once again hold the fish in his hands.

"Did you see me, Bram!? I did it! I caught the biggest fish in the whole world!" I was dancing and jumping at this point, unable to contain an ounce of my overwhelming five year old joy a single moment longer.

"Didyouseemehuh!Ican'tbelieveIcaughtafishonmyfirsttry !Dadisgoingtobesoproud!" I jumbled out in my excitement.

Bram, always calm, said nothing as I zipped around him in youthful bliss. He retained an ever charmed smile on his face as he watched me. I'd seen the same look on my parents' faces, and guessed that that is what adults did when children were so happy they could scarcely breathe.

"Alright Daine, let's get this cleaned up." He withdrew a long and sharp knife from the sheath on his belt and crouched down as he cradled the fish over the water. "But, before we do anything, we need to thank the fish for giving himself to us."

I nodded and solemnly bowed my head. With my face lowered, Bram began to again speak in a language that I didn't know.

I eyed him from under the cover of my dark hair. *What on earth is he saying?* I wondered as I watched him and listened. I felt what I can only describe as a warming, or a tingling, that grew and seemed to fill the world around us. The air suddenly felt alive. I looked around. Everything shimmered with life, colors, and depth that I had never seen before. My head came up, and I marveled at the scene around me.

When Bram was done with what I believe was his prayer, I could have sworn that it almost felt as though the earth sighed in sadness that his words were not continuing.

"Daine," Bram's voice now said in its usual timbre, "come close, I want to show you how this is done."

I quickly crouched beside him in the mud and forgot everything I'd just seen in the experience of learning how to gut a fish.

*   *   *

My parents were rendered entirely speechless when they saw what lay on a bed of grass in a basket upon their table.

"I've never seen a fish like that come out of a pond," my dad finally managed.

"Nor have I, Robert," my mother added absently. Her eyes and mind were unable to truly tear themselves away from my fish.

Myself, well, I practically overshadowed the sun radiating with my pride.

"Daine here is one amazing fisherman. He just threw his line in, zigged it a bit, and within a minute, had this beast on his line. Ha, if he did not have the chance of gaining an education or of learning from a master carpenter, I'd say he'd have quite a future in fishing," Bram boasted as he ruffled the wavy hair on my head.

Mother just shook her head in disbelief, and went to work cooking the brute for us for lunch. To this day, I don't think I've ever had a fish that tasted as wonderful as that one did. When we were through eating, stuffed so full that our bellies hurt and all of us were eying the massive quantity of fish that remained upon the platter unenthusiastically, Bram stood and informed us that he would be leaving us for the next few weeks. It was necessary he explained, to acquire some oddities before he felt comfortable in beginning my instruction. But, as he assured me, he would most definitely be back for my birthday.

With Bram gone I was entirely left to my own devises. I spent the next few weeks causing mischief around my father, annoying my mother, and generally acting the biggest pest that I possibly could. As such, it was a relief to my parents to know that in only a few short weeks, I would be away for most of the day doing something constructive with Bram.

Chapter Four

The day of my fifth birthday dawned, and to my disappointment, was not marked by anything spectacular. I spent the morning completing my chores with my mother, and then by helping my father in his shop with anything he could find to occupy me. Lunch came and went, and still there was no sign of Bram.

I left the house in hopes of finding something that would allow the rest of the afternoon to pass with ease – hopefully relatively free from boredom. Aimlessly, I took the path that rounded around the corner of my father's shop. I hadn't gone more than a few steps when, suddenly, an idea stopped me in my tracks. I knew exactly what I was going to do. I turned on spot, and ran as quickly as I could into my father's shop. Inside, I found him bent over, meticulously carving a door.

"Papa! Do you have a fishing pole?!" I startled him with my unexpected outburst. Luckily, not enough to cause the sharp wood chisel he held to mar the wood's face. He looked at me, both relief and the slightest hint of annoyance showing on his face.

"Yes, I do. You'll find it back there somewhere," he used his thumb to indicate the haphazard collection my parents stored in a back corner of the barn.

He watched me as I zestily climbed on and over trunks, barrels, crates, searching wildly for anything that resembled a pole. Finally, I found it, wedged between two trunks and under a crate. Seeing that I was unable to get it myself, my father silently stepped up and moved things out of the way so that I could lift it out of the mess myself.

In a moment of triumph, I raised the pole over my head and relished, "Yes!"

My father snorted back his laughter. "Let me look it over, Son, just to make sure that it will work properly."

I handed my new treasure reverently over to him. After climbing down from the mountain I had just ascended, I followed him over to his work bench.

He had it laid on the table before him, inspecting the line and the hook. He then picked it up and tested its flex before turning back to me with a look of fondness, "Happy Birthday Daine! Your mother's going to be very disappointed when she finds out about this - she wanted to give it to you tonight at dinner. But, I don't see any reason why you shouldn't be able to use it on your actual birthday." He handed it over to me tenderly and rumpled my hair.

"Thank you, Papa!" I exclaimed, throwing my arms around his legs for the tightest hug I could manage.

"You're more than welcome, Son," he said while looking down at me, my arms still locked around him.

"Now, if you give me an hour to finish carving that door, I'll come out with you. Maybe you could even show me how it's done."

I pulled back from him, dejected. How would I ever survive having to wait a whole hour? I thought miserably.

My father must have seen my despair because he quickly amended, "Or, you could go now and I'll catch up to you when I'm finished . . ."

I nodded, smiling in favor of this option.

He chuckled, "Just go down by the stream in the back, okay?"

I nodded so enthusiastically that my neck hurt.

"Well, what are you waiting for?" my father asked. He leaned back against his work bench and folded his arms over his chest expectantly.

Needing no further encouragement, I was instantly out of his shop and running toward the stream. Behind me I could hear my father's gentle, amused snigger sounding from inside the barn.

The wind rushed through my hair as I sprinted toward the stream. My bare feet seemed to barely even touch the ground. The stream was not far from our house, but to a five year old with a new fishing pole, it was absolutely too far. However, that day the wind seemed to lift and carry me, and I ran there faster than I ever had before.

I looked over the river, making a keen inspection of all its ripples and currents. I found a spot where the water seemed to gently pool before moving on, and decided that it would be the perfect place to try out my new pole.

I kissed its wooden handle lovingly and looked carefully over the line, as I'd just seen my father do, and then down to where the simple hook hung weightlessly dangling on the line.

The hook! I almost forgot.

I didn't have any of Bram's fancy flies, but I could find something that would work just as well. I propped my pole up against the closest tree, and began to search for a stone that I could overturn. Finding one, I crouched down and moved it easily. I peered into the impression eagerly, hoping to find something that could be used to lure a fish.

Vaguely, I became aware as the same warm, tickling sensation that had filled air when I had last fished with Bram, began to grow. It diverted my attention away from the rock's hollow. I looked up, and excitedly searched the woodland for Bram.

He was not here.

However, the air continued to administer its glistening, genial caresses.

I was at a loss to explain it, so I shrugged it off, and went back to looking for the perfect piece of bait. In my moment of distraction, everything that I might have used had managed to disappear. *Stupid*, I thought to myself as I moved over to another rock that was not too far away. I overturned it, and found that there was nothing there either.

"Damn," I murmured aloud.

Guiltily, I checked around me to make sure my mother had not heard me. There was nothing to be seen but the trees, river, rocks, and grass. I blew out a sigh of relief and stood to look for another rock.

I spotted one, closer to the water this time. This one was stuck good. I tried to twist the rock and loosen it from the mud, but found it was impossible to do while standing. I kneeled in the river bank, my toes digging into the silt as I worried the rock back and forth, back and forth. I worked until my arms were sore, but the rock just wouldn't budge.

Sitting back on my heels, I wiped my muddied hand across my forehead. Something in the air changed. Throughout my entire search the air had shimmered with an affectionate tingle, but now, the tingling had become more of a smoldering sting. It didn't burn, and it didn't hurt, but it felt like a direct rebuff against my skin.

I looked around again, this time with suspicion. There was still no one else but me.

But, the eyes can deceive, and I couldn't shake the feeling of being intently watched.

My brow furrowed as it became difficult to concentrate, the sensation continued to increase in its intensity. Shakily, I stood up from where I had crouched over the rock, and staggered away as I made my way up the river bank to where I had left my pole. I clutched it tightly against my chest and then attempted to walk away from the river.

I had moved, but I wasn't sure how far. A pair of leather shoe clad feet stepped purposefully onto the sloped trail not far ahead of me. I blinked heavily; nothing seemed real in this sparkling world. When the feet remained where they were, I dragged my eyes up from the shoes until I found brilliant green eyes glaring murderously at something behind me.

The charged air cracked violently around Bram, and then all the more, as it seemed to expand outward, enveloping me within a protective stronghold. Removed from the oppressive disturbance, I could once again see and think clearly.

This Bram was even more ferocious than the Bram I'd seen through my mental haze. He radiated absolute and unchecked fury from every inch of his deceptively elderly body. I shrank back from him as I saw something truly ancient in his gold and green searing eyes.

"Daine," his calm but unnaturally forceful voice resonated throughout my bones, "stand behind me." He continued to glare menacingly at something beyond me.

I took a step toward him and heard the most beautiful voice that I had ever heard sing in reply, "Daine, you have not yet caught any fish. I could help you acquire as many as you wish. Just come back to the river. I am waiting for you."

I spun around searching through the crackling air for the voice that both beckoned and alarmed me. My barefoot involuntarily took a step toward the stream. I stopped, waiting for the repercussions of my disobedience to manifest. Just when I was about to take another step away, a strong and familiar hand was placed very gently upon my shoulder.

"Daine, do not heed her. Though she possesses the voice of an angel, that she is not. If you follow her, you would find out all too tragically that the *Sidhe* would use you for nothing more than its own ugly purpose. That is not what I want for you. You are more than that. Come, we've a birthday to celebrate."

His eyes were no longer livid with vibrant green fire, but regained the kindness and concern that I had known all my life. His gentle voice shattered the longing I felt for an unknown, and instead reminded me of my home, parents, and of trust. I took his hand in my own and allowed him to lead me up the path, the steps no longer difficult to take. Neither of us spoke a word to the other, we simply walked. My hand remained in his, and he, deep in thought.

My mother interrupted our silence. "There the two of you are! Happy Birthday my very Good Sir! Come, wash up, dinner is ready."

I had forgotten.

I grinned from ear to ear and ran right past her as she swatted at my backside. She had a bucket of water and soap waiting for me on the bench that rested beside the door. I laid my pole against the house and hurriedly began to clean myself.

"Bram!" My mother greeted him affectionately, "It is so good to see you. Robert and I didn't know what to do with ourselves while you were away. We expected you to show up at our door every morning and evening, and were greatly disappointed when you never did. The next time you feel it necessary to leave, please, don't let it be for quite so long."

Bram returned my mother's embrace and greeted her with a kiss each of her cheeks, "Ah, Carine, you think too much of this old man. But, I am still vain enough to be pleased to hear that I have been missed. Where is your husband? Would you like me to collect him before our supper gets cold?"

"Yes! Please! You know how absorbed Robert gets when working on a new project," my mother allowed.

Bram nodded, his hand going up to tip the rim of the forest green felt hat that I hadn't noticed he was wearing. He hurried off to remind my father that there was a birthday celebration waiting entirely on him.

39

I finished up washing and I heard my father and Bram coming toward the house. Apparently my mother did too, and she hurried into the house, the sound of plates being placed on the table was soon coming from the door.

My father and Bram walked up the flagstone walkway to our door. Stooping down to rough me up a bit, my father mussed my hair and then quickly worked his way down to pinch my neck. I giggled freely. Of course, my laughter just encouraged further assault, and he tickled my ribs with abandon. Through my laughter, I heard him roughly wonder, as he worked my sides over, "Did you catch any fish Daine?"

"No," I gasped out between giggles.

He smacked my bottom lightly. "That's all right, maybe you'll have better luck the next time. Quick, let's get in the house, I'm starved," he said with a smile.

I ran into the house with my father and Bram following just behind.

My mother had made a wonderful meal of lemon sage hen, watermelon, roasted potatoes, green beans, and even to my surprise, a small chocolate cake. We feasted in companionable conversation and company, the warm summer day giving way to a mild summer's night.

After we had eaten, my mother stood in the kitchen cleaning the dishes and my father, Bram, and my self continued to sit at the table. The lamps had been lit, and the warm glow added to our contentment. Father and Bram talked of nothing but

Bram's trip to Paris. We'd just learned that was where he had been, and as he'd just announced, he'd brought gifts. At Bram's insistence, Mother left her pots and pans and joined us at the table.

From a leather satchel that had been hidden beneath his coat, Bram removed a large paper covered parcel wrapped with twine. His mouth bore and amused smile as he caught sight of my parents attempting to mask their curiosity with mature indifference. He cut the twine with his iron dagger, the wrapping fell away revealing three other similarly wrapped packets, each of varying size and shape. These, he divvied out.

The package he placed on the table before me was quite small, but I paid little mind to that fact as I made quick work of the fastening and paper. Once opened, I stared wide eyed at what lay before me.

Inside of the wrapping were two very unexpected things.

A large, meaning both in mass and that it would fit a man well, and heavy metal ring. The entirety of which was ornately carved with connecting Celtic knots and almost nonexistent symbols that I couldn't decipher let alone be sure were actually there. On what was to be the front of it, a substantial oblong sapphire had been set.

Surely this was meant for my father and not for me. I looked at Bram and found him watching me. His head gave only the slightest of nods.

41

Tentatively, I took the ring. I held it in my small fingertips, raising it toward the light and marveling as the sapphire sparkled in the lamplight. Gently, I slid it onto my finger. Instantly, I felt the all too familiar hum begin to echo in my bones. I placed it back on its wrapping, breathing heavily with confusion. I turned to my parents, seeking their reassurance, but found them otherwise occupied.

Bram had given my father two new books, a gift he considered worth more than was measurable. To my mother, he'd given a delicate gold and diamond cross, as well as a note indicating that three bolts of expensive fabric would soon be arriving for her directly from Paris.

It was with reluctance that I turned my head away from my parent's happiness, to look again at Bram. He eyed me expectantly. The shadow of the ancient being I'd seen before lurked plainly in his eyes. I was sure of it, he had known what I'd felt when I'd put the ring on my finger. But, my parents had not noticed a thing.

I swallowed heavily, looking away from his relentless stare, and back down at the ring on the paper. That was when I discovered his second gift, the twisting silver chain of a necklace.

I was afraid to touch either of them.

Bram's voice then came to me solidly, though it was scarcely more than a whisper, "The chain is for the ring to hang upon, to be worn always around your neck – until you are able to wear it upon your finger."

I raised my eyes to his, and noted that they were now only slightly softened. They still were lit like embers. He opened his mouth to speak, but thought better of it. When he did speak, it was with an air of gravity. "Keep it close, Lad. You will find that it will help you focus. To magnify your abilities. You may also discover that it will serve as a shield to you when you have nothing left to give."

I cocked my eyebrow up at him in question. To my surprise, I watched as Bram silently lifted his hand from under the table, and placed it upon the table's surface.

On his own finger was a similar, but uniquely different sapphire ring.

He remained motionless as he regarded me scrupulously. Finally, in that moment of deafening silence that grew between us, he offered only the slightest of nods, before bringing his examination of me to an end. As if it our private exchange had never taken place, he removed his hand from the table and once again hid it beneath.

And then whatever the spell was, was broken.

"Oh, Daine!" my mother exclaimed as she finally noticed my gift.

Her hand rose to her cover mouth in her surprise. Her amazement had drawn the attention of my father away from the pages of his books and to me. He looked at the gift with wide dark eyes, and then looked at Bram with astonishment. His eyes only briefly darted to my own before they locked again onto my ring sitting on the table.

My mother carefully reached along the table and took the ring in her long fingers. I winced as she touched it, expecting her to experience the same sensation I had. But, nothing happened. She turned it over in her hands, admiring the stone and the Celtic pattern aloud.

My father then stood and reached across the table to my mother, who herself, reached her hand toward him and gently placed it in his waiting hand. He looked at it while he sat, his face warring with emotions. No one said anything as we watched him, waiting for him to speak.

"Bram, this is quite the birthday gift for a five year old boy," my father said humbly while staring deeply into the ring's large sapphire.

Bram simply shrugged and gave a slight smile when my father momentarily glanced up at him from under his concentrating brow.

Father cleared his throat. His voice was graveled, "I'm sorry Bram, but I cannot allow Daine to accept this. This is too valuable of a gift for a common working man, let alone the son of one. This is the gift of kings," he held the ring out to where Bram sat at his right, "and I just cannot permit anything of its worth to be given."

"Robert," Bram said tenderly as he took the ring from my father with his own worn hand, "as you well know, all of my family is in Ireland. It is rare that I see them, and when I do, it is only upon the occasion that I venture across the continent and the sea to go to them."

"They do not reach out to me out of love and familial ties, but instead, only when they've found cause to want something that only I may provide. But you," he looked around the table, meeting our eyes as he indicated all of us, "you have taken me into your hearts and into your home freely. You have never expected anything of worth from me, nor have you ever asked for more than any loved one or friend would ask of their own."

"You have done this despite the fact that you have undoubtedly known that I am a man of very considerable means. These past five years have made us a family," he continued, now focusing entirely on me, "and I have come to care for, love you, and claim you as my own." His eyes looked up from mine, and with a smile he met the emotionally touched expressions of my parents.

His eyes found mine, with a warm smile of encouragement he raised the ring up so that we all could see, "Daine, I want you to have this." He reached across the table from where he had been sitting across from me, and gently replaced the ring on the paper and silver chain. He sat back in his chair, the picture of ease and joy. "That ring has been with me for a long, long time, waiting to belong to someone who is as good as you."

I just sat there, unable to say or do anything but stare helplessly between Bram, my parents, and the ring.

My mother extended her hand toward me, and softly placed it on my own. Her thumb lightly rubbed a reassuring motion on the back of my hand. She looked at my father and gave him an almost imperceptible slight of her head.

Taking her lead, my father, proud, kind, and in this moment extremely humbled, began to speak. "Son, I . . . I . . ." he ran his hands through his hair, shook his shoulders and cleared his throat, though it had little effect on the timbre of his voice. "Daine, Mr. Macardle has bestowed you with an incomparable gift. And although I believe the sentiments between us are the same, I have not changed my opinion that his gift is too valuable to be given. However, if you'd like to accept it, I will support your decision entirely."

I felt the huge responsibility my father had given me. Did I accept this gift and become steward of something priceless? Or, did I leave it to remain in the hands of someone who had proven capable and worthy of bearing its burden?

I looked away from my father and found my mother's face. Her beautiful hazel eyes were loving as her hand continued to gently knead my own. She delicately bit her lip, nodding understandingly to me.

Bram gave all appearances of remaining impassive, but I had come to know him well enough to see that he too was anxiously awaiting my decision.

I returned my sight to my father. He sat aloofly in his chair, absently biting his nails. His dark eyes watched me carefully.

I looked back at Bram, took a deep breath, and dipped my head in assent.

Instantly, my mother was to be found standing behind me. "Here, let me help you with that," she offered kindly.

When I did not decline her offer, she reached for the ring and the chain, threading the chain through the ring effortlessly before she astutely fixed them to hang from my neck. She patted my back, and leaned around me to look at the ring as it lay against my chest. "It looks wonderful, Daine." And with that, she kissed my temple.

My father shifted uncomfortably in his chair, "Carine, there wouldn't happen to be any of that delicious birthday cake left, would there?" he inquired hopefully.

My mother smiled at him, "Of course there is. I'll get you some. Bram, Daine, would either of you care for more?"

I, of course, told her that I did, and Bram, though he promised he'd have had more if it were in any way possible that he could fit it in his completely full belly, politely declined.

"Well, I think I'll be going. It is getting late, and we've a busy day tomorrow, Daine." Bram stood and began to put on his coat. "Thank you, Robert, Carine," he had returned the green felt hat to his head and tipped it to each of them as he said their names. "The food was extraordinary and the hospitality unparalleled. Happy Birthday to you again, dear boy. Enjoy your cake and sleep well. I will be by just after breakfast to collect you for school in the morning."

"Good night, Bram. Thank you for your most thoughtful and wonderful gifts – though, I doubt it needs mentioning, that we consider you to be gift enough." My mother said, her smile catching.

My father stood and stepped toward where Bram was waiting at the door, "Yes Bram, thank you. I am greatly looking forward to reading my new books. And even though I think you've given us too much tonight," his hand placed on the old man's shoulder, "it honors me that know that you consider us your own. I hope you know that we think of you as the same." He clapped Bram's shoulder fondly.

Bram lit his lantern, and left. I watched his light out of the front window, noting that his lantern did not take the path to his own home, but instead disappeared around the corner of the barn on the path that led to the river. Rather than think on that, I turned all of my attention to the piece of rich chocolate cake that sat so invitingly on the plate before me.

Chapter Five

I must confess I was expecting school to be some kind of magical, otherworldly, experience – and that, it was not. The next morning, Bram arrived slightly before the appointed time to collect me for my first day of school. I had no books or writing materials, so all I had to do was simply walk out of the door with him. The experience the day before by my mother's stream had led me to assume that I would be learning something by way of explaining what had happened. But, my assumption was just that.

However, discovering Bram's house was extraordinary. Up to this point in my life, I had never been there. His home was palatial, and a French country manor to the very description. Large trees obscured the house from view, while well appointed and manicured gardens flanked the house on all sides. It was two stories of perfectly hewn pale stone. Inside, it contained a full library, more art than I had ever encountered or imagined existed, and of course, innumerable rooms and chambers. Strangely, for all the space to attend to, Bram did not employ a single hand to maintain either himself or his property.

Immediately, we set upon the basis of all learning – the alphabet. Bram taught me to read, and just as he'd promised, to do so efficiently. Once I had that mastered, he also began teaching me Latin, mathematics, history, and science. Homework usually consisted of reading one of the various novels from Bram's personal library, memorizing large tracts of Latin which I'd then be required to translate and recite perfectly back to him. Of course, it was also required that I accurately label the various fauna and flora on our outings.

There was nothing spectacular about it. That is, until I was twelve.

One spring afternoon without preamble, Bram stood looking down on me from where I sat at his drawing room table. He cleared his throat roughly. His hand went to stroke his still immaculately groomed mid-chest length beard. The sapphire of his ring glinted in the sun and firelight, while his lips remained pursed as if in thought.

"Daine, seeing as how you have mastered everything that I promised your parents I would teach you, I think it time that you learn the real purpose of your education." His green eyes regarded me stoically as he began to unfasten the buttons of his shirt. His face remained expressionless as he dropped it to the floor. He moved his beard away, and exposed the skin of his upper body.

A heavy iron torque lay about his neck. Its ends were open, the tips adorned with what appeared to be iron balls etched in symbols. Between the ends, twisted iron roped its way around him. Although a Celtic torque was an unexpected thing to see on the old man's neck, it was discovering that his entire torso and arms were fully covered by swirling black tattoos that I found to be most unnerving.

Bram remained impartial and unmoving despite my critical gaze. When he next spoke, it was methodically, "You do not truly know me."

I allowed my face to show my confusion.

Bram continued, "You know the man, Daine, but you do not know *me* - neither my purpose nor my passion. You have come to know a portion of me, but, you must know some of what I consider to be sacred and secret to really know me." His white bushy eyebrow quirked up in question, wondering if I understood.

I gave no reply, maintaining the mark uncertainty.

He sighed and lowered his arms from the raised position that he had been holding them in. "Daine, my name is Bramwyll Áedán Roithridh Muireach Macardle," the ancient being in Bram's eyes now considered me openly for the first time in seven years. "I was born in Drumcliff, Ireland, one hundred and sixty-nine years ago. I am a Druid, born to one of the four original bloodlines. Of those four bloodlines, only two remain - and you, Daine *Caradoc* Dalton, are the only male with potential to be born to yours in generations."

I looked at him incredulously, unconsciously toying with the heavy silver ring that hung from the chain around my neck.

"Daine, I speak honestly. Do not think that I cannot see the disbelief in your eyes. Consider a moment, if you will, would your ring respond to you if you were not a Druid?"

I paused to consider it. I had no other explanation for the way my cells vibrated with life whenever the ring slipped onto my finger. I didn't know what a Druid was, so perhaps it was as good a reason as any. However, it was entirely impossible for him to be as old as he claimed. Seventy-nine or eighty-nine, either of those or some where in between he could easily be. But, one hundred and sixty-nine . . . My spirits began to lower as I realized that age was clearly beginning to take a toll on his mind.

"Bram, I don't know what to say." I said as I shook my head somberly.

"I know you do not, Daine. You have not been taught. History has long forgotten to include our stories in its pages," Bram sympathized. He stooped and picked his shirt off the floor, returning to his well groomed self before my eyes. "But remember, knowing nothing of something does not make it false."

I raised my eyes and looked into his plainly. "Yes, that is true. It's just that . . . well . . . ," I looked back down at my hands resting on the table top as I confessed, "I have to be honest. What you've said just doesn't seem to be in any way probable. You cannot be one hundred and sixty-nine years old, Bram. You just can't," I managed to squeak, my voice coming out in barely a whisper.

I mustered my courage, swallowing the lump of sorrow that had started to form in my throat, and slowly stood up from my seat and began to gather my papers and books from the table.

"Daine," Bram said softly, stepping forward but keeping the table between us. "I know what I have just told you would seem to be unreasonable. But, I have never said anything to you that was not true. I am a Druid. You are a Druid - and an uncommonly strong one at that. You have been able to memorize and recite all of the Druid texts in half of the standard time, and I have seen you harness the earth and her elements for your benefit. You just did not know what it was you were doing. It is second nature to you."

"Bram, I don't even know what a Druid is, so how can I know what you have seen me do that supposedly makes me one of them?" I didn't believe him.

"A Druid is a keeper and protector of the earth. A wielder of her elements. As for seeing you, I have seen you demonstrate many talents. But, the one that you will most easily recognize is using the wind to run faster than any other boy of your size is capable of doing."

I looked down sheepishly. There were times when I felt that I wanted to run faster, and so, I did. The wind would blow steadily at my back, seeming to press me forward. My feet would hardly touch the ground. There was never a time that I felt so free.

Then Bram leaned forward, placing hands on table. His countenance was genuinely intent as he said in a low voice, "And, most astoundingly, I have seen you bear the presence and full glamour of the Sidhe and walk away entirely unphased. What's more, you did so when you were scarcely outside of your infancy. Now *that* is something that should be impossible. Had I not witnessed it with my own eyes, I would have never believed it myself." He then pushed himself away from the table and stood resolutely while waiting for my response.

The air grew heavy around me. It pushed at me, emphasizing the validity of Bram's words. My mind and heart raced. I stood steady but entirely speechless, and could concentrate on nothing more than breathing in and out through my panic. Gradually, the atmosphere returned to its normal condition, and it became easier to work through my thoughts of astonishment and disbelief. Just when I was about to open my mouth to speak, Bram turned away from me and walked toward the fire. He grabbed the iron poker and adjusted the logs so that the fire would burn hotter. He then turned his face in my direction.

"Daine, I have taught you all that you need to know in order to succeed at whatever endeavor you should choose to pursue in your lifetime. You can read and comprehend the old masters, as well as being able to use mathematical skill and science in contemplation of the world around you. I have taught you everything I originally promised to, and heretofore, I will no longer serve as your teacher in these matters."

He began to pace before the fire, his hand thoughtlessly caressing his beard as he added, "If it is your desire to continue your education at higher institutions of learning, I will provide for everything that you should need financially in order to do so. You may attain whatever the degree or degrees you desire - it will have no effect upon my support of you or your decision."

Abruptly he stopped pacing and walked to stand close to me, his eyes refused to hide the ancient awareness inside. He smiled familiarly and warm, and placed his hands on my shoulders while he stooped a little to be able to look me in the eyes.

"However, if you would like to be instructed on how to become who you really are, a Druid, I will agreeably consent to your request and from that moment forward, consider you my apprentice." He patted my shoulder lovingly and added as he stood up straight, "You have quite the decision before you. Think on it well. If I do not see you for studies tomorrow morning, I will not regard you any differently for your decision."

I nodded unseeingly. I walked past him without looking at him - I just couldn't. It was with great sadness that I left his drawing room, crossed the foyer, opened the heavy old door and stepped through, hearing it close solidly behind me. I closed my eyes and breathed in deeply, opening them again as I exhaled. Slowly, I began the walk home.

Bram must be going mad. That was the only reason for it all. I kicked a fist sized rock down the trail in my frustration and anger. The birds happily sang in the warming spring sun. A light breeze blew through the greening tall grass and the new leaves on the trees. It was a beautiful day. However, I was so flustered worrying about Bram that I couldn't think of anything else but what he'd just told me. And, more importantly, what I was supposed to do about it? I needed a place to think, somewhere I wouldn't be bothered. I was reluctant to think of it at first, but admitted that it would be the perfect place for undisturbed solitude.

I hadn't been back to our river's side since the afternoon of my fifth birthday. I was scared of it. But, no one else ever went there either. So, instead of continuing on the well used path that would take me home, I turned left into the tangle of grass, brush, and weeds, and made my way toward the river.

I held my breath when I first saw it, waiting for all of the horrors the imagination of a twelve year old boy can conjure to magically appear. But, it was completely ordinary. The birds sang, insects buzzed, and the wind flowed through the trees. I chided myself for being so ridiculous. I continued walking until I found a large flat topped boulder that looked down upon the river flowing gently ten feet below. The warm spring sun shone through the trees above and gave the rock a bright speckled appearance as its rays fell and warmed it. I climbed up its side, and after surveying all that was around me, sat down in peace.

I listened to the river running by, the birds singing overhead, and soon felt drowsy. Thinking better than to use a boulder for a pillow, I removed my jacket and balled it up under my head. Lying down, I closed my eyes and breathed easily as the sun shone down on me, perfectly content. My thoughts did not organize themselves easily as I lay there. Instead, I found that I had entirely forgotten what it was that I had so desperately needed privacy to think about. Rather than try to remember, I drifted complacently into a warm and lazy sleep.

I awoke uncomfortable. In a way I had yet to ever experience.

It wasn't unpleasant, but I felt desperate to relieve a need that I wasn't able to articulate, let alone know how to alleviate. I moved to stretch my legs, and groaned in pleasure as my pants rubbed against me. I opened my eyes, shocked. The air once again was humming, the wind had ceased to move in the grass and trees, and the birds and insects had disappeared and were entirely silent.

I froze in absolute terror.

Everything I saw shimmered and seemed more richly colored than I'd ever remembered it to be. It was difficult to breathe or think. I remained still, attempting to remember where I was and just what was happening.

"Daine," a rich and sensual feminine voice purred.

I gulped the air as my every cell trembled with arousal.

"It has been too long. Why have you stayed away from me for all these years? I have missed you exceedingly." The voice pouted as it grew nearer.

I looked around for its source but couldn't see anything amiss in the now sparkling world. "Who . . . who are you?" I gasped as I strained against the sexual awakening that was almost too much for me to bear.

"It is I, Daine, your forgotten friend and lover. Maurelle. Surely you cannot have forgotten about me, have you Daine?" Her voice caressed every inch of my body, inside and out. She was nearly beside me. I shut my eyes fiercely in a single futile effort to protect myself against a force I knew I was powerless to resist.

"Come, Daine. Take my hand. I will teach you wonders that you have not yet even begun to dream about. It can be just you and I, forever."

I opened my eyes, and was nearly blinded by the vision that knelt beside me in loosely draped ruby colored silk.

Her long blonde hair shimmered like a many faceted yellow sapphire in the sunlight. Her pale, glowing skin, was the perfect setting for radiant azure eyes, and her plump rosy lips promised both passion and pleasure. Although she was lean, she was still supple. A delicate hand with perfectly groomed nails begged for my own, as a smile that promised unthinkable experiences splayed demurely on her lips. Her brilliance put the sun to shame. She was too beautiful to be a part of this world.

Only in visions or dreams could something even remotely close to her exquisiteness be created. I breathed in her heavenly scent, and shuddered as my young body released everything that it's pubescent form could manage. Her hand came up to caress my face, and came away smeared with red, though she seemed not to notice. I myself did not care either while she knelt beside me. My eyes were bleeding purely by the sight of the undiminished glory of her.

At her slightest touch, I again lost myself to her. I was unable to move. Despite being frightened, I lacked the will or the capacity to do so. I was completely at her mercy lying on top of the boulder in the sun. She smiled bewitchingly, as her hand then went down to the bottom of my shirt and pulled it over my head and tossed it aside.

I smiled at the sensation of it and was completely surprised when she winced, pulling her hand away with a grimace.

"What's wrong, what is it?" I implored her, anxious to resolve whatever was causing her discomfort.

I followed her eyes. They were fixed on my ring that lay on my chest, still fastened around my neck by its simple iron chain. She moved gracefully, positioning herself a few paces away from me.

Beguilingly she spoke, "Daine, would you mind removing your necklace for me? It is such a beautiful piece, that I believe it would be best for you to place it somewhere that it cannot in anyway be damaged by our play. Perhaps wrapped in your shirt so that you will not lose it?" she offered.

If that was all she wanted, I was more than happy to comply. My hand went to the ring around my neck. I pinched the band of it and began to lift it, its chain rising in slightly delayed unison up toward my head. The world lost most of its glittering haze as my fingers moved to allow for greater contact with the ring. I blinked profusely as my eyes worked to acclimate to their new way of seeing. My breath hitched, and my hand holding the ring abruptly stopped moving.

Maurelle seemed to be glowing with an effervescent light. As did everything she touched, or had touched recently. The rest of the world, though clear, was dim in comparison.

I closed my eyes in an effort to re-center myself. When I again opened them, it was to look directly at Maurelle. I blinked, and found that she now stood even farther away from me, close to the trunk of a tree in its prime.

Anger from an unknown source burned furiously inside of me. I glared maliciously at her as I sat up. I removed the ring from around my bare neck and chest and slid it with the chain still dangling from its band, onto my still too small finger. I clenched my hand tightly closed to hold it in place. With the ring on, her beauty was still unrivaled, but it did not cause one's eyes to bleed from simply beholding it. Furthermore, I could see where her sparkling glamour abruptly disappeared. It was as if a large glittering bubble covered the landscape, and everything within it was under her rule and domain, and therefore subject to the manipulations of the Fae. That was exactly what she was, an unwelcome visitor from Faery - the *Sidhe*.

"Daine," her perfectly feminine voice petitioned from beside the tree, "Remove the ring from your finger, please. I cannot be everything we both desire me to be with it remaining anywhere near you. Come, let us leave this place and create paradise together." Her voice echoed loudly in my brain.

Compulsion. I was sure that was what she was doing. She was trying to force me to do her will with influenced words. They rattled in my mind in an effort to control me. Had I not had the ring on, I would have unthinkingly done whatever she wanted me to. But, for whatever reason, the ring served as a buffer against all of her powers of persuasion and deception. There was no way that I would be taking the ring off as long as I was still breathing.

Something else fluttered in my mind; a memory, or perhaps a knowledge that was embedded so deeply inside of me, that I had never noticed it was there. It tensed, and I felt a sense of recognition dawn. I knew Maurelle, from somewhere, or sometime before. I knew absolutely that she wanted nothing more than to destroy me, and would use whatever means necessary to do so.

Outrage boiled in my heart. I had done nothing to provoke such murderous intent. Aside from refusing to remove a seemingly innocuous ring, I had obeyed her in everything. It didn't matter. I knew now of her intent. Like a wolf, cunning as it silently stalks its prey in the night, my dormant Druid flexed with power in a long anticipated awakening.

"No, Maurelle," I said coldly, "I do not think I will." I stepped toward her, my eyes focused and intent. "In fact, I have every intention of leaving this place without you, immediately. Should you try to move me as your kind is prone to do – to sift me, or in any way hurt me, I will guarantee you a very, very long time in an even smaller confinement."

Her beautiful face imperceptibly wavered, before she resumed her game of persuasion. I took another step toward her and the path, and saw as her pretty fingers briefly tense.

"Daine, I am hurt." She cooed, "I have done nothing to warrant your callousness toward me. All I have done is offer you limitless delight. Any mortal would exchange their soul for such promises. But for you, and only for you, I have asked nothing in return. I offer myself to you freely." Maurelle spread her hands at her sides in an action of mocked, but innocent pleading.

"No, Maurelle, with you there is nothing that is free." I watched her carefully as I stepped back and began to climb down the rock to the ground. Deliberately, I choose my steps on the path as I backed away from her, watching her intently.

She never moved, remaining always next to the tree. However, something about her perfect face had changed. I knew at once that she had given up on trying to tempt me. Instead of seduction, she had assumed her true attitude of superiority and complete annoyance. She leaned against the tree with her lean arms folded against her chest.

"Ha! Insignificant mortal. If you think that you, a mere human child, can dismiss or think to threaten me, you are greatly mistaken." She sifted and instantly stood on the ground before me. Her flawless face looked down on my own as her long fingers tightened around my throat. She pressed me backward until I was firmly against the trunk of another tree. Her perfectly straight and white teeth clashed together.

Prettily, she growled, "It has been a long time that I have awaited your coming, Daine. Never forget - you belong *to me*. Neither you, nor anyone you call your own, will ever be free from me. So do not think that you can simply walk away. You. Are. Mine." Her pouty lips formed themselves into a smile fit only for the bedroom.

My hands fumbled uselessly at the hold Maurelle had on my throat. She was stronger than anyone I had ever known. She held fast, amused that I would even try to loosen her hold, and tightened her grip instead. I was beginning to see dark spots randomly in my vision. In a desperate last effort, I opened my fist and pressed the sapphire of my ring against her bare skin, just below the bow of her collar bones.

She shrieked with an unearthly scream, as the scent of burned flesh filled the air. She withdrew from me, holding her hands protectively over her brand. The radiant light that silhouetted her body briefly flickered before it disappeared. She removed her hands, looking down vainly as she tried to see what I had just done.

All I saw was the prefect imprint the ring's stone emblazoned on her chest.

I did not wait to see what Maurelle would do. I turned and ran as quickly as I could up the path toward what appeared to be the boundary of her realm. I willed the wind, currently absent from this place, to carry me faster than I was able to move on my own. Behind me, I could hear her shouting words from a language I couldn't even begin to recognize. It grated in my ears. I kept going, afraid that if I faltered now I would not be permitted to live a moment longer. If she caught me, I was positive that my death would be torturous.

I burst through the transparent wall that separated her from the rest of the world with a stumble. I looked around me, taking everything in. There was nothing that was vibrant, or richer in tone than it should have been. Nor was any of it sparkling, and for that I was eternally grateful.

I turned, and staggered backwards as I saw that Maurelle glared inhumanly at me from behind the wall. Frantically, I looked up and down the length of the barrier to find its end. Glowing blue symbols marked the rocks, ground, and trees at varying intervals in every direction I could see along her prison line.

Maurelle stepped mere inches closer, and I fell back, preparing myself to run if I needed to. She reached a hand toward the wall exactly where I'd come through, and instantly withdrew her fingertips as if wounded. She regarded her fingers, but her eyes made little pause before they shifted back to mine. "I may not be able to remove myself from this place as of yet, but make no mistake, you will always be mine." Her eyes blazed an incandescent blue in her otherworldly beautiful face.

I shuddered in revolt. Boldly, I looked directly into her glowing blue eyes. "By the time you've finally managed that, I will have become something you will have every reason to fear," I retorted tersely.

"Ha! Again with your distorted bravery. Your false courage is amusing, *human*." She sneered the word, as if there were not a caste or creature in all existence that she found to be more insignificant or disgusting. "I suspect that you are depending upon Bramwyll to instruct you in how to becoming something formidable?"

I said nothing but my defiance gave me away.

Smiling, her voice lost its terrifying tone, and again became warm and alluring. "I see that I am right. Remember this well, just as Bramwyll counseled you against consorting with the Tylwyth Teg, I too must advise you to use caution in trusting the old Druid. He too will only use you for his own ugly purposes."

And then she was gone. Removed from this place or only invisible to my own eyes, I did not know.

I breathed raggedly. I looked away from the hazy wall and down at the ring I still wore and held clenched in my palm. Shakily, I removed it. The blue symbols that I saw along the line disappeared, along with the visible boundary that had separated Maurelle from me. So too went the unmistakable presence of my long unrecognized acquaintance. No longer called upon, the Druid inside of me directly returned to slumbering in my soul.

I noticed with sharp clarity that I could hear the birds chattering away, and feel the cold spring breeze on my skin. I shivered, realizing that I was completely drenched in my own sweat. My face felt cool and tight. I touched my cheek, and my hand came away with the slightly tacky blood that my eyes had shed upon seeing Maurelle in her undampened form.

I returned the necklace to my neck, and turned away from the river, running as quickly as I could toward Bram's home. Nervousness and fear pooled in my stomach, and I pushed forward all the faster. He was the only person I knew that could wake me from this nightmare.

Born of Oak and Silver

Chapter Six

"Bram?!" I yelled, as I burst into his house. He did not answer. I could not find him in the drawing room, nor was he in his study, library, or kitchen. Frantically, I ran upstairs.

I found him sitting upright and fully clothed on the bed in his room. His gnarled hands tightly gripped the blankets, and his wrinkled, caring face, was as white as his beard.

"Bram . . . " I said, my voice full of concern as I rushed to his side.

His eyes were closed and his breathing was so light that I would have never noticed it without putting my hand under his nose. Panic filled me. Bram was never sick; I'd never even seen him catch a cold. I placed a trembling hand on his forearm and gave it a slight squeeze. When he didn't respond, I shook him urgently. My fear grew rapidly as he failed to respond.

I stopped shaking him, it was useless. I sat in the chair next to his bed and watched him carefully. Minutes later, his eyes slowly opened. They were as vibrant as ever and clear, but did not immediately see me. I began to shake his arm desperately. "Bram," I shouted again, my voice cracking with emotion.

This time, he responded. He shook his head, as if to removing himself from a heavy daze. He made a small groan as he brought his hands up to gently cradle his throbbing head. "Daine," he gingerly whispered. He closed his eyes, but continued haltingly, as if the words hurt his mind to form them, "I felt you enter the wards. I had no conception of what Maurelle would do. I feared the worst, Lad. She is evil." His old wrinkled eyelids slowly opened to reveal watering eyes. "I thought I'd lost you."

He blinked against his tears, as well as the fading brightness of the room. "When I realized that you were on your own, I used the earth to know what was happening. From so far away, it was . . . draining." Bram began to massage his temples tenderly, muttering something occasionally from under his breath. I retrieved a small leather pouch for him, filled a glass with water and a small amount of the pouch's white powder. I stirred them briefly together before handing him the glass. He drank it quickly, and then resumed rubbing his head.

It didn't take long for the powder to take effect. He winked at me, and that was all the reassurance I needed. I was angry.

"Bram, why didn't you tell me that there was a Fae living by the river!? She tried to seduce me. ME! I'm still a boy!" I said exasperatedly. And then my shame overtook me. I looked down at my dirty shoes as I quietly admitted, "She violated me Bram. I . . . I lost myself to her . . . twice." I turned red with embarrassment.

Bram surprised me when he chuckled mirthlessly. "Daine, all men lose themselves when they see her - especially, when she is undiminished as she was with you. You met her in her true form. Whenever she is near, we become mindless, bumbling, buffoons before her – slaves to her every whim. One look," he snapped his fingers, "and we're done for."

He tentatively stood and walked slowly over to the washbasin. Pouring cool water into it, he began to wet his face with hands cupped full of water. The color began to creep back into his face. He rolled his dampened shirt sleeves to the elbows, revealing iron bracelets on his wrists and swirling black tattooed forearms.

"Daine," Bram interrupted my contemplation, "you'd better come over here and wash up. Your mother cannot see you this way."

I obediently walked to where he had just stood before the water basin, and was startled to see my reflection in the mirror before me. My brown wavy hair was limp, knit through with sticks and other debris. It lay plastered to my head with sweat. My hazel eyes were large, and appeared impossibly hollow in my face. Blood, now dry, had cascaded from my eyes and down my cheeks. Droplets dotted my shirtfront below. I turned my head and noticed that my ears had bled as well. *Must have been from her scream,* I thought. On top of all of it all, I was dirt smeared and undoubtedly smelled awful. I began to wash in the basin with ardor.

Bram had disappeared downstairs to assemble a few things for us to eat. I was ravenous, and he knew that I was all too well. I joined him in the fire warmed kitchen, and with him began to devour everything he had thoughtfully placed on the table.

"Daine, I have never been a subtle man. I may choose to not say things, but when I do, I am always honest and direct . . ." He leaned back in his chair, his right ankle resting on his left knee, with his hands folded neatly in his lap. His worn face was absolutely sincere. "Which, is why I see no reason to be indirect with you now. What have you decided? Surely you must now see that what I say is true. Do you choose to continue your studies with me and complete your training in Druidry? Or, have you chosen to continue your education elsewhere?" His green eyes were earnest as he sat quietly waiting for my response.

I had left his home earlier that morning with no intention of ever returning again as his pupil. Though, Maurelle had convinced me otherwise. I shuddered once again as I remembered our recent encounter. I sat up a little straighter, perhaps even puffed out my chest a bit in an effort to appear older and more mature before I spoke with a forced deepened voice, "Yes Bram, I have come to a decision; one that I would have thought recent events would have made clear to you." I looked at him squarely as I continued in sobriety, "I would like to do whatever is necessary to become a Druid."

"Good decision, Lad," Bram's eyes anciently gleamed. The slightest hint of a smile could be found on his lips beneath his beard as he leaned forward to take a drink from his wine glass on the table. He then returned to the same relaxed position, the merest hint of satisfaction still evident in his demeanor. "It will be a difficult, and oft times tedious. Mastery requires a minimum of twenty years of apprenticeship. However, considering that I have thought of you as my apprentice for the last seven years, we are left with a mere thirteen years. During which time, I must teach you everything that I know."

I nodded my head solemnly - my life had just been mapped out clearly before me.

"The first thing you must know, is that Druids and the Sidhe, or Fae, or even Fairies if you will, have always been at war. The Sidhe would like to take our world for their own, and *we* will do anything and everything to prevent that from happening. We fight to protect what is ours. This is why the earth permits us our power – so that we may keep Faerie and our world *permanently* separate."

I swallowed as I realized that I was about to join the ranks of a long-standing war. I nodded my head slightly and he continued. "Secondly, you may not tell anyone what you are. The exception existing only if revealing your position has direct importance to an immediate or future cause. Two examples of this might be for finding an apprentice of your own, or uniting with other Druids for your work. For the most part, it is rare that you will ever discuss your true calling with anyone outside of your known Druidic clan." He took a deep breath before adding, "This means that your parents may never know what you are studying to truly become."

I opened my mouth to protest but was cut off.

"I know, believe me boy, I know it all too well. It is a heavy burden that you must bear." His hands affirmed in the air emphasizing his point, "But, it is for their own safety. The Sidhe have a way of finding those we love the most – and killing them in a most horrific fashion."

My eyes went wide, and I looked away. A secret like this would create an invisible wedge between my parents and I. One that I felt was already growing larger with every measure of new knowledge I acquired. I closed my eyes and grimly nodded my head. I knew that Maurelle was not lying when she had threatened me and all that could be considered mine. "Bram, will I learn how to kill them?"

He looked at me, unwavering in his gaze, for what nearly spanned an eternity. I fought the urge to stir in my chair as his eyes bored into me uncomfortably. I determinedly held his stare, and watched as the ghost of a smile could again be found in his eyes. Soon it was on his lips, though they were hidden behind his beard. "Yes, Daine, I will teach you how it is possible to kill them. I will also teach you how to bind and withstand them."

I was just about to ask him how, when a knock came at the door. My father entered the house. "Robert," Bram called out to him, "we are in the kitchen."

I could hear his heavy boots as they walked on the marble and then wooden floors. He smiled largely when he saw me. "Just where have you two been all day? Your mother and I had to go ahead and eat without you, and even then dinner was on the cool side." He ruffled my hair that had the same wave as his own. He was as warm and familiar as he had ever been.

I had been afraid to see my parents; scared that somehow my encounter with the Fae and my decision to become a Druid would have made some visible mark on my soul. I was relieved to see that there was no perceptible change, and the solidity and comfort of my father's presence made tears begin to trickle from my eyes and run down my cheeks.

My father squatted down to look concernedly into my eyes. Seeing him so caused the flood of emotions I had been holding back all that day, to rush out of me in a violent torrent.

I leaned into my father's strong arms and sobbed.

He held me, unsure what might have caused me to react this way. His eyes turned to Bram questioningly, and Bram responded quietly, "The boy has been feeling out of sorts today. Take him home Robert, and let him rest. I suppose I pushed him too hard with school today," he said in feigned guilt. "Let's take the rest of the week off, and resume our studies again on Monday."

My father nodded against my head, and I heard the wood creaking as Bram stood up from his chair. My father pulled back slightly, looking at my eyes which had started to puff and my tear stained face, "I just don't feel very well at all, Papa," I said to him in a cracking voice, "Can we go home, please?"

He lingered over my face a little longer before being satisfied that there was nothing else wrong. He stood and took my hand and he led me through the house and toward the front door. "Thank you, Bram." My father said as he reached Bram who was waiting for us in the foyer. "Hopefully this is nothing serious."

"Ah, Robert, I highly doubt it is." Bram assured him. "Nothing that sleep and a break from studies will not cure. Do you need any help with your workload?"

My father looked uncomfortable, as he ran a hand through his hair. "Actually, I could use your help Bram. I have more orders than I can finish by myself."

"Why didn't you simply say so, Robert?!" Bram reached out and clapped him on the shoulder. "I will be there first thing in the morning. I ask only that Carine have some strong coffee available."

My father rocked back on his heels as he laughed, "Bram, you know that is the only kind of coffee that Carine knows how to make. But, I'll make sure she knows that you requested it. Who knows, she might try to purposefully make something 'strong' and neither you nor I will be able to even drink it from our cups it will run so thick." My father and Bram both laughed, and then my father looked down at me and shook my hand that was held in his, "Ready to go home, my good man?" he asked me.

I nodded my head pitifully, my attention fully focused on the room's wood floor.

"Well, we'd better be going then. Thanks again Bram, and I'll see you in the morning."

We left, and quickly walked home as the first of the spring crickets chirped joyfully in the grass around us. The sight of my mother waiting patiently for us in the doorway brought on a new surge of sobs. Unquestioningly, she hurried to embrace me, and quickly whisked me away from the cold world and into the protective shelter of my room.

She lay beside me sweetly singing lullabies, smoothing my hair from my forehead until I had fallen asleep. It was the last time that she would lie beside me in order to comfort me. After this moment, I became a man in my own mind, and no longer wanted my mother to comfort me - although there were moments where I desperately needed it.

Chapter Seven

"Daine, do you know what the Curse of the Four Fathers is?" Bram asked, standing contentedly dry on the banks of the pond on his property.

He was impeccably dressed in a three piece suit, despite the sultry summer sun. The only thing about him that may have seemed amiss to the casual observer, was the fact that he was using a closed umbrella as an un-necessary walking aid along the pond's slippery and mossy banks. The oddity in this being that there was not a cloud that could be found in the bright blue sky.

I was to be found waist deep in pond water. I was attempting to master water well enough that I might be able to call it down from the skies. In order to do so, as an apprentice it was necessary that I be touching water. Druid masters, such as Bram, simply had to ask and the water would have happily appeared no matter where they were. As of yet, none of my efforts had been successful. But today . . . I was determined that today would be different.

Bram was ever patient as I tried to learn the art of Druidry. More often then not I found it to be nearly impossible. He pressed that it could not be forced; pointing out that frequently it was the most powerful of Druids that experienced the most difficulty in bending the elements to their wills.

"No, Bram," I said in consternation. My hands, with the ancient sapphire ring fitting now nearly perfect on the middle finger of my right hand, hovered inches above the water's surface. "I can't say that I have heard of anything referred to as 'The Curse of the Four Fathers'."

Bram could be horribly distracting at times. I'd been focusing for hours on this, giving myself a pounding headache in the process. But just before he'd started talking, I was beginning to feel a recognition, or acceptance, between myself and the water.

I was seventeen and I had by that time grown to my full height of six feet. I kept my wavy dark hair long enough to be plaited, but short enough that it wasn't either a nuisance or what I considered to be feminine. My face had become a mix of both my father and mother's features. I had my father's pointed nose, dark wavy hair, and cleft chin. Of my mother, I had her full lips, hazel eyes, easily quirked eyebrows, and high appled cheekbones. I was very lean, and had not yet developed the muscled bulk of my adult form. Though, I had lost all of my boyhood's softness. Frankly, I was gangly, and for the most part awkward and clumsy as my brain fought to gain control of its elongated self.

"Daine, you're trying too hard. Just take hold of the water. It's willing. I can feel it patiently waiting for you," Bram instructed me from his perch.

I raked my wet hands through my damp hair in frustration. Regardless of what he said, I could not feel anything waiting for me. *Aside from perhaps, some lunch and dry pants*, I thought to myself sarcastically.

I closed my eyes and took a slow and deep breath, held it for a moment, and then released it just as gently. I repeated this again. I felt my heart beating strongly in my chest, measuring a few of its long measures before I opened my eyes. When I did, it was to turn my full attention to Bram and away from the chilly water that had wrapped itself around me. Although it was a hot summer day, spending hours in the cold water, hardly moving, had chilled me to the core. I shivered as I continued to stare at Bram with what I hoped was a look of complete misery.

Bram regarded me, clearly amused from the shore. He removed a sweet from his vest pocket and popped it into his mouth. He then stepped forward, finding good footing on the muddied rocks before extending his hand out to me.

I quickly left the water's cold embrace, and came to stand beside him, shivering. I was now five inches taller than he was, and I looked down at him now. He handed me a candy and wrapped an old blanket around my goosebumped shoulders. Together we stood side by side looking out over the pond.

"It is as I keep telling you," he said around the candy in his mouth, "you already know how to call the water to you. You only need to allow the long dormant center of yourself to fully awake and take hold. Cease trying to resist it. It will not harm you. You are as much a part of it as it is of you."

I wore my confusion plainly on my face, but without even turning to acknowledge it Bram continued, "I know you fight because it is in your nature, it is who you are. You battle everything, good and bad, and you always will until you willingly allow *all* of yourself to become present. When you do, it is then that you will be able to harness anything."

We continued to look out over the water in companionable silence, eating a small bag of candies that Bram had withdrawn from his vest. It was a very warm day, and even standing in the shade of many trees, my pants had dried almost completely within a few moments.

"What is the 'Curse of the Four Fathers', Bram?" I asked him abruptly after remembering that he had mentioned it.

Bram regarded the water carefully, and let out a steady breath before he answered me.

"A very long time ago, the Celts went to war. It has never been known exactly with whom, but only that the battle was long and bloody. During this war, among all other atrocities, four men in their ferocity had barbarically placed live infants upon the tips of their spears. The poor babe's were run through until the point that they reached a specially crafted holding plate. Mothers were made to watch on in abject helplessness, while their child's shrill screams drove them to heartbroken madness. These men then left the impaled children's remains stacked upon their spears. They marched from battlefield to battlefield, using these gross implements to serve as both an honor to themselves and a warning to others."

The pond had grown still and quiet. Not a single fish jumped, nor did even a single insect dare to interrupt the horror of Bram's recollected history. He turned, looking at me pensively as he continued, "Because of this appalling deed, every fourth generation bearing their blood has been cursed. Over the years, this has grown to be many. As such, disease, war, pestilence - all calamity always occurs every four generations."

"Why are you telling me this Bram?" I asked him with my face bearing the mark of deep consideration.

Instead of answering me, Bram looked up at my face studiously, nodded his head as he agreed with his own private thoughts, and then began to walk away from me. "Come," he said over his shoulder, "you may not need to rest, but my old bones need to sit down for a moment before I relate the entirety."

I doubted that Bram needed repose at all. If anything, he wanted to be within the security of his wards, elaborate and therefore impenetrable by any and all unwanted guests. I stood briefly, shaking my head lovingly at the absurdity of my old mentor. I hurried to collect my shoes, and then jogged to meet him.

We sat outside. Despite his large home's design which allowed for the maximum amount of breezeway, it was still uncomfortably stuffy indoors. On the few and occasional days of the year that were like this, Bram preferred to sit well within the shade of the many trees at the back of his house. We sat together eating large chunks of bread with a yellow cheese, our glasses full of a light summer wine.

"Your great-great-grandfather, have you ever heard him spoke of?" Bram questioned me while he absently twirled wine around the bottom of his glass.

"Ummm . . . no, I can't say that I have ever heard anything about any of my great-great-grandfathers. For that matter, I can't say that I know much about any of my grandparents, regardless of their degree of kinship," I told him as I tore another hunk of bread off of the quickly dwindling loaf.

"I thought as much," Bram said with a sigh. His right hand went up to rub his careworn eyes before he continued, "Tell me Lad, do you at least know where your name comes from?"

"Daine? Well, I would guess it comes from Denmark or somewhere there abouts." I told him easily.

"No, it is not Daine that I was inquiring about. Though, it may surprise you to learn that Daine was your maternal grandmother's maiden-name, and she was French. But, back on point, it is Caradoc that concerns me. Do you know where the name of Caradoc originates?"

I honestly couldn't say that I did. It was always just my name, and an old sounding one at that. But where it had come from, or how I had received it was something that I had yet to consider. Rather then relate this to Bram, I simply shook my head in the negative.

Bram sat up a little straighter as he drained the last of his wine from his glass into his mouth. He cleared his throat, and then informed me, "Caradoc was your father's paternal great-grandfather. He too was Irish, and was also a Druid - an exceptional and gifted Druid. I knew him quite well. Well enough to consider him a dear friend."

Bram's eyes took on the look of someone reflecting on the past, as he continued to inform me of a grandfather I had never heard of. "He was born in Drumcliff when I was thirty or forty, I'd suppose. I didn't think much of him at the time, as I had a family of my own and other matters to attend to. Within a few years of his birth, he too began showing signs of having the Druid in him." Bram leaned forward with a look of warning as he took the last remaining portion of the bread. I laughed, and gestured that I would not fight him for it. At this he too chuckled. He ate a mouthful and began his story again.

"Caradoc's father was also a Druid. As were all the males in your line as far back as we can trace. As for why none of Caradoc's sons, or grandsons showed to be gifted with the Druid until you, I cannot be so sure. But, I do have a theory. In Drumcliff village there once lived an old widow. She was widely considered to be a seer of sorts. One night, a few years after Caradoc's passing, a most urgent messenger arrived at my door. He requested that I attend Mrs. O'Carroll immediately. Never one to take the woman lightly, I took my cloak and slipped hurriedly into the night behind the boy."

"I found Mrs. O'Carroll knitting before her fire as she hummed a now forgotten folk carol. A steaming teapot and two cups sat atop the table beside her. I had expected to find her on her death bed for all the pressing nature with which the boy, her grandson I later discovered, had addressed me. But, I sat down in the chair that had been placed opposite of her all the same."

"I was caught off-guard by the casual and easy manner in which she bantered – nevermind that it was 3am and not 3 in the afternoon. *Blasted woman,*" Bram muttered underneath his breath with smile he did not try to conceal plastered fondly on his face. "Despite the strange hour, Mrs. O'Carroll and I shared a congenial cup of tea before her fire. It was only after our tea and cordialities were completed, that Mrs. O'Carroll informed me that she had received a forecast that she believed was of the utmost importance. One that she knew could only be shared with me -

When out of Caradoc, Caradoc comes
To barren parents, the ritual of mistletoe the Druid must
aid.

85

The walls will crumble, the earth will weep,
The Sword of Caradoc held anew, will hold that evil be
staid.

He leaned forward and regarded my face, searching for the evidence that indicated I was considering what the widow's prophecy might have meant specifically for me.

"Bram, are you implying that I am the Caradoc she spoke of?"

"Yes, that is precisely what I am saying. You are the only male born with the gift of Druidry, as well as being the only one of his descendants to bear his name." Bram replied solemnly. "We have been meticulously tracking every birth born throughout the branches of his bloodline. At no time was there ever a single Caradoc born to the line before him, nor after him – until you that is. Moreover, never was there a married couple that failed to produce living children – until your parents."

"But," I countered, "my parents weren't barren, Bram. My mother bore three children before me."

Bram nodded his head; he knew that as well as I did. "Daine, to be barren does not necessarily mean that you are incapable of conceiving children. It may also be interpreted to mean that a woman is unable to bear viable offspring. This, as you know, was how it was with your parents."

"If that were true, then what is 'the ritual of mistletoe' that Mrs. O'Carroll told you would need to be completed?"

He repositioned himself in his chair before nodding his head in approval of my question.

"As you know Daine, a Druid draws all of his ability and power from the earth. The Ritual of Mistletoe is a long practiced fertility rite. Among other things, it requires an oak tree upon which mistletoe grows. A mistletoed oak is a valuable, but exceedingly rare, thing. In order for the ritual to be performed, a Druid must have access to one of these trees. At present, I am aware that there are only six of them in existence throughout the entire earth. Of those six, one is located in our friend Maurelle's personal prison." He gestured absently toward the river and to the prison that was too close for my comfort. The smallest thought of its proximity always left me feeling uneasy.

"I was taken quite by surprise when I discovered that one of Caradoc Dalton's male grandchildren was living in a home right next to my own. I confess, I had been losing faith in the Widow O'Carroll's words, but upon discovering your parents, I was again filled with an inextinguishable hope. However, rather than immediately introduce myself to them, I thought it prudent to keep my distance and instead watch for the signs that would indicate your parents were who I suspected them to be."

"Not too long after this, I discovered that Maurelle was watching them too. I could not abide it, and immediately confined her within the area that I found her. I placed wards about its perimeter that would keep her in, as well as those that would repel, doing my best to keep humanity safe from the machinations of the Sidhe."

Bram sighed and chuckled a bit, "They just didn't seem to work so well on you, now did they?" His eyes brightened with humor, and he chose that moment to extend his glass towards me in request that I again fill it with wine. He saluted my stupidity and dumb-luck before he drank appreciatively, set down his glass, and gently brushed away the last crumbs of bread that had littered his beard and shirt front.

"I left for Ireland as soon as I was able to ensure that Maurelle would not be able to escape her hold. It was pertinent that I advise the High Council that I had a newly married Dalton male living adjacent to me, who just so happened to have a mistletoed oak on his property. The presence of a member of the Fae's Royal Court demonstrating an expressed interest in the Caradoc male and female was also of especial note. These revelations had the chamber echoing with new and ancient excitement, and fear."

"I could not get back to France quickly enough. I was eager to meet these Daltons, and to establish provisions that would guarantee Maurelle was firmly fixed within the keep. When I learned that your parents had been unable to bear a child, I knew that I had finally found where Mrs. O'Carroll's Caradoc would be coming."

"To gain access to the Mistletoed Oak, it was necessary that I enter Maurelle's confinement." Bram shifted in his chair uncomfortably, "Our meeting was most unpleasant." He cleared his throat and took another hearty drink of his wine. He would not look at me. Sensing his discomfort, I thought to spare him and looked aside as well. He coughed before he continued, "Maurelle was quite upset at being limited as she was, and in order to complete the business which I had come for, it necessitated that I do things that are not the way of the Druid. I relied on darkness to render her immobile, so that I could use a gold plated knife to cut the mistletoe I needed away from the tree."

"After I released Maurelle from the dark charm, I used the mistletoe leaves to make a tea that both your father and mother drank, unbeknownst to the other. However, in order for the ritual to be complete, under the same mistletoed oak a blood sacrifice had to be made in the light of the full moon. I took a young white bull to the tree, again bound Maurelle, and slit the bull's throat while I said:

> *sanguine purus nunc effundendum*
> *ad redimendos steriles,*
> *enutristi utero, veluti terra.*

Your parents conceived you while they were drinking the mistletoe tea. As an added bonus, they also had quite a lot of beef that winter too."

"Never before have I related what I have just told you, nor have I ever spoken of what I am about to say." His green eyes bored into my own, his bushy white brows lying heavily knit over his vivid green eyes.

I swallowed, and nodded to him in understanding. My own dark brows lowered over my eyes, knowing that whatever it was that Bram was about to relay would weigh heavily upon me. I looked at the large sapphire ring on my right hand as I clasped my hands together and lay them in my lap. My gaze remained there as I waited patiently for Bram to continue.

When he didn't, I lifted my eyes to find his own. He held my gaze for a long moment before he began.

"Daine, there are moments in life that define us. They reveal our potential, and if you believe in this sort of thing, our destiny too. It is then left up to you to determine whether you will do as these revelations would have you do, or not. Regardless of that final decision, either way you are brought to an awareness of who you are." His voice grew slightly bolder, "Daine, *this* is one of those moments." Bram viewed seriously. His left hand was poised thoughtfully under his chin. His right thumb rubbed the band of his own sapphire ring, worn on his middle finger, as his hand rested upon his knee.

"Upon the earth exists items that were created by the Sidhe. Their origin makes them effective weapons against our enemy. There are two which can kill anything, mortal or seemingly immortal, when used by the hand of someone very skilled. One, is known as the Sword of Light. At its blade, entire nations have been destroyed. The other, is the Spear of Truth. You may have heard it called by other names, the 'Spear of Destiny' or perhaps, the 'Lance of Longinus'." He paused as he registered my disbelief.

"Bram, do you mean to tell me that the spear that pierced the side of Christ as he hung on the cross, was actually a Sidhe weapon?" I viewed him skeptically.

"Yes, the very same," he confirmed easily. "There was also a slingshot. You will recall that it was favored by a young boy named David who used it to kill a giant, as is mentioned in the Bible. However, it is no longer relevant because David destroyed it when he recognized the amount of unearthly power it lent him. Exactly how he managed that, I have never been able to figure, I just know that he did."

"These 'airm a scrios', Objects or Weapons of Destruction, are dangerous because they permit the bearer ultimate skill and prowess. A man will become nearly invincible as long as an Object is retained. In order for this to be possible, the weapon must have a carrier capable of drawing energy from the elements, as well as having an energy store of what I will loosely term, 'the magic of Faery'. To hold one of these Weapons would mean the scales of the war would be shifted in our favor."

I regarded him carefully, paying special note to the way his voice was incapable of masking his hope. I nodded my head in understanding.

Bram continued with his lecture. "In addition to the Sword and Spear, there is also the Stone of Fál and the Cauldron of the Dagda. However, considering that neither of the two are weapons, I do not find it pertinent to include them in our lesson."

Bram sat up a little straighter in his chair, cleared his throat, and said quite softly, "Caradoc held the Sword. With it he presided as High Master over the Council of Druids for thirty years. During his stewardship, we were peaceful and our families were protected. But, of far greater importance was the fact that we had driven all of the Fae back to Faery. At the next Autumnal Equinox we were to complete the ritual that would prevent the Sidhe from ever entering our world again."

"However, it did not happen as we had planned – there were . . . complications," he hesitated. "Caradoc used the Sword as the ritual dictated, and in the process was himself destroyed. Though, losing him was not the worst of it. Whether by repercussion, or independent circumstances of the ritual I am not sure, but, the moment Caradoc ended, the boundaries separating the Faery from our own world rapidly whittled away until they had been reduced to nearly nothing."

"Those of us who were present worked fervently to intervene before the walls collapsed entirely. We continue to watch them with the utmost of diligence, but we do not know how much longer they will hold. The walls, after all, are only material manifestations of our wills. One can only add so much to them before they become so, heavy, we'll say, that the added precautions become too heavy for the walls to bear any longer. This is the present state of the walls."

"You see, Daine, there are different castes of Fae. Some of the lowest castes have managed to come through. Brownies, Sprites, Bogarts, Pixies, the Wee Ones, there are many names for them. And although these creatures can be quite pesky at times, they are not much of our concern. It is the Royal Court and its minions that would destroy us all should they manage to enter our world. They are older than we can comprehend, powerful beyond our own capabilities, and have allure able to enslave all of humanity."

"You have met one of them, Maurelle. Though, she is one of the lowest members of the Royal Court and her superiors would make even her seem lackluster to say the least. That is speaking only of their glamour, and saying nothing of their own magical capacity and immortal comprehension."

My mouth hung agape. When he put it that way, what could we possibly do to protect ourselves if they ever did make it through? We had nothing that would stop their advancement except for a set of eroding barricades. The very idea filled me with despair. Not only for myself, but for all of those whom I loved that would be utterly defenseless against such abominable power. But a weapon, a weapon that could actually hurt them was something worth holding at all costs.

"Bram," I asked through my muddied thoughts, "where is the Sword now? You say Caradoc was destroyed, but was the Sword destroyed with him?"

Bram sat pensively, his fingertips meeting in a steeple before his mouth. It was a while before he chose to respond. "The Sword vanished at the passing of Caradoc. I do not know where it has gone."

I was left feeling the effects of what appeared to be a hopeless situation. My association with the Fae was limited to my experience with Maurelle, and the knowledge that Bram had thus far imparted to me. It was not nearly enough, but it was enough for me to know that we were in trouble.

"But, if you were able to physically bind a Sidhe royal to the very place that she stood, couldn't the same be done to all Sidhe who were able to slip the wards and enter our world?" I asked him optimistically, but felt as though there was none.

Bram attempted to begin speaking, but then closed his mouth to again return to thinking of what he might say. Choosing his words most carefully, he said, "Maurelle and I have a special bond, one that does not come easily. What I did then has only been accomplished at one other time in the history of the earth, and again, only between a human and Fae that had been somehow linked through previous ritual."

I nodded my head grimly. "What of the rest of the Widow's prophesy . . . 'The walls will crumble, the earth will weep,' do you know when that will happen?" I asked hastily.

"No, I only know that the walls will fall, and they will do so soon."

"Was the Widow ever wrong?" I asked hopefully.

"No."

Bram deflated me entirely.

"Daine, you asked me why I told you about the Curse of the Four Fathers, and thus far, the reason seems to have wholly escaped your attention. So, I will be blunt. Yours is the blood of the fathers. All of them. You are the fourth generation. It has been four generations since Caradoc passed, and knowing that the Curse falls upon you, in addition to the prophesy, I fear that fate has dealt you an extremely difficult hand. Be that as you will, as I mentioned before, it is nonetheless your portion to do with as you will."

I swallowed heavily. "And, what of the last bit that she told you, 'the Sword held anew,' and 'peace be staid'?" I asked him a little too frantically for my liking.

"It is your only hope, as well as mine. Unfortunately, we have not yet been able to locate the Sword. All the same, I am confident that we will."

Bram's fingers thrummed on the arm of his chair as he studied me carefully. "Daine, I have come to the conclusion that the remainder of your instruction would best completed among

95

the other Druids in Drumcliff."

I was startled. I had been fully expecting Bram to continue in his bleak history lesson.

"There would be some around your age, other apprentices and such. Though, the making of acquaintances is not my primary objective in asking you to accompany me there. I believe the influence of other Masters would give you greater control and skill as you are exposed to their individual strengths and weaknesses. You would have no choice but to challenge yourself in order to master *them*."

"Additionally, they may instruct you in matters that I have unintentionally forgotten to teach you." He paused for a moment, allowing me to see the humor in his eyes before adding offhandishly, "*And*, I have been away for quite some time. Despite having kept regular correspondence with the Council, I find the information shared to be lacking in its depth and current relevance by the time it reaches me. It is time that I went back, and I would like for you to accompany me."

His green eyes looked at me expectantly, searching my face for any sign of my agreement and commitment to his proposal. The years of our interaction had allowed me the rare gift of being able to see his hope and desire in his seemingly emotionless and proper façade.

"Bram, I am speechless, not just by this but with everything," my hands circled aimlessly in the air. "I cannot make this decision now," I told him gently. He'd just extended me an opportunity unlike anything I'd ever encountered. In my seventeen years, I had never left Strasbourg. "I will need some time to consider it, and to discuss it with my parents."

Although I was now considered to be a man, in good conscience I could not leave my parents without extending them the courtesy of expressing their opinions on the matter before I made my own decision. It was also prudent, that I inquire if they might aid me financially in getting to Ireland.

Bram nodded his head in agreement, and moved forward on his chair before gracefully lifting his old body out of his seat. "Well then, I think that is enough talking for today." He walked to my chair and extended a strong but old hand toward me to help me from my seat. I took it, and stood up gingerly. My foot had fallen asleep and had turned to lead. I shook my leg to resume the circulation, before noticing that my old friend still lingered close to me.

I was assuming that he would add a monumental final stone to the preposterous mountain he'd just given me. But, I was pleasantly surprised when he smiled and stated reassuringly, "I know you will make the right decision. Now, go home, think it over, talk with your parents, and then give me your answer in the morning." He patted my arm, and without waiting for my response walked toward his house.

I remained where he'd left me, watching him leave. When he disappeared into the house, I slowly exhaled a long held breath. I had a lot to contemplate and none of it had to do with going to Ireland. I shrugged my shoulders, and turned away from Bram's large manor heading toward my parent's comfortable stone cottage.

My parents would be excited about the opportunity. It was one that they themselves would not be able to provide. Although my father's carpentry trade was doing exceedingly well, he and my mother both lacked the desire that pushed for change. They were comfortable in their situation, as they should be, they'd worked hard for it. But, their complacency led them to assume that I would be equally satisfied to remain in the same situation I had been in since being born to them.

As I reached the edge of the clearing that held the house and the barn, I stopped and attempted to imprint every fragment this place upon my very genetic makeup. I swallowed, slightly nervous, though already resolved in my decision. I went quickly up the well worn stone steps, and into the house. Together, my mother and I prepared dinner in the late summer afternoon that was just beginning to cool.

Chapter Eight

It went as I had predicted. Both of my parents were filled with sorrow that their only child was now choosing to go off on his own, a sentiment they both managed to mask quite well. But, their sorrow was easily overshadowed by their excitement for the adventure and opportunity I'd been given. Granted, I doubt their reaction would have been as positive had it not been Bram who was asking me to leave. They viewed it as both a means to finish my education, as well as the opportunity to see the continent chaperoned by my adopted grandfather.

Without my asking, they offered to pay all of the necessary travel expenses on my behalf. The matter arranged, my father clapped me on the back, and shook my hand while he quietly remarked something about my having become a man. My mother stood not too far off smiling as she saw my father luminous with pride, and the way my no longer boyish features mirrored his almost perfectly. Though she put on a brave front, her eyes glittered in the firelight as she fought to save the tears that I knew would be seen only by my father.

The next morning, I arrived at Bram's big house at the accustomed time for school. He was waiting for me on the front porch eating an apple. I could tell by the light in his eyes and the smile that was showing through his alabaster beard, that he already knew my decision. Seeing his reaction filled me with such joy, that I could not help but beam back at him the smile I'd held in when he'd extended his offer for me to accompany him to Ireland.

"As I said earlier, I knew you would make the right decision, my Lad!" Bram happily exclaimed as he took my hand and pulled me in for a quick hug and pat on the shoulders.

His enthusiasm was catching, and I found it nearly impossible to remove the massive smile that had plastered itself to my face. "When do we leave Bram?" I asked him excitedly.

"Tomorrow," he said, as he took a billfold of papers from his inner vest pocket and placed them into my own hand.

My heart beat heavily in my chest. There was so much to do in that amount of time, and I doubted my parents, let alone myself, had expected me to be leaving so quickly. In my attempt to grasp the immediate proximity of our voyage and all that I needed to do beforehand, Bram had turned and was now walking away from me and through his house.

"I expect you'll need some luggage," he called loudly to me though the open front door.

I nodded my head up and down, eyes wide, and I quickly jogged after him into the house. I was completely surprised to see that all of his furnishings, paintings, sculptures, and light fixtures were covered by white sheets. The windows had all been shuttered and reinforced. I could see from my place in the foyer that the fireplaces in both the drawing room and library had been cleaned and were now barren. The iron firewood grates waited empty and desolate in their places while a meticulously stacked bundle of wood had been placed neatly beside the hearth for future use.

"Bram?" I called to him as I rushed past the large staircase and into a backroom which overlooked the seats that we had been sitting in the afternoon before.

The little, but ornate and well appointed room served as his personal study. It was generally used for his "business dealings" and correspondence with his family and associates. But, at the moment, it was also serving as a sorting room as Bram prepared himself to leave. Just to the right of the door was a large trunk and a small handheld suitcase.

"Use the smaller one for the day to day things that you may need while we are travelling, and the trunk for everything else." Bram instructed aside as he gathered and sorted papers into leather bound carriers.

"Bram, my parents have agreed to pay for my travel expenses. I need to know how much to reimburse you, as well as how much I'll need for the remainder of our journey," I said as I stooped to pick up the small suitcase from where it was standing on the floor in front of the trunk.

Bram stopped sorting the papers and regarded me with an incredulously raised bushy white eyebrow. His mouth pursed in absolute rejection. "Go and ready my wagon, Boy - we'll take the trunk to your parent's home immediately. We'll be traveling by train to Paris, and from Paris to Le Havre. From there, we'll take a ship to Dublin. I have some business there, but once it has been concluded, we'll proceed by coach to Drumcliff."

It would appear that he was going to neglect the question of reimbursement entirely.

"Bram?" I asked as he again returned to sorting the papers on his large mahogany desk, "What if I had told you 'no'?"

Again, he looked up from the papers, only this time it was with a smile instead of a gruff scowl, "That would have been the wrong decision, and I have always taught you to choose what is right."

I too smiled at his absolute logic, and left him happily to do as I'd been instructed. I readied the horses and carriage, and then re-entered the house to get the trunk and smaller suitcase from Bram's study. Surprisingly, they were already waiting beside the door. Bram exited his house just as soon I'd discovered the luggage, and sprightly jumped up into the driver's bench.

I struggled as I loaded the heavy trunk alone, with Bram watching amusedly from his perch. *The trunk must be lined with lead*, I thought to myself as I strained to lift it off the ground. After I had managed to wrangle the massive piece of luggage onto the luggage platform on the back of Bram's carriage, with no help from Bram besides the occasional chuckle I might add, I jumped up into the seat beside him. Without further delay, we were on our way to my house.

While my father helped me laboriously bring the trunk up to the house, Bram sat comfortably at our well used table enjoying coffee and a pastry with my mother. Once we had the trunk inside the house, my father sat down at the table with a great huff.

I was too excited to sit, and set to busying myself in my room gathering my things together. Upon opening the trunk, I discovered multiple large leather portfolios, in addition to several extremely heavy small sculptures and silver serving items.

Bram called for me to bring the trunk's contents in to them, and so I did so as quickly as possible, setting every thing on the table before rough hewn table before them. Once the trunk was empty, I became so intently focused on packing the trunk that I failed to notice the conversation of Bram and my parents. It was only when the room fell silent that I attuned my attention to discovering the cause for the lag in discussion.

Bram was going over several of the legal documents detailed in the leather bound portfolios, which gave the horses and wagon to my father the moment we stepped foot on the train leaving Strasbourg the following morning. He then continued to relate that his large, and beautiful manor house, as it stood at this very moment with all the furnishings, ornaments, and property, was to be theirs the dawn of my twenty-fifth birthday.

I grinned stupidly. At hearing this, I poked my head out of my bedroom door in order to see my parent's reaction.

Both of my parents had been struck dumb. My father barely managed a slight nod in Bram's direction as he attempted to swallow heavily.

I returned to look over my room, smiling to myself at the wonder that was Bram. I continued to anxiously busy myself, packing everything that I thought I could possibly need in an unknown place and future.

I cannot say that Bram, my parents, or I slept at all that night. My mother fretted over me endlessly, mending my clothes, and even trimming my unruly hair, while my father and Bram spoke of things I was not able to hear due to my mother's ministrations.

*　　*　　*

Just after dawn, the four of us stood on the platform next to a waiting train. It was a mild summer morning. Other passengers crowded the quay, forcing us to stand in close proximity as we prepared to voice our good-byes.

Remarkably, I saw no tears in my mother's eyes. Instead, I saw nothing in their depths but pride, love, and hope. She held my father's arm tightly, hardly speaking, and had barely uttered a word all morning.

My father too was unable to hide his pride in, and hope for, his son. He was effulgent, and seemed to stand taller. For all of this, He, however, was less able to hide his emotions and ran his hand frequently through his slightly graying hair.

When it was announced that our train would be leaving, Bram quickly bid farewell to my parents and left us to ourselves.

"Good luck, Son," my father said as he extended his hand out to me. "Make sure you study hard, stay out of trouble, and listen to Bram in all things." He paused in the shaking of my hand and held it firmly as he told me, "You have always been an exceptional boy. I know that you will become an even more extraordinary man."

I began to shake his hand slowly, unwilling to look him in the eye for his touching words. I was grateful when my father pulled me in for a hug. I hugged him back, and only pulled away after he'd patted my back and whispered in my ear, "Don't be afraid to do something great."

When I looked at him, he was smiling, radiating with encouragement. My father then reached into his coat pocket and retrieved a large bundle of folded bills. He slid them firmly into the inner breast pocket of my jacket, and solidly tapped my chest reassuringly with his palm.

He reached back to my mother's waiting arm and pulled her forward to face me.

She smiled warmly, looked me over from head to toe, and studied my face most carefully. "Daine, be careful while you're away," she said quietly as she focused on straightening my coat, "and make sure that you haven't gone away forever." Her auburn hair was warming in the dawn's growing light when she added, "And, if you happen to find yourself a wife, make sure she's someone that I'll approve of." She lifted her haughty brow in emphasis while giving her head a definite nod of absoluteness.

A grin spread widely across my face, and I laughed at the outrageousness of her statement. I pulled her in for a deep hug, her head leaning on my chest as she tried to breathe me in.

She looked at me, and with a final act of courage dismissed me. "Now go, quickly, before I'm never able to let you go." My mother stepped away from me and into the support of my father's arm wrapped around her.

My father then took the simple dark gray felted dress hat off his head, and placed it on my own. They both seemed to like what they saw as they began to chuckle in a private sentiment that only the two of them could enjoy.

I looked at them for a moment, and finding that I was at a complete loss for words, gave them a curt nod of my acknowledgement, approval, and love, and then quickly turned and stepped up and into train car that had been not far from my back.

I found Bram sitting comfortably not far from the entrance. Upon seeing me, he gestured for me to take a seat on the bench directly across from him. I took the seat quickly, and turned to look out of the window on my left. My parents still stood together, the picture of parental love and support, with the morning light rapidly growing at their backs to give them an almost angelic appearance.

I couldn't help but feel a deep sadness at the imminent departure of my childhood, and the constant presence of both my mother and father. And though I fought to hide it, at seeing my mother and father both attempting to act so bravely for my benefit, but failing to hide the tears that now escaped both of their eyes, I too allowed myself to fully mourn the passage of what once was.

The train began to move slowly forward.

I raised my right hand, and planted it spread on the window pane beside my face. My parents both raised their hands in farewell.

I watched them fade away until I could no longer see them on the quay huddled together and waving. When all signs of them were gone, I leaned back and drew my hat down over my face feigning sleep. The hat my father had just given me conveniently hid the flood of tears that now coursed down my face.

*   *   *

It didn't take long for my sorrow to pass and for my excitement of the new journey ahead to become my entire focus. Bram laughed good naturedly at my inability to hold still, or to refrain from asking him innumerable questions about what might be in store for us. He bore the onslaught patiently, and related in detail everything he knew I would find either interesting or important.

My excitement lasted the first twenty-four hours. After that, it faded and fizzled into absolute boredom.

Bram kept me occupied with a stack of ancient and dull texts he insisted I memorize. I stared blankly at them as my focus wandered aimlessly over random daydreams, or to stare blankly out of the window at the passing scenery. Frequently, Bram would interrupt my reveries, insisting that I at least attempt to complete the task before me. But, as he well knew, it was a futile effort, and chivalrously he accepted defeat.

When all was said and done, we arrived in Dublin in a little over a week. I was in awe of the city. Like Strasbourg it was teaming with life, though of a different kind. Dublin seemed to consist of generations of pure-bred natives, whereas Strasbourg was always repopulating with the influx or disappearance of trade, and its citizens could be from any number of origins.

The same could be said for Dublin as well, though the city possessed an unnamable charm that I couldn't resist. Perhaps it was the Dubliner's accents, or maybe it was simply that the people I encountered were genuinely good. Whatever the case, I found myself absorbing every detail of the place with ardor.

Bram quickly adapted, and like his fellow Irish men quickly fell into a language that sounded occasionally like English – though of that I couldn't be sure. Despite my best efforts to understand and communicate in return, my proper and meticulous English grammar failed me quickly. Rather than continue to ask people to repeat themselves, or to clarify and speak more slowly, I decided it was much simpler to remain mute and instead focus on the details of the world around me while Bram conducted his easy conversations.

We were not in Dublin long. After disembarking the ship, Bram paid a porter to collect our trunks and to have them transported to a nearby pub and inn he favored, The Rusted Wardrobe. After being permitted a few hours to clean ourselves up, it was there that we met Bram's youngest son, Darragh Macardle.

I did not know much of Bram's family, only that he had four sons, all of whom were married and had children of their own, and that all of his sons were Druids. Bram had never given me reason to be nervous about the meeting, but I couldn't help but feel a sense of anxiety about it. After all, Bram had spent more than the last seventeen years dedicated to me, and in so doing had left his own family behind.

I had assumed that Bram's sons knew of his reasons for staying in France, but even to myself, they seemed hardly acceptable to leaving one's own life and family behind. So, while feeling inadequate and restless, I dressed and groomed myself to the best of my ability.

Bram also dressed quickly. I could tell by his demeanor that he was greatly looking forward to seeing his family once again. We repacked our suitcases, and hurried to the bar. Bram surveyed the room before walking swiftly toward a well dressed man with slightly graying hair. They embraced, and as I looked at his son's pleasant face, I knew that his mouth and teeth were the exact duplicates of those hidden by Bram's own pale beard. They stood together in a moment of joyful reunion, before Bram remembered that I was an unknowing bystander, and stretched out his arm to bring me forward.

"Daine, I'd like to introduce you to my son, Darragh Macardle." Bram said by way of introduction.

"It's a pleasure to meet you, Sir." I extended my hand to Darragh.

"I assure you, Daine, the pleasure is all mine. From what my father has told me, you have quite the innate talent and potential." He stopped shaking my hand to motion toward his father, "Father's told me much of your abilities, and has kept all of us abreast of your development in Druidry. I myself am still amazed that you've managed to survive, and come away unscathed from the close proximity of one of the higher Sidhe in full glamour. That is quite the accomplishment."

Darragh gave me an appreciative smile, reminding me again of his father. He spoke to Bram while clasping his Father about the shoulders, "Come Father, Daine, my carriage is out front. Aileen has been anxiously awaiting your arrival since you told us of it months ago. I do believe that if we are even a moment late, she'll have An Garda Síochána sent out to collect us."

He herded both Bram and I out of the inn's door and into his waiting carriage. Our trunks and luggage had already been loaded and secured, and not a further moment was wasted in seeing us off to the home of Darragh and Aileen Macardle.

They lived in a village, or perhaps even suburb, not far from Dublin. Their home was located on the sea coast in an area that is still called Killiney. The bustle of Dublin Port quickly fell away, and revealed an idyllic scene before us as the coach moved steadily forward. Rolling verdant hills could be seen all around. The sky was clear except for a few high clouds that scarcely seemed to move. It was beautiful, and greener than any place that I had ever imagined.

The Macardle home was set back from the village proper on a large expanse of land that overlooked the sea. We turned onto a gated drive which seemed eternally long before emerging before a massive grey stone Georgian mansion. It appeared to be two stories when standing at the front of the house, but the hillside dropped away to reveal a lower level in the back of the house. Large Roman pillars formed a beautiful portico entrance. The shrubs were perfectly hedged, the lawns pristine and lush, and the trees were plenty. The sea breeze blew through the leaves on the trees, creating nature's perfect melody in harmony with the waves that crashed gently on the shore not far beyond the house providing tempo. All of this was lit from above by a cheerfully warm afternoon sky.

Bram looked at the house nostalgically as he stepped from the carriage and onto the paved drive below. I moved out of the enclosed coach behind him, and breathed deeply of the heady air. Darragh instructed his coachmen where to remove our trunks, while simultaneously moving his father tenderly toward his front door. I followed in silent awe and contentment, not far behind.

We entered the princely home through a heavy wooden door hung with solid iron fixtures. The hair on my body tingled as we stepped through a line of invisible protection runes and into the home. The interior was just as grand as the exterior, though where the outside of the home was breathtaking, the inside, though no less magnificent, hummed unmistakably with the comfortable sounds of home and family.

Aileen was a slender dark haired woman with a demeanor that was both confident and friendly. Darragh and Aileen smiled brief affections to one another before Aileen reached Bram and caught him up in an immense embrace.

Behind her trailed six children, four daughters and two sons. The youngest I guessed was around twelve, and the oldest near twenty. The couple's oldest was a son, who was followed by a daughter, another son, and three more daughters.

I stood away, a silent observer to the reunion. Bram was answering all of Aileen's rapidly fired questions, while Darragh spoke aside to his sons. I was invisible to all but the youngest, a little dark haired girl with hair of long ringlets and eyes that were as green as Bram's. She stared at me curiously.

I smiled at her, and gave her a slight nod of hello. She quickly turned her head away as a blush seeped across her porcelain skin.

Aileen noticeably startled when she realized that she had overlooked me. She apologized profusely, and enveloped me immediately in an equally all encompassing hug. She felt my shoulders, and called to the nearby housemaid to promptly have tea and sandwiches ready for an impromptu luncheon. I was thrilled to hear that I would soon be fed, and cheerfully endured all of Aileen's questions about my likes and dislikes, as the lovable Irish wife sought to make my stay as enjoyable as possible.

It was at our spontaneous meal that I finally became acquainted with the two who would become my closest friends, Bram's grandsons Gairnan and Cian Macardle. Gairnan, or Gair, was the oldest with sandy hair, brown eyes, and a bit of a ruddy complexion. He was heavy set, though it was all muscle and not an ounce of fat that gave him his strong bearing. At just under six feet tall, he was only a bit shorter than I. And, although I was quickly working to fill out my lanky frame, at twenty, he easily outweighed me by at least seventy-five pounds of solid muscle.

Cian, was also seventeen with dark auburn hair that you could only tell was red when the light hit it just right, blue eyes, and was of the same build as his brother. When I first met him, he was about an inch or two shorter than me, though within the year he grew to be nearly my height.

Both, Gair and Cian were Druid apprentices. Although they should have been at the castle studying, Darragh and Aileen had both thought it more important for them to see and meet their grandfather, and myself, than to continue their studies. They would be returning to Drumcliff with us.

I found it was relieving to be with young men who were of my age. My childhood friends had consisted primarily of Bram and my parents, and although I found them to be great company, family is no substitute for friendly companions. The brothers took me instantly as one of their own, and together we set about planning fantastic exploits for the days that we would remain in their home.

It was also during this meal that Bram took notice of his youngest grandchild. While she and her older sisters seemed to be unable to take their eyes off of me and their brothers, Bram only had eyes for Ayda.

She was slight, but not in a sickly way, more of a fine boned beautifully delicate manner. She held herself upright with full bearing and self-possession, and despite her young age, rivaled her older siblings in maturity and comprehension. Though, it was not her demeanor alone that made Bram make special note of her. It was also her looks that roused his full attention. Her dark, nearly black hair curled wildly about her head in a way that was all its own. Her large shining emerald eyes were fringed by long dark eyelashes, which promised to be both devilish and stubborn despite her refined nature. And, her smile of rosebud pink lips managed to light up the entire room. In her young age, she already showed the signs indicating that she would be extremely beautiful when grown.

I soon learned the reason for Bram's fascination. Ayda was the spitting image of her grandmother in look and action. Her grandmother was no other than Bram's late wife, Anne. Either because of herself or her ties to the past, Bram was captivated by her. He spent every available moment enthralled by her every temper and comment. Ayda was most definitely fiery, and she knew exactly how to get her way with both of her parents, her older siblings, and now her grandfather. I, for the most part, found her to be bothersome and bossy, and chose to avoid her whenever it was possible.

In spite of her brothers and I's obviousness in not wanting her company, Ayda meddled unconcernedly in the manly affairs of her brothers and I – regardless of what it was we were doing. Always, we kept a wary eye out for her. We might not see her, but we had come to know that she was never far away. It would mean our hides if the innocence of one very pesky sister might somehow become corrupted at our own hands. She greatly diminished our fun.

My days were filled with adventure and endless entertainment with the Macardle boys, but it was the nights that I most looked forward to and enjoyed. Brigid was the Macardles' middle child. She was sixteen, with strawberry blonde hair and eyes as blue as a raging sea. Her temper, like her younger sister's, matched the passion that burned in her eyes. Her lilting voice undid me, and every night, I would sneak out to spend the night on the beach, in the gardens, or among the trees with Brigid.

Nothing more than talking, laughing, and shy kissing ever took place, no matter how badly I wanted it to. I could not bear the idea of dishonoring Bram and his family - no matter how willing the partner. So, in the morning while lying in my bed, I would think of Brigid and vigorously work to remove the temptation from my mind and body.

Bram was busy throughout our stay attending to various matters. Darragh was never far from his side. We stayed in Killiney for two and a half weeks before Bram had concluded his business. Then, it was time to return to Drumcliff.

The parting was somewhat sorrowful for everyone. I had come to have a strong fondness for Brigid, and was sorry to be leaving her for any length of time. Of course, it was promised that we would return, and soon. We took a few longing looks behind us as we set off for the by-road journey across Ireland and north to Drumcliff.

Travel was slow, and exhausting.

When we entered Drumcliff a week later, it was just as the night began. Firelight glowed within the village homes, falling obscurely onto the quaint cobblestoned streets. I could not wait to jump out of this carriage and stretch my legs. However, my excitement soon turned to wild apprehension as the carriage moved through the town and back into the country. Doubtful, I checked the faces of my companions. They seemed not the least bit surprised, and were relaxed even. So, I did my best to appear content to still be still driving onward.

Another half hour's ride up the coast led us eventually to our final destination.

A magnificent old castle stood in the midst of a heavy stone blocked wall that secured the entire perimeter of the structure. Both were massive, and the very things that come to mind when imagining fantastic tales of knights, dragons, and damsels in distress. The coach continued to approach, halting just before the heavy wooden doors in the wall. Passwords were exchanged, and finally the doors opened for us.

The courtyard was immense. The Druid stronghold had looked massive from the outside, but I was shocked by the amount of spatial distortion that had occurred. Inside of the castle gates, countless acres of fruitful farmland were enclosed within, along with multiple water sources, and a naturally fed pond that more closely resembled a lake. Moreover, the castle gates enclosed a fully functioning, pristinely kept village with innumerable individual households laid out in a perfect grid.

There were men, boys, women and young children. All of Drumcliff Castle's inhabitants were presently found hurrying to finish various tasks before it grew too dark to complete them. A multitude of torches were scattered about, lending light where it was needed.

Cian and Gair both gave a whoop of excitement. Gair leaned across the space where our feet and legs were to give me a solid thump in the arm, "Welcome to Drumcliff Castle!" Their excitement was contagious, and I found that I could hardly wait to explore what was to be my home.

All of us exited the coach, and began to stretch. Finally, our journey was over.

I breathed deeply of the night air. Cool, with a slight presence of the sea mingled with the earthy wetness of agricultural prosperity. It filled me with peace. I was happy to be here, and my inner, more knowledgeable Druid, agreed with the sentiment entirely.

Men approached Bram from all sides to extend warm greetings at his return. Soon he was completely lost in a mass of well wishers. Cian leaned close to me and to mention something about a kitchen. Immediately, the three of us were off with one purpose in mind.

Having eaten well in the bustling kitchen, Cian and Gair took me up several flights of stone stairs to what was their room. It was a large 4 room apartment. A bed, dresser, desk and chair, and washbasin had been added into once vacant bedroom specifically for me.

I washed quickly, happy to remove my dusty clothes and free myself from all the grime of travel. I was absolutely exhausted from our month of traveling. I fell into my bed and was soon immersed by an instantaneous and deep sleep.

Chapter Nine

Life in Drumcliff was busy, but also very fulfilling. Every moment of everyday was in one way or another geared to educate and strengthen the Druidic body living there. I remained at the castle year round, with only a few stints made to visit the Macardles in Killiney. During which time, Brigid and I stayed in as frequent communication could be managed between our sporadic visits. I was eight years in Ireland, but it did not take me that long to discover that I loved her. I had every intention of marrying her as soon as was possible.

However, life always has a way of altering our plans.

At age twenty-five, I was the youngest Druid Master we had on record. Once the High Council had voted to award me the status of Master, I had been given an intricate iron torque to wear around my neck as a symbol of my status. But, the significance of that moment was surpassed by my excitement at having nothing stand in my way of taking Brigid as my wife.

I had to leave Drumcliff, and soon.

Bram, who like his son and grandsons, knew of my unabashed attachment and fondness for his granddaughter, quickly intervened to thwart my immediate departure. He found me in the Castle's stables, hastily saddling the horse I had chosen to take me to Killiney.

"Daine, before you take your leave, there is something of importance that I must discuss with you," he said conversationally as he walked toward me and the horse. In the quarter of a century that I had known him, he had failed to age even a single day. The reasoning for this was something I had yet to figure out.

I continued to ready my horse, setting my roughly unshaven jaw in resignation as I knew whatever he had come to say would indefinitely delay me.

He stopped a few feet from me, stroking the horse's shiny and tawny head, as he muttered ancient words of affection to the animal. He patted its jaw for good measure. "Are you planning on going to Killiney?" he asked me, though I was sure he already knew as much.

"Yes, just as soon as I am able to get this horse ready I will be off." My father's felt hat rested once again on top my head, and my wool coat was already worn comfortably on this brisk late fall afternoon.

Bram nodded. He knew that I was leaving, and moreover, the where of it before he'd ever asked me. I just couldn't understand why he was making an effort to exchange small-talk. I paused in what I was doing, and regarded him expectantly.

Seeing this, he looked at me with eyes that seemed to momentarily glow with compassion before he pointedly stated, "Daine, you can not marry Brigid."

I closed my eyes feeling my heart constrict. So this was what it was all about, the family did not approve of the match or my intent. I turned back to the saddle I was working on, and was about to resume where I had left off when I felt a gentle hand on my shoulder slowly turn me so I was once again facing him.

"At least not right now," Bram added softly, seeing plainly both my reaction and aching.

"Why is that?" I asked him gently, though I was unable to mask the stab of pain from my voice. Did I really want him to tell me that I wasn't enough?

Bram spoke brusquely. He had my attention; there was no longer a need to draw me in. "The Ben Bulben Silver has torn. I need you to accompany Cian, myself, and a few others to that gateway, so that we may permanently seal it," Bram informed me. His tone masked something else.

This was not the explanation I had been expecting. Frankly, I was a bit chaffed that he had not told me earlier when there had been several opportunities to do so. If he was wanting dramatic impact in finding me just before I ran off and married his granddaughter, he'd found it.

"Why did you not tell me this before?" I asked him with annoyance.

"I only just learned of it myself. A member of the Bulben watchmen arrived only a few moments ago to inform us of the rift. He has reported that many Sidhe, of all castes, have managed to slip through. Apparently, it happened sometime during last night, and the members of the Ben Bulben Guard have since been busy attempting to contain the situation. It has been disastrous. Ennis was only able to slip away a few hours ago in order to ride here and seek our aid. I am reluctant to admit, that it does not bode well for any of us. I need you to lend your strength to us. We must shatter the Silver before it again becomes active at night fall." He scarcely whispered, "A moment later, and I believe it will be too late."

I could sense the strain and potential fear in his voice. What I did not know until I had arrived in Drumcliff, was that Bram was the highest ranking Druid among any of the known orders throughout the world. This made him the presiding officer, or even chairman, of the entire Druidic Order. If Bram was showing any evidence for a need of concern, there was no doubt in my mind that things were more serious than he was willing to say.

"Bram, of course I am willing to offer whatever aid I may contribute though, I doubt I'll be of any help at all. I have barely been recognized as a Master. Shouldn't only members of the High Council be accompanying you?"

"I've trained you personally, and I know your methods, just as you know mine. We can have no room for mistake if we are going to shatter the Ben Bulben Silver."

He regarded me confidently, extending his arm to rest his strong hand on my shoulder as he added, "We will be leaving within the next twenty minutes. You are ready for this, never doubt that my boy. Finish saddling your horse and then meet me in the courtyard."

There was no need for him to say anything more, and having much to attend to in a few short minutes, he strode lithely out of the stables. Soon I was leading my horse into the courtyard, where Cian and many others were already assembled and waiting for Bram.

Bram reappeared shortly, his white beard and age wizened skin completely at odds with his wildly flashing green eyes. He climbed effortlessly onto the back of his horse, and motioned for us to move out of the already opening castle gates. As one, the group of ten men that he had gathered began to move forward. However, Bram and his horse remained where they were, watching as the group he'd personally selected left the protection of the castle wards.

When I approached, bringing up the rear, he moved his horse to a trot alongside my own. His face was full of humor, though he spoke to me without looking at my face, "Furthermore

Daine, if you think that I would permit you to marry my granddaughter without a proper wedding, you are sorely mistaken." His eyes twinkled briefly as he allowed a momentary glance my way, "Aileen would skin us all and then force us to lie upon hot coals if that were to happen."

I cringed inwardly as the visual of his words bloomed in my brain.

"Though, not that you need it," he added, "as patriarch of the Macardle clan, when the time is right, I give you my full blessing and permission, and wish you and Brigid a long and happy life together." He urged his horse forward and took the lead of our group.

Simultaneously, we all spoke the well known incantations that invoked the earth and wind to move. Our horses began to run faster than what would have ordinarily ever been possible as the wind carried them, and the earth moved to lift them.

Sligo and Ben Bulben were not far from Drumcliff Castle. It was not long before the massively out of place plateau could be seen growing ever bigger against the darkening horizon. We continued forward despite an unspeakable sense of wrongness that grew stronger with every gallop toward the Bulben watchmen's stronghold. The already gloomy October's sky took on a deeper, and slightly unearthly shade of violet, as we came to a stop just at the base of Ben Bulben. A cluster of weary and bedraggled men were circled around a roaring fire, seeking both the blaze's warmth, and the reassuring company of their trusted companions. This was all that was left of the Ben Bulben Guard.

We dismounted our horses and allowed them to wander freely toward a gently running stream. I found myself alongside Cian at the back of Bram's group as we made our way toward the blaze. In total, including what was left of the Bulben watchgroup, we were fewer than twenty men. I was disheartened by so little a number. If what we were about to attempt had Bram feeling unsettled, the more of us we could manage, the better.

I kept my fears harnessed deeply inside, and joined the ranks surrounding the fire. I glanced over the circle of Druids, scanning faces to locate Bram in their midst. He was crouched, and speaking with another man whose face was turned towards him. The men were quiet, listening intently as Bram, and who I would later learn was the Ben Bulben Guard's Captain, spoke.

"It was so sudden, and there was no preamble to its opening," the surly Scotsman named Liam told Bram. "I've never seen anything like it, the Silver was *gaping* Bramwyll. I don't know how it happened, neither I nor any living member of my guard was present to witness it," Liam said in exasperation before he continued. "It was a typical night, nothing was out of the ordinary, when without cause, there was this massive, rolling wave, of something . . . I don't really know what to call it, but you could feel it building as it approached."

"I didn't know what to think, and I called all of the watchmen together as we rushed for the Silver in arms. After we'd broken through the fennel, this energy surged forward from the direction of the Silver, and passed through us – like a wave. No one was harmed but by the time we'd checked everyone that was when we noticed that the Silver no longer resembled a mirror. Gone too was the boulder we've always associated with the door. In its place was nothing but a massive yawning hole showing us a plain view into Faery."

Bram was made entirely speechless. He remained motionless except for his right thumb which rubbed at the band of his sapphire ring. His brow furrowed.

"I couldn't believe my eyes. I know I've already told you that it was like nothing I've ever seen, but I just don't know what else I can say about it. We were nothing more than a bunch of staring statues gazing into the wonder that revealed before us - it was impossible to do anything else. The colors and the beauty of the place are just . . . indescribable," Liam's eyes lit up dreamily, his voice coming from somewhere far away. "It is like looking at, the very least, a waking dream." Liam's eyes regained their focus and regarded Bram fully, "I'd say it was nothing less than looking into heaven."

Liam paused for a moment, lost once again in his remembrance. He swallowed heavily before being able to haltingly add, "We all know what effect the Sidhe have on mortals, and so there is no need for me to detail it. Looking into Faery has very much the same effect, one loses his will and mind entirely. He can think of nothing more than stepping through to leave the cold harshness of mortality behind him forever."

"Thank the gods that the Druid was frantically roaring inside of me to shake me from my rapture. I'd almost lost any ability to think at all . . . but blessed be the Druid! Without its constant ruckus, I would have never had the sense about me to mind what happened next."

"There the Guard all stood, in various states of unconsciousness, when much to our horror a massive outpouring of Fae came forth - some of which I've never seen or heard of before. There were hundreds of them. Caught unawares as we were, most of us couldn't rouse ourselves quick enough to react. Hideous, monstrous, troll like creatures came forth and grabbed fourteen of my men before turning and running with them back through the Silver. As soon as the last of the trolls had entered, the Silver closed behind them."

"If that weren't enough, we found ourselves surrounded by these grotesque . . . winged . . . gargoyle like creatures with black iccorous hides that were as hard as rocks, and a mouth of innumerable needle like teeth. We banded together, in hopes that if we were together, somehow we might be able to create some kind of a defensive attack. They launched themselves at us, either flying through the air, or running on four fiercely taloned legs. The only saving grace we were permitted was fire and iron."

"A few of us were able to link and create a dome of fire around us. This seemed to repel the beasts, saving the few of us that had been able to centralize together. Those who were outside of our blazing shield would find themselves caught up in the gargoyles' teeth. Pressing their iron rings and bracelets against the creatures' mouths would have the animals screaming blood-curdling shrieks of pain, as smoke and iccor erupted from wherever they'd been touched by the iron. Our men would then be released and left to die upon the blood soaked ground."

"Those poor souls would drag themselves toward us with fear and desperate pleas for help bellowing from their mouths, their faces unutterable masks of terror . . . Gods help them. Those who had been held and pierced by those mouths of thousands of needlelike teeth suffered irreparable damage. It was too late that we learned the beasts' saliva was a venomous poison. Men bled to death amid screams of agony, as an acidic residue burned through their veins. It rendered any aid we might have been able to give them entirely useless."

It was at this time that Liam stood, the thick blanket that had been draped over his shoulders fell away. Under the blanket his upper body was complete bare. Multiple large lacerations had been crudely stitched with the Druid's healing ointment generously slathered over the wounds. It would stave off infection as well as speed up the healing process. If his battle wounds were not a disturbing enough sight, the intricate scrolling dark marks that sleeved his shoulders entirely, were. His large hands trembled slightly as he gestured to them.

"These were not here yesterday morning Bramwyll," Liam said somberly. "I feel I have been tainted, forced to dance with and be touched by Darkness. Though, I suppose when you call upon heaven's aid, one must pay their own pound of flesh. If this is the price required to save the nine of us that remain, I am happy to have been able to pay it."

At this, Bram stood and looked closely at the swirling marks that wound their way just under the iron torque etched with runes that hung around Liam's large neck, and down and across his shoulders.

"These marks are different than those that come naturally through Druidic rituals and stewardship. See the pattern here," Bram indicated, "this is the archaic symbol for the Sidhe, the Abjure. These patterns and the extent of their intricacy can only come from encountering the Fae, and in risking all to resist them. Generally, they only appear when against all odds you've managed to survive. Your assessment is correct - you have been touched by Darkness. " Bram closed his eyes briefly and nodded.

"Tell me," he said when he'd reopened them, "are there any others who are now thus marked?"

"Yes, all of us who remain now bear them."

The group of bedraggled watchmen remained incommunicative despite their mention. It was obvious to us all, that last night's encounter had shaken these seasoned men greatly. None of us failed to notice their nervous glances made toward the sky, noting that soon it would be darkening. It made all of us shift uneasily where we stood.

Liam's strong body gingerly lowered itself onto the stump he had been using for a stool. He reached down to retrieve his blanket from the ground and sheathed himself again with its warmth.

"That was not all Bramwyll," Liam said, clearly exhausted. "We believed ourselves to be truly doomed. None of us had ever called and summoned the strength of fire for that length of time. As the hours passed, it took all of us to be able to keep it burning about us. Those gargoyles were continually circling on the ground and flying overhead, searching, always searching for any lapse in our shield."

"I do not believe that any one of us believed he would live to see another dawn. But infinitesimally, the gods showed mercy and the night began to recede. With the light ever so gradually beginning to grow, so too did our hope. We dove and reached into the recesses of our souls to maintain our fire. Somehow, it held until the dawn had broken."

"Just before the sun crested the horizon, the Silver again opened. Through the fire, and with all of our Druidic ability employed, this glimpse into Faery was painful . . . too unearthly to be appealing."

Bram nodded his head in silent understanding.

"While we glanced into Fae, fearing what might come out of the Silver next, a voice . . . a voice like silken honey, or pure loveliness, spoke saying, 'The Curse of the Four Fathers is now upon you'. As soon as she had finished speaking, the Silver began to tremble, and a loud, inharmonious noise that made you feel as if your skull might crack, sounded from Faery. The creatures turned, and bounded away like loyal hounds to their master."

"Now, Bramwyll," Liam asked, "I do not know what 'The Curse of the Four Fathers' is – it's not referring to this, is it?" Liam asked quickly, allowing his blanket to slip to show the swirling marks on his shoulders.

Bram stroked his beard pensively, remaining silent while he stared into the fire. He was deep in troubled thought. He abruptly looked up and aside where he found me and stared at me with his all-knowing eyes. I knew that whatever the Curse entailed was now going to begin.

He left his eyes on me while he addressed Liam's question, "No, Liam. Your markings have no correlation to The Curse of the Four Fathers. That is another, and separate matter entirely. Rest assured, my friend, I do not know what repercussions it will bring, but it is burden that only myself and another must bear directly." His wild eyes looked me over, waiting for my acknowledgement of what he'd just said. I felt Cian's eyes turn to look at me as well as he followed his grandfather's line of sight. I did not look at him.

Bram returned his attention to Liam and the others who now made up what was left of the Ben Bulben Guard.

"Gentlemen, we have quite a momentous task ahead of us. Please, go and ready yourselves to the best of your ability. I will allow you a quarter of an hour to do so. We will reconvene here before we make our way to the standing stones atop Ben Bulben. Then, the task is ours to shatter the Silver - regardless of whatever else may be waiting," Bram instructed us authoritatively.

We dispersed somberly, no one wanting to be here anymore than the next. I broke away from Bram and Cian to walk to my horse alone. Mechanically I went through the motions of preparing myself for a fight. I withdrew my daggers from my saddle bags, ensuring their sharpness before returning them to their scabbards. I strapped one at my ankle and another at my waist, before beginning the mental check list, assuring myself that all of my iron was in place. My torque hung coolly around my neck, the circlets around my wrists were both secure, and the sapphire ring around my finger thrummed a silent reassurance.

Inside I was a nervous wreck. Never had I been party to anything remotely as dangerous, or complicated as this was likely to become. All of my apprenticeship had focused on mastering the elements, as well as healing the earth and using its bountiful gifts for the purpose of man. Granted, Bram had insisted that I read a vast majority of the texts in the archives, stressing that their importance would undoubtedly come to mean more to me in the future. Evidently, I had not read enough because I was entirely out of my league on this one. Of course, I had dealt with various minor Sidhe in my training - containing them, or transferring them mostly. But, shattering a Silver was unprecedented. I did not even know if it could be done.

I leaned against my horse and drummed my fingers on the saddle, trying vainly to center myself. My horse's muzzle moved against my hand. I smiled, grateful for the carefree interruption. I again returned to my saddle bag to retrieve a pouch of oats for his perusal. When he had finished, I rubbed his neck, speaking words of comfort as much for his sake as for my own.

The moment was too short. It was with great envy that I watched him as he turned away from me, and trotted happily off to where many of the other horses now grazed on winter grass, far from any danger. It was at this time that I noticed Cian as he walked toward me. Despite the circumstances, he was remarkably jovial in nature and tone.

"Can you believe this!? I'm completely buggering out over it all. I don't know whether to say my prayers or wet myself," he said in a completely serious voice, though he could not remove the amusement from his eyes.

I permitted him a small chuckle before conceding, "I was thinking much the same, myself. How did you manage to draw out for this one Cian?"

"It was none of my doing. Grandfather thought that it would be 'good practice and experience in the application and theory of ritual on a necessitated basis'. Or, at least that is what he told me. Personally, I think he's just ashamed at the thought of having one of his own still an apprentice, and anything he might do to speed along that process is fine by him. I'm just sorry to have to be at the receiving end of his determination. Now I know what it feels like to be you – and I can't say I like it a bit."

"Ha, you have no idea," this time I laughed and meant it. "Try living under his complete focus at least twenty years and then see how you like it. It is only then that you will have something to complain about – ye poor wee lamb," I mocked him, receiving a good natured punch in the arm for my teasing.

"Oww, that was a good one!" I said while rubbing just below my shoulder.

"Serves you right, 'ye poor wee lamb.' Good thing I didn't hit you any harder, or you wouldn't be able to hold Brigid for a month." He removed my father's grey felt hat from my head and placed it on his own. His eyebrows waggled, managing the same expression his grandfather had given me in jest my whole life.

"In any case," he added casually, "Grandfather insisted on dragging me out here, only to decide that it's too dangerous for someone of my 'skill and talent'. But yet he is again insisting, no, mandating, that I remain in camp to help those who are too wounded to aid the situation . . . or to defend themselves, for that matter. Of course, I am asserting my own adult decision making prowess, and am ignoring his counsel entirely." Cian looked at me, hoping for a reaffirmation indicating that he was justified in his determination to join us.

"Cian . . ." I didn't know what to say. In all honesty I believed anyone who did not have to risk being present in an unknown, but sure to be dangerous situation should most definitely avoid it at all costs. I paused, looking at the ground while struggling to think through the right thing to say. I decided that honesty would be best.

"Cian, Bram has the most experience of anyone in these types of situations. There is no one I'd listen to concerning these matters, but him. However, you are a man and can choose for yourself. Whatever it is that you decide to do, I will have your back indefinitely." I offered him a reassuring smile.

"Good, it's settled then," Cian said with a large smile of his own and a resounding thump on my back. Despite his slightly above average size, Cian was like an ox. I would never want to be on the other side of a fight of any kind where I stood against him. As it was, even a playful slap left me hunched over and coughing, slightly winded.

Righting myself to stare directly at Cian's largely grinning face, I feigned look of blatant menace. I sighed, shaking my head at my best friend's sheer stubbornness, or stupidity, in deciding to ignore his grandfather's council. Whatever it was, his presence was soothing and I breathed deeply of the crisp winter air. It was time.

"Come on, we wouldn't want you to be late for your 'experience in the application and theory of ritual on a necessitated basis'."

He nodded, clearly amused, and together we strode quickly to the still blazing fire where the others would be gathering.

Cian and I both knew that we extremely under qualified to be numbered among the ranks of such practiced masters. If anything, we were a liability to their objective instead of a benefit. Still we held our heads high and tried to pretend confidence in nothing else but ourselves.

"Why are Darragh and Gair not here?" I asked Cian as we walked, "I would have thought that if there was anyone Bram would want by his side, it would most definitely be them."

"They are in Gort," Cian said matter-of-a-factly. He turned his face to mine and whispered, sharing a secret that not many other people knew. "If you can believe it, they're investigating the possibility of a Nuckelavee."

I stared at him momentarily in disbelief. If a Nuckelavee had managed to come through a Silver, things were much worse than what I knew. The problem with the Silvers, was that not only did they open randomly, but we also did not know where all of them were. It was no wonder that Bram was on edge.

Lost in our own thoughts, Cian and I closed the final distance that remained between us and the meeting area. Men had already begun to assemble.

Soberly, we walked amass up the well warded path to the top of Ben Bulben. The wards hummed with the warning of something being amiss as we passed them. I was surprised to find that the hike was much shorter than I had expected. Before I was ready, the rocky path ceased in the midst of a cluster of carefully cultivated and uncharacteristically massive fennel bushes.

I looked took in my surroundings. Aside from a few random bushes, grass, and protruding rocks, the top of Ben Bulben was relatively flat. This gave a stark contrast to the imposing set of standing stones that stood as dark sentinels, surrounding a massive boulder that lay directly at their center.

"Come, we do not have much more time." Bram motioned for us all to follow him as he walked briskly toward the standing stones.

I followed, looking uneasily at Cian who was still wearing my father's dark grey felt hat. I was grateful that he had not left my side. He looked as distressed as I felt.

"Stay close to me, Cian. If anything goes wrong, I'll shield us both," I told him. I was not a coward but even then I did not want to face something so unknown alone.

Bram's voice broke the silence as he instructed us further. "Fan out around the stones, each of you stand with a stone at your back. Be sure to always keep that stone there, and stay within the circle of the standing stones."

Without hesitation we all obeyed.

I found myself in front of an unparticular stone, Cian on the left and Liam on my right. A sliver of sun still remained on the horizon. A biting wind whipped over Bulben that had even the most stoic of men setting their jaw fixedly against its chill.

In the center of our circle, Bram walked thoughtfully around the massive boulder that was sunk into the center of the standing stones. This boulder held a Silver that linked our world to Faery.

I could feel the earth under my feet, almost undulating in revolt of what it knew was most assuredly about to happen. The Druids were the protectors of the earth, and she welcomed our care. What I was currently feeling was directly related to the Silver and what had already, and might again, come through. The earth was not pleased.

There were thirteen of us standing before the thirteen stones. Bram at our center made fourteen. Bram had included his two oldest sons, Braesal and Ewan, as well as three of their own sons in our numbers. The others were men that I had come to know through my time at Castle Drumcliff as an absorptive apprentice. Bram had chosen well in balancing the Master's strengths and weaknesses. The only two links in this chain that I doubted were standing side by side – Cian and myself.

Bram again circled the stone, this time regarding every man in the eye as he passed them. When he came to me, his look was both wise and knowing, speaking silent volumes of his confidence in my abilities. I didn't believe him. Before I could show him as much, he passed his gaze on to the others.

"Gentlemen, luck is with us," he said. "Fourteen is the number of Masters necessary to afford us the greatest potential for success - one of us for each stone. As I dictate, please focus and lend your energies to what I shall be commanding." Bram then turned away toward the Silver.

From where I was standing, I was able to view him from the side. Still, I was able to see his face, and more importantly, what he was doing.

He took a long and extremely sharp blade from the sheath at his belt. The runes that had been etched along the blade seemed to glow as they caught the last rays of the fleeting sun. He began the invocation, speaking loudly so that all present could hear. He asked that the earth allow us her power, that we might be permitted to protect and serve. And, remarkably, he prayed that God would be with us as we attended to this most grievous task at hand. When he had finished, ever so slowly, he ran the entire length of blade against his wrist.

The blood instantly welled and flowed from the wound. He pointed his fingers toward the earth, allowing his blood to drip freely on to the dark soil. He then lifted his completely bloodied fingers, and began to draw runes in an arch on the boulder's surface before him.

When he had finished, the façade of a rock no longer remained. Instead, within the runes a reflective silver surface, much like a mirror, loomed ominously before him. The Silver was not yet open, and showed no signs of being in the same state as Liam had described it before. No glimpse into Faery could be seen. We assumed silvers were like one way mirrors. Anything on the right side of the doorway could see into our world without obstruction, but, we could never see them. Bram was taking a marked risk in so plainly standing before the Silver just as night was about to ensue. From the moment the sun fell, the Sidhe would be able to come through at will.

Bram pulled a handkerchief from his trouser pocket, and swiftly bound the wound at his wrist tightly. However, he never permitted the dagger to leave his hand. Just as the sun finally dipped below the earth, he stood upright, the dagger held at the ready in his right hand, and in quick succession he began to call the elements.

The earth was already at hand, wetted with a sacrifice of blood, and so it did not require much effort to ask for its compliance.

Next, he called fire. Originating from nothing but appearing instantly on the ground before Bram's feet, it consumed the entirety of Bram's offering.

Wind arrived, bursting forth from the sky in a single cyclone. It fell upon fire with a massive "whump" that you could feel echoing in your heart and head. My ears popped from the massive concussion.

Finally, came water. In a similar fashion to fire, it welled up freely and pooled upon a ground that was undoubtedly solid rock.

With water now present, the ground before Bram's feet began to boil.

Bram coaxed, and soon the boiling earth began to churn and ball. The mud soon peeled away, revealing a swirling mass of swelling colors. Bram stooped down and gently took the color infused lump into his hands. Speaking in an ancient and all but forgotten language, he moved toward the Silver and reached forward to press the seething conglomeration into the doorway.

The mass attached itself easily to the Silver, and began to spread of its own volition. It covered everything within Bram's bloodily drawn runes. Bram stepped back, a greater distance than what he had before, and waited while the surface of the Silver began to emit sounds that sounded much like logs within a crackling fire.

"My warmest greetings to you, Gentlemen," a sensual female thrilled from somewhere in the shadows. All of us started, and looked around frantically as the scent of jasmine and sandalwood filled the air.

I looked at Cian, and then to the others. Even without seeing her, I could tell that they were lost to her already. The only one who seemed to be all together immune to the voice and heady scent was Bram. My reaction, although different from the rest, still consisted of a twinge of desire in my loins, but unlike everyone else, it was followed by an almost over-powering revulsion.

"How perfectly fortuitous for me to have found so many handsome, powerful, and capable males virtually knocking on my door," Maurelle stepped fearlessly from the shadows, and into plain view within the circle of Druids and standing stones.

The moment they laid their eyes upon her, all of the men dropped to their knees. They reached worshipfully toward her perfect body.

Bram failed to notice. He remained focused on the crackling Silver, continuing to mutter his incantation despite Maurelle's proximity.

As one of the only two of us who were able to remain standing, I once again looked over our fallen group of men, and swallowed the knot of terror that was rising in my throat. All of their eyes spilled great tears of blood.

"Bramwyll, how wonderful it is to see you again. I trust that you are doing well," Maurelle waited patiently for his response.

When Bram failed to turn and look at her, she was piqued.

"Bramwyll, I am disappointed in you. It is very rude not to greet so close a friend as I after we have spent so many years apart. Especially, when we consider how gracious and kind you have been to me in the past," Maurelle chided.

She was as beautiful as ever. The wind toyed lightly with her long curling blonde hair as she gracefully moved. Her smile was exactly as beguiling as I'd remembered it to be, and her eyes, still that same iridescent shade of ethereal blue that both beckoned and promised paradise. She was supple, but lithe and tall – a typical characteristic of the Fae.

My boyish self had remembered her as a giant, unequalled in size, irresistibility, and loveliness. But, to the man that I had become, she was now a few inches shorter than me. Somehow, this small leniency allowed me some tether to resist the complete embodiment of femininity and desirability that she was.

All this time, Maurelle had been slowly walking toward Bram. But, suddenly, she stopped. She stood no less than ten feet away from him, so entirely still, that she gave up the pretense of needing to breathe. Her head tilted slightly to the side as her smile changed from one full of promise, to another that was completely filled with joy.

I wasn't sure which was more damning to a man's soul.

Her eyes turned toward me, locking me within the full rapture of her elation. "Daine, ah, I had hoped that I would find you here." She sifted so as to be instantly in front of me, moving so quickly that I was not able to mentally register her moving.

"My, my," she breathily whispered, pausing to nibble her delectable bottom lip as she looked me seductively over, "What an unequally handsome man you have become. Even as a child I found you to be absolutely tempting, but now . . . now I am delighted that I find you to be utterly intoxicating." She leaned forward, pressing her lush breasts against my chest, and looked up and into my face dreamily. She lifted a hand to seductively trail it along my face.

I shivered; deep and into every recess of my core I felt her touch.

"And look, no tears," she pulled her hand away from face to show that it was not marred by a single drop of blood. "I have waited an eternity for a mortal who was male enough to endure me in my untempered state."

My hands wrapped around her waist, pulling her forcefully toward me. She pressed against my body. I heard her faint gasp of surprise and pleasure, and smiled my own back at her. Slowly, I tipped her chin so that her face would meet my own. Her mouth parted in eagerness, and I felt my own willingness stirring undeniably throughout my mind and body. I looked at her plump lips, and then into her bewitching eyes.

I dipped my head low, running my lips and nose along the side of her neck and up to her ear. I breathed deeply of her scent. It was more arousing that I could have ever imagined. I paused by her ear, nuzzling her a bit before I whispered as softly as my voice could manage, "Not a chance in Hell."

I lifted my head away and smiled down at her sincerely, still twirling a lock of her golden hair between my fingers.

She laughed, entirely amused at my unexpected rebuff. "Do not be so sure of that, Daine. You forget that you are marked as mine," she countered, still wearing that joyful, but yet completely undoing smile as she slipped elegantly from my hands. "However, contrary to your assumption, you are not presently the most pressing man of interest." She turned and moved a few paces away from me.

I watched in absolute horror as she began to reach down and offer comfort the entirely incapacitated Cian. He lifted his face to her's, shuddering with convulsions of rapture at her briefest touch.

When I was able to see his face as he adoringly looked up at her, it was marred by an unstoppable river of bloody tears. I stepped from my place before a standing stone. I would not allow her to toy with him a moment longer.

"Daine! Do not move from before the shadow of the stone or you will break the circle!" Bram commanded me from where he stood still watching as the Silver slowly fractured. Great beads of sweat dripped from his face and beard with his effort.

I was torn, Cian was in severe danger. But, I knew that if I broke the circle, so too would be the rest of the human population. Against my instincts and loyalties, I returned to my place before my stone and watched helplessly as Maurelle hovered affectionately over Cian.

Maurelle began to speak to Bram and me, "As you can see, Daine, Bramwyll has graciously provided me with several choice examples of his own to choose from. It would be tremendously rude of me not to partake of the gift he has so generously offered - wouldn't you have to agree, Daine?" She looked down at Cian, her gaze full and tender. "And, I must confess, the allure of youth is simply undeniable." She smiled at him and Cian replied with a grotesquely bloody and contorted smile in return.

She helped him to stand. Magically, she suddenly held a square of shimmering fabric. Most tenderly, she wiped the blood away from his face. Her long and delicate fingers then proceeded to smooth his hair. "Come Cian, there are needs that we must attend to." She swept her gaze down to his tented pants, and looked up into his eyes under the hooded fringe of her long lashes. Her hand slid down from where it had rested over his heart, trailing down across his abdomen, and teasingly close to his aroused sex.

He throatily moaned and worked to press himself against her. She smiled most cruelly. Leading him by a single hand, Maurelle began to move him forward. A dumb and thoughtless smile was pasted to his face.

As she approached the Silver, Maurelle sifted so that she was now behind Cian. She pressed her body into his from behind, and wrapped her arms around him before again urging him forward. She was using him as the shield between herself

147

and Bram as she moved ever closer to the Silver.

A tingling started up through the ground at my feet. It pulled on me. Bram was drawing from my Druidic powers to complete the fracturing of the Silver. I paid it little notice. My heart was in my throat as I watched the man who was my best friend reduced to cattle.

"Cian!" my voice croaked, I cleared it and yelled even louder at him, "Cian! No! Fight her! I know you can hear me Cian! Fight!" My anger and even greater desire to protect my friend, had finally allowed that I disregard Bram's instructions and find the strength to move my feet. I did not care if the circle was broken, this was Cian. I'd told him that I would protect him, and thus far I had failed. I would not stand idly by as he was taken advantage of by something as vile as the Sidhe.

I started toward them at a run. The air was charged with the energy that Bram had collected in order to crack the Silver. The hair on my arms stood on end as I requested even more be given, calling fire, and seeing how instantly a swirling ball of intensely hot flames willingly formed in my waiting hand.

The Silver began to stretch and open to allow Maurelle entry. The binding, cracking elemental substance, stretched further in order to recover the Silver's newly growing form.

I was now within an accurate range, and raised my arm launch to the ball of flames I held at Maurelle's back. I paused mid-motion as Bram stepped between myself and Maurelle. The flames still burned in my hand. I shouted my vexation, "Bram, what are you doing!? She's going to take Cian! Move!"

I fought to move around him, but was met by his countering of my every step. Two old hands shot out quickly, and held me in firmly in place. I struggled against him, and watched with wide-eyed dismay as my hand that held the fire was pulled down, and locked down at my side. The fire began to sputter and threatened to go out.

Anger turned into frantic desperation as I realized that Bram had succumbed to her influence as well. With all of the others under Maurelle's spell, I was Cian's last hope for release. However, Bram held me fixedly in place, his old limbs like that of an iron aged oak. Fighting him was useless.

I looked down at my mentor's face. His too was lined with by the tracks of blood before they stained and receded into the extreme white of his beard. I attempted to compel him as I looked into his eyes, pleading with him in my frantic fury, "Bram, let me go. Please. We must help Cian." I struggled futilely against him again, willing that the strength of my words would over-ride the all consuming influence of the Fae.

I saw as his own ancient eyes began to blaze in defiance. He was fighting it. I moved to test his hold, and his hands tightened painfully as they held me locked into place. "Bram, please, help me." I begged him one last time.

Maurelle laughed mirthfully, "Ah, Bramwyll, I assumed you would be less susceptible to fall under my glamour. Do you never learn? Though, I will admit that I do find the knowledge of falling so easily to be quite . . . arousing." A wave of provocative sandlewood washed over us. "I will make sure to remain undampened around you from this moment forward." She again filled the men's loins as she giggled merrily. "Come Cian, I have needs which I think you will attend to nicely," she spoke against his ear, feigning privacy when she had spoken loud enough for everyone present to hear. She bit his earlobe softly, and Cian groaned audibly.

Maurelle resumed pulling him backward.

"Bram! Let me go, you fool!" I fought wildly, void of any effect on Bram's seemingly supernatural strength.

"Farewell Daine, I shall look forward to seeing you once again and soon. Bramwyll, I thank you wholeheartedly for allowing me the use of one of your blood. I promise you, he will die . . . slowly," Maurelle laughed again, her cruelty being disguised as joy.

I felt as though I was crumbling inside as I watched helplessly as Maurelle's heel crossed over the Silver.

"Cian, I am so sorry," my regret and sorrow laced my words. I lowered my head in defeat.

It snapped up abruptly as Bram suddenly spun around with the iron dagger that had remained in his hand poised for throwing. I watched in disbelief as he threw the knife at them, sure and quick.

The dagger flew swiftly, flying through the air with a slight whistle as it cut its way through the night and toward its target.

It landed true, protruding squarely between Cian's eyes.

He crumpled, though still being held up by Maurelle's preternatural arms. She chuffed disapprovingly, and threw his body to the ground with a sickening thud.

"No!" I shouted as I pushed futilely against Bram who was still preventing my flight toward my friend. He was immovable.

"I do not give you or your kind any that I consider my own - nor will I ever allow it to be so," Bram told her calmly in a voice that echoed off the standing stones around us like thunder.

My bones rattled inside of my body as his words ricocheted off them.

Maurelle seemed completely unaffected, "Ha! You have missed your target then, Bramwyll. Never will I stop pursuing the bloodline of the great Macardles. Heed my warning: Gather them close Bramwyll, and make sure that it is there that they always remain. Your vigilance cannot extend everywhere." With her final words, the Silver shattered irreparably. Maurelle had been well enough inside to have been spared.

The slivers of Silver began to smoke and burn as they touched the earth. Several fell onto Cian's body, and burst into flame as soon as that made contact with his flesh.

Bram finally fell forward, brushing the flames off and away from his fallen grandson. He took Cian's lifeless body into his arms, and sobbed with heart wrenching agony.

His tears were free of blood.

My father's ruined hat lay upon the ground in the growing pool of Cian's blood. I fell to my knees and felt as the world began to crumble beneath me.

Chapter Ten

The funeral was a silently marked vigil – there were no words able to express our grief. We stood much like standing stones ourselves, guarding and watching over the shrouded figure in the midst of the burning pyre.

I mourned alongside Darragh's family. My arm around Brigid as she sobbed quietly against my chest, and with Ayda weeping on my shoulder as she tightly clasped my hand.

It was Bram, the family's patriarch, who touched his torch to the prepared mound on which his grandson's body lay.

We mourned as sparks and ash rose, caught by the cliffside wind, leaving a flickering trail behind them as they were led down to the sea below.

Chapter Eleven

"We should prepare ourselves for the worst - fortify the wards, and move everyone into Drumcliff," a Druid of about fifty, who was not a resident of Drumcliff, was voicing to the assembly of Druid masters.

Two and a half weeks after Cian's funeral, we had gathered at the request of the High Council in order to discuss the events of Ben Bulben. The presiding members of each watch group were present.

Our discussion focused upon the potential repercussions of the rifting Bulben Silver, which had permitted an unprecedented, and diverse, number of Sidhe into our world. Furthermore, it was hoped that the gathering of many, with a wide variety of skill, talent, and insight, might enable us to discern how it was that Maurelle had managed to escape her highly warded prison.

"At this time, we do not know if that is necessary. We have had no word from the other Watches that would support anything further having occurred. To date, the strangest report we have received was from a small village here in Ireland. They purported to have a Nuckelavee riding about. We sent two of Drumcliff's best to determine if the claims were valid, but neither Darragh nor Gairnan were able to find any evidence of the creature's existence," Ewan, Bram's second oldest son related.

Darragh and Gair were not present to add their own testimony to Ewan's, as they had returned to Killiney to grieve in the familiarity of their own home.

"Yes, but the very fact that there was a rumor at all should serve as a warning to us that something is not right. There has not been a single report, or even rumor, of Nuckelavee being in our midst for centuries," the fifty year old Druid countered. "Furthermore, we have no means by which to attribute the escape of one of the higher Fae from wards created by Bramwyll. Containment wards failing should be reason enough for all of us to exercise extra precaution. It would be foolish to ignore what is so blatantly happening before us. We have strength in numbers. The Watches should be banded together before it is too late for us to do so."

Bram sat silently at the head of the chamber, his fingers steepled before his mouth as he heard and pondered all of the points presented by our congregation. He had said very little throughout the meeting's run, and by turn, the conversation had done little more than repeat all of the same concerns over, and over again. It had been this way for most of the day before Bram finally cleared his throat and decided to speak.

"Gentlemen, the same distress fills us all. Those who are uneasy about the safety of your families are more than welcome to gather them in Drumcliff." This admission brought many nods of approval from the men in the crowd. "However," Bram interjected, "those of you without familial dependants, or those of you who are comfortable doing so, I would strongly encourage you to remain at your posts until we are better able to ascertain the severity of the situation." This made some shift uncomfortably. Bram had posed a direct conflict between their senses of duty and self-preservation.

"In the mean time," Bram continued, "I will be leaving directly for France in hopes of discovering how it was that Maurelle removed herself from my wards. If none of you object, Daine Dalton will be accompanying me." He looked over the group of amassed Druids for signs of disapproval. His gaze lingered briefly upon my face until I gave my assent before it moved on to the others.

When no one opposed his proposal, he stood up abruptly. His heavy wooden chair squeaked in protest at his quick removal from its seat. "Very well, in my absence I appoint Braesal to fill my seat in the High Council." He nodded to his son, who nodded back in acknowledgement. Bram then strode promptly from the room.

I extradited myself from our group as quickly as I could manage, moving through the castle randomly, searching all of Bram's usual resorts. I found him in the final library that I came to, the one that contained the oldest reference that the Druid possessed. Bram stood in the center, bent over the room's only table. He was reading a yellowed scroll of leather, his lips moving soundlessly as his eyes moved over the ancient words. I entered the room, and came to a stop opposite of his studiously bowed frame.

"Get your things, Lad, we will be leaving within the hour," Bram uttered as he continued his search.

I was frustrated. There were so many things that I wanted to ask him, but, being unable to articulate anything, I simply turned away and went hastily to my room to gather my things.

My apartment had taken on an air of reverence. Neither Gair nor I had slept in our room since the night before Cian and I had left for Ben Bulben. I stood in our common room, looking over the living space to Cian's chamber's doorway. Part of me fully expected Cian to emerge from his room, text in hand, and give me another discourse on the finer pleasures of Miss Rosie Calhoun.

I breathed deeply; it still smelled of him here.

I crossed the sitting area to my own room and found it stagnant and lifeless. I sighed heavily as I entered - too many now sad memories accompanied this place.

In my wardrobe I found my leather riding packs. I did not know by what means we would be traveling, but decided that it would be best to travel as lightly as possible. I stuffed a few items of clothing in to the bags, my daggers, and the book that I was in the process of reading weeks ago. As a second thought, I also brought out all of the money that I had stored away in a small pouch, and stuffed it into the bottom of my bag. If it came to it, I would buy what ever else I absolutely needed.

I left my room and apartment without a single look back, shutting the heavy wooden door firmly behind me, feeling my skin prickle in recognition of the wards. It was a strangely reassuring sensation in a time of so much possibility. Either things would continue as they had thus far, or they would become strikingly different.

I made my way back to the library where I had left Bram. At first glance, I did not think that he was any longer there. I hesitated briefly beside library's entrance before turning to resume my search elsewhere. A soft rustling prompted me to enter the dim and cold room.

I approached the littered table, noticing Bram slumped over on the floor as his hands cradled his wizened head.

"Bram!" I rounded the table and crouched down beside him. I tilted his head back, fearing the worst. I found his eyes reddened and tearful.

"I have no inclination as to how it was possible, Daine. I made those wards myself. They were unbreakable and irreversible to any but me. And now . . . now, I no longer possess the answers or explanations to anything. And they are all depending on me!" he shouted as he hit the shelf beside him, causing all of the books which it had been supporting to crash to the floor.

He looked directly into my eyes, his were vulnerable, "What's worse, is that I do not know how to protect them. And Cian ..." He shook is head tragically. His hand lifted to clamp tightly on my shoulder, "I fear for you boy. Run. Run away from all of this as rapidly as you may. Take Brigid, and hide away with her. Have a chance at happiness - even if it is only for a moment. Any chance at happiness is worth any and all sacrifice to possess it."

I looked at my care worn friend and felt nothing but a heart-wrenching pity. He took responsibility for the survival of the entire human race upon himself. "Bram," I said to him placing my own strong hand on his somewhat feeble shoulder, "you are not alone. We will find the Sword. We will ensure that no Sidhe will ever claim the earth - ever."

My assurances seemed to make him a little less burdened. I decided to lighten the mood further. I offered him a large smile as I added, "And, considering how long I've thus far had to wait, I think it best that you not tempt me with running away with Brigid."

I clapped his shoulder once, shaking him lightly in an effort to lighten his mood enough that he might be able to simply move forward. "No one knows how everything will unfold, and no matter how much it seems so, nothing is impossible. Now, come," I stood and used my right hand to clasp his and lifted him to his feet, "we have traveling to attend to."

He dusted himself off. "Yes, it is high time that we were off." He gave me a curt nod, and strode past me and into the hallway.

I was surprised when he did not stop at his rooms. Instead, he went straight to the stables where we found his and my own horses saddled and waiting. Liam sat astride his horse. He would be accompanying us to Sligo, and then would return with our horses once our arrangements had been made. Mounting up, we trotted out behind Bram. The gates of the castle opened, and Bram's horse immediately took off in a gallop. Liam and I invoked the wind in order catch up with the already far ahead Bram.

Bram brought his horse to a canter just outside of town, only seconds before a cart loaded with barrels rounded the bend ahead of us. It was now night and most of the town had closed its doors for the evening. All the same, we rode purposefully through Sligo before Bram dismounted his horse in front of a small sea-worn office on the docks. Liam and I waited outside. We did not wait long however, before Bram reemerged with a time hardened sailor trailing closely behind him.

"Come Daine, it is time for us to go," Bram told me as he passed.

Liam dismounted, and stood waiting beside my horse. I swung my leg over the saddle and allowed my feet to fall to the ground. I placed my reins into Liam's hand, patting a fond farewell to my horse, before I loosed my leather packs from where they had been strapped behind the saddle. I took off in a sprint, following the direction I had seen Bram and his companion heading. I found them already on board a small single mast skiff preparing to make sail.

"I thank ye much, Mister Macardle, for yer most generous payment," Seamus, the captain of *Helena's Light* said in a gruff Irish accent as we were readying the sail.

Bram only briefly acknowledged the old captain's gratitude before returning to his preparations. Covertly, he invoked the wind and immediately the sail was filled. We were all taken off guard as the boat leapt forward, eager to cut through the water as a knife through warm butter. We sped through the night, making our way around the southern coasts of Ireland. We did not slow until just before dawn, soon coming to a complete stop beside a small and clearly private landing.

The land beyond the coast was untouched aside from a simple path that leisured its way up a gently sloping hill sheltered by trees. I knew at once exactly where we were, and smiled at the thought. Bram had brought us to the Macardles' home in Killiney. My heart jumped in anticipation of seeing Brigid.

Bram and I quickly left the boat, feeling slightly off balance from a night spent sailing as we walked. The favorable breeze continued to blow, so fortuitously shifting direction in order to carry our grizzled captain back home to Sligo.

We walked hastily in the night's dim but faintly growing light, Bram in the lead and I bringing up the rear. The dawn was growing before us just over the hill.

Bram unexpectedly stopped, and I stumbled clumsily into his back.

"Wait," he held his hand out in a motion of stopping.

We remained still, listening and feeling intently for anything that was amiss. Bram's suspicion pushed aside all of my excitement, and allowed me to sense what it was that he had felt too. Everything was still and static, almost as though it was locked away deep inside of something dark and impenetrable. We heard nothing. Not a breeze rustling in the trees as it came off the sea, nor any birds scavenging in the winter morning. Not even a frost had gathered here.

The earth that gave us our first inarticulate warning, telling us that something was most definitely wrong here. The wind shifted, blowing down the hill and the path toward us. Our nostrils filled with the stench of acrid smoke.

My eyes widened, as I finally realized that the dawn's light upon the crest of the hill was not the dawn at all, but fire's light. I rushed past Bram and broke into a wild sprint, frantic to make my way toward the Macardles' home. I ran, as feelings of dread grew heavily with every pounding heartbeat. I broke through the edge of the trees, and gasped. My very lungs seemed to collapse, and I found it nearly impossible to regain the ability to breathe again.

I found misshapen devastation, now charred and smoking and in some areas still burning. I found the remnants of Darragh Macardle's magnificent home. I was entirely frozen, unable to do any more than begin swallowing gulps of smoked clogged air. My eyes began to water, from emotion or the hovering smoky air I didn't know.

Bram arrived only seconds after myself, and took a horrified step backward upon realizing what he was seeing. There was nothing left but discordant rubble. He fell to his knees, and with a trembling hand, reached for the ash flecked earth. He gently placed his palm on the ground and fanned his fingers as wide as they could spread. "Lower yourself, Daine, the air is slightly more breathable down here," Bram said weakly.

I looked down at him, and soundlessly did as I was told. It was a battle not to lash out at him when every instinct I had was demanding that I rush down there and look for Brigid, not kneel passively in the dirt. Still, I could not begrudge him, and placed my palm upon the soil. I was instantly overwhelmed by the warnings of the earth. Something unnatural had been here. The earth herself felt defiled where its footsteps had fallen.

Darkness crashed into my brain, permeated by sharp outbursts of emotion - terror, pride, horror, and grief - all locked away inside of the dust at our fingertips.

I felt my gut twist with worry in response.

"Bram, there is something not right about this." I told him while I remained crouched with my hand pressed into the earth. My eyes refused to open by choice. I fought to breathe steadily and evenly.

"Yes, the Sidhe have been here; though it appears that several days have passed since their coming." Bram stared at the ground, also unwilling to acknowledge the tragedy sprawled out before him.

"But, there is something more Bram. It almost feels like . . . I don't know . . . as though there was a human who was willingly working alongside the Sidhe." I opened my eyes to look at Bram's now standing frame. I remained crouched, seeking for more from the earth as I continued to speak. "I do not recall having learned of humans aiding the Fae of their own volition." I swallowed and looked across the still smoldering ruins, "but, as contrary as it may seem, that is exactly what I am sensing. Whoever it was, wanted to be here and wanted to be a part of this." I told him softly though my voice was now roughened from the smoke.

I was now fighting to restrain the panic that threatened to smother me, as well as the smoke which promised to do the same. I found it strange that there had been no one, until us, to disturb the scene. *Where were the people of the town?* I thought. If I had seen a massive pillar of smoke and possibly the glow of flames anywhere in the approximation my neighbors' homes, I would have investigated it immediately. As counter-intuitive as it was, there was not a single indication anywhere of that having happened.

The earth, although unable to express herself as humans do, retains vast stores of information about past events. One just needed to know how to read and understand it to gain access. What you found there was the truth, as a thing incapable of deceit cannot be made of anything else.

I noted that not even a single breeze had been permitted to interrupt the consumption of the family's home and property. The smoke hovered strangely in place, like dark lofty clouds that were unable to lift or remove themselves. They just grew and remained. The entire situation made the both of us extremely uneasy. We'd just found what would be the future of our world if we did not find a way to stop it.

Bram refused to look again at what was left of his son's home. He continued to look down at me, shifting in place, "Are you certain, Daine? I was not able to ascertain as much from my own interpretations. Although I confess that I may not be the best of judges at present, as my emotions have rendered me . . . compromised," Bram admitted shamefully.

I stood slowly to face him, "Yes, Bram, I am sure. It scares the hell out of me."

We stood there a few moments longer, unsure about what we should to do next. Our family could be down there, but it could also very well be a trap. The fact that a human was willingly working with the Fae, without any coercion or glamour used by the Sidhe, was unheard of and called for much cause for alarm. It baffled me to think what could have possibly motivated any individual to do so. The Fae's promises were all false, and any reasonable human, capable of their own thought, would be able to know as much.

I looked at Bram. His eyes were now unabashedly reddened and watering as well. I turned my face again to the destruction. Nothing was left but massive piles of entirely blackened stones, and some random bits of devastation that were still burning days after the incident – whatever that was.

"Bram, I have to find Brigid," I said to him without turning to face him. My eyes were widely surveying the hazy landscape for any signs of life. By the shore I thought there had been birds, but here, there was nothing.

I did not wait for his approval, but sprang forward, wanting to waste no further time in finding her or her family. The earth had told me that there had been none to come or go with the exception of the Fae and its human companion. If that were true, it meant that Brigid and her family were buried somewhere in this mess. I held to a spark of hope that somehow they'd survived, despite a sense of foreboding that said they had not.

I began to call out her name hoarsely as I stumbled my way through the smoke. It was thicker here around what had once been the house and its outbuildings, hovering like a shroud about the entire property. I stretched my mind, searching for anything that might be living. Again, I was met with nothing.

I moved to the closest pile of debris and began to rifle through it. The possibility of having lost Brigid forever was causing a sickening ball to expand in my gut. I found nothing in the mound I was currently working on, and moved a few feet over to begin desperately working on the next. I worked frantically for what seemed an eternity. My fingers cracked and bled as I tore into the fractured stones, digging tirelessly, searching for any sign of life . . . and hope. When I began making choking noises, I knew that I needed to move from the smoke or I might soon suffocate.

I felt a firm hand take my elbow. I looked first at the hand and followed it up until I found Bram's face. His was somber as he began to shake his head sadly.

Without a word I knew.

Bram moved away, making his way back toward the hill and away from the congealing smoke. I followed him with my eyes downcast, my handkerchief held over my mouth and nose as I stumbled over the obscured ash and soot covered ground. We made it to the hill, and both of us fell to ground.

On my knees, I began to sob; my upper body crumpling forward so that my forearms supported my body on the soot covered ground. I remained that way until there was nothing left inside of me to express. I was a dry and empty river. I mourned not only the woman who would have soon been my wife and the mother of my unborn children, but also the entire family who had made me one of their own. I had lost a father, mother, brothers and sisters – an entire family that I cherished as blood.

I had become so lost in my grief, that I had entirely forgotten I was not alone. I raised my head from my hands, and found Bram just over the crest of the hill, staring blankly into the sea. He looked as bedraggled as I felt. His soot covered face was streaked by trails of tears, and his impeccable clothing was now stained varying shades of gray. Even his beard had turned to the ugly color of ash. I couldn't look at him any longer, and made a careful study of my cracked hands - of the dried blood that was obscured and dirtied by grime.

"They are all there." He gestured unspecifically behind him toward the ruined estate. "They have been lain out together. I cannot figure out by what … party," he coughed the word, "… most of them died. Had you given Brigid a ring?"

I felt sick inside, and had to force myself to speak. "Yes. I did."

Bram nodded, and with a cracking voice managed to barely get out, "And, did she wear it around her neck?"

I couldn't speak, I knew that whatever it was Bram was about to reveal was going to be something I wasn't going to like learning.

He choked on a sob, trying to compose himself enough to tell me, "She was the fortunate one." His turned to me, his brilliant green eyes made all the more so by his tears, "She was killed by fire."

I felt as though I had had the wind knocked out of me. I had expected him to deliver such a blow, but I was not fully prepared for it. No one ever could be. In that very moment, I believe I felt it as my heart broke into jagged pieces. I then realized what Bram had inferred, and I asked him quietly, "And, the others?"

He cleared his throat, and looked down at his right hand where he was fidgeting with his sapphire ring. He cleared his throat a second time and began, "The others appear to have been completely . . . sucked dry." He now chose to turn and stare directly into my eyes, "That is the most accurate way that I am able to describe them. There is nothing left to them but their shriveled remains, devoid of all resemblance. I," he looked at the ground and shook his head a bit before returning his gaze to my own, "I have never seen anything so appalling. They were relinquished of their life forces in a most horrifying manner, and were then reverently laid upon the ground in their birth order. All, but Ayda - her body was not with the others."

I had to swallow a fragment of my heart before I was able to speak. The idea of the deaths the Macardles must have endured wounded me even deeper still. For the first time, I began to feel angry. Anger soon turned to rage and then a scorching fury.

"Let's go and find her then." Without waiting for Bram's direction, I reached inside of myself and called the wind. I felt a stirring deep inside, the energy of the earth being pulled up through the burned soil beneath my feet. Without preamble, a forcefully blustering wind rushed off the sea, swooping up the hill, and shrieked past Bram and I as it gained force and speed and surged toward the Macardle's smoke obscured estate.

The smoke and wind clashed, the wind rebuffed.

The smoke remained unmoved by the wind, strange and unnatural in the wake of such strength against it. However, as I directed, the wind began to circle the perimeter of the property, again gaining speed as it constricted, closing in against the smoky front. Soon, the smoke and wind were beginning to spiral, escalating higher and higher until it appeared as though a massive tornado hovered precisely over what had been the Macardles' home. The wind whipped the smoke upward, dispersing it as it carried it higher into the atmosphere.

The sky was overcast, and rain began to fall heavily upon the earth. With the air now clear I breathed in deeply in an effort to clear my lungs of the soot that had collected inside of them. I coughed heartily, and began to feel whatever had decided to lodge itself in my breathing ways loosen. The rain was an equally welcome addition as it began to wash my dirty hands and face.

Bram was speechless.

I did not know what was crossing his mind, but I did not ponder upon it long. I was still incensed, and as soon as the wind had cleared the last of the smoke I ran headlong through the pouring rain, once more into the wreckage. I did not know exactly where Bram had been searching, so I went to the closest area that I had not yet been to. Bram did not accompany me, and so I searched recklessly alone.

I did not have to look long.

I found the Macardles' bodies just as Bram had described them. To the far left was what I believe could only be Darragh laid alongside his wife, and followed by Gair and the rest of their children. Bram's description had been perfectly apt. Their bodies now resembled shriveled grapes. Even their bones had taken on a different state, where if they existed at all, it was surely only in a powdered form.

I found myself involuntarily gagging in disgust when I saw the collapsed and shriveled faces of my adoptive family. Puckered, unnaturally large gaping holes remained where their eyes, noses, and mouths had once been.

My eyes then found the remains of my beautiful Brigid.

I had avoided looking at her despite her place in the center of her family's lineup. Her body was burned beyond recognition, but mercifully lacking the collapsed and shriveled characteristics of her family. Only a simple diamond ring, which had melted into her flesh as she'd burned, provided the only recognizable characteristic of familiarity.

She was gone, and I turned away from the tragic demise of the Macardle family as my body sickly purged itself of everything that could be found be rid of. I allowed myself a moment to steady myself, with my head lowered almost to the height of my knees as I tried to regain my composure. The stench of the place was horrendous, death, burned flesh, and something sulfuric in nature. I found myself retching again.

I tried to inhale, but couldn't without feeling that I was being smothered in rot. I scrambled away as quickly as I could manage through the now slippery ashen mud, blinded as my eyes watered profusely from both being sick and the smell, meddled with the heavily falling rain.

I looked up through my tears to see Bram making his way around the burned and mud-covered landscape, moving for me, his eyes resembling glowing emeralds as he neared. He immediately reached down and pulled me to my feet, my skin feeling charged where he touched my arm as he pulled me up.

He looked beyond me, toward the bodies of his son and grandchildren. I could feel his readiness, charging and electrifying the air between us. I immediately turned to face the direction he faced, preparing myself for the worst.

We stood, side by side, peering into the trees that were just beyond the Macardles' remains. Nothing appeared, the rain continued to fall extensively upon us, but we remained fixed in our positions, waiting and listening for what, I did not know. Just as I was beginning to consider letting my guard waiver, was the exact moment that something did.

It was worse than I had expected. I was quickly beginning to realize that legends just might be long forgotten truths. I held my breath as the Nuckelavee pushed its way through the trees, filling the air with the most terrible odor I could have ever imagined. The ground withered with its every step, and every bit of verdant foliage began to instantly rot the moment he, for it clearly was a he, passed by.

The beast was truly a terrible sight. Upon the back of what could have once been the frame of a great horse, sat a creature with no legs. Its arms were long and sinuous, stretching almost down to the ground with fingers that resembled claws more than human appendages. The torso led up to a sickly skinny neck that was unable to hold up a head that was at least three times bigger than that of a man's.

Because of the inadequate neck, the creature's head lolled, from side to side as it walked toward us. It smiled a nasty grin with a mouth that was similar to that of its steed. It had no hair, as it had not a single strip of skin upon its body. Reddened and raw infected muscles and tendons pulled and flexed to our plain sight; made all the worse by yellow veins through which its black blood flowed. The poor creature that served as its mount suffered a similar appearance.

Every instinct was telling me to run from the terrible beast, that is, until I saw that one of its scissor like hands held the limp body of Ayda in its grasp. It dragged her along the ground, much like a child would with a rag doll. Her body was still partially covered by a ragged, dirty, and tattered dress. I held my ground, feeling again as my own inner beast raged at the atrocities that had been done. That such a base creature should dare to touch even a single hair on her head, sent me beyond what I was able to contain.

I searched Ayda through the pouring rain, looking for any sign that she might still be alive. I prayed that she was. Under my heightened scrutiny, I noticed that both the Nuckelavee and Ayda seemed to be shielded by some invisible means, so as to not be bothered by the rain.

"Release your hold on the child!" Bram's eyes flared, and I felt the air begin to vibrate with his words.

A painful sounding laugh whined from the porcine-like jaws of the overly large head. It was followed by a scraping, guttural sound as the Nuckelavee attempted to speak, "Silly human. Think to challenge th'Nuckelavee. I crush y'bones, drink y'innards, all th'while, you still living." The creature then produced a smile full of jagged, swine like teeth.

Bram was about to speak but I stepped before him before he could counter. I spoke low, my own eyes flashing murderous retribution at the creature as I commanded it, "Let her go now, or I will personally ensure you a more painful death than you will already be receiving." I seethed with anger and adrenaline that fueled my body for the upcoming battle.

Again, the Nuckelavee attempted what can only be described as a laugh, filling the air with foul venomous breath. It lifted Ayda to its snout and smelled her skin, then ran a long sore covered tongue over her bare neck and arms. Her chest rose and fell ever so faintly in an effort to live. My skin crawled at the sight of such befoulment.

I called forth fire. It shot forth from the trees behind the Nuckelavee, and hit the creature with full force in the back of his upright torso. The Nuckelavee stumbled forward, catching itself with one hand and the horse's knees. I realized that the leg-less rider was somehow fused to the actual back of the horse, making them one in body and mind.

I did not hesitate before another blast of fire issued forth from the trees to land again on the torso's back. The smell of the creature's slightly charred flesh tangled with its already acrid reek, made it so that Bram and I had to fight not to choke.

The Nuckelavee emitted a snarling growl as it attempted to use its overly long arms to help right itself. It released Ayda, and left her in a crumpled heap as it again began to stand.

Fire came from behind me this time to hit the beast square in the chest. It stumbled a few paces away, its raw muscled chest smoking from the blast. No very serious damage had been done by the fire. If both Darragh and Gair had succumbed to the Nuckelavee, then it was without question that Bram and I were in for a very difficult fight.

A gross infection began to seep from the sores in the creature's body. It dripped onto the ground as it pooled around its feet. Everything living thing that had been grass, flowers, or brush, dried and withered instantaneously as the infection touched them. It moved out and away from its creator, making its way toward us.

I was oblivious to anything but the Nuckelavee, watching its every move in an effort to not be caught off guard. I was unsure of just how I was going to fight it, much less destroy it. The ooze that was moving toward me was an obstacle that I was defenseless against. It was a consolation that in the very least, I had been an adequate distraction. Out of the corner of my eye I saw Bram lifting Ayda and carrying her silently away. I had not even known that he had left me.

The Nuckelavee had not either.

I stepped toward it, my inner, ancient beast shining visibly through my eyes. I decided to try something a bit more continuous than a single blast. I extended my hands and called forth both wind and fire. They shot forward from behind me, merging together to envelop the Nuckelavee in a swirling, bellowing, pillar of flames. This seemed to have more of an effect on the creature. It howled and growled as nearly every surface of its bare tissue was unceasingly burned. It moved toward me, and stopped as the fire moved with it. Distracted by the current assault, its infection stopped moving forward and seeped into the earth, killing the soil as it went, but losing its ability to any longer be a threat.

The fire and wind that surrounded the Nuckelavee not only singed its flesh, but also caused that the barrier that had existed between the Nuckelavee and the rain to no longer be available. In one massive leap, the creature jumped from the pillar. The wind and fire had no way to track such an immense change of place that they simply ceased to be. However, as the rain fell upon the beast, it shrieked in pain. The moisture was acid upon its tissues. Every drop caused the already burned flesh to sizzle and melt away. The creature charged into the trees, seeking shelter from the rain.

With a flick of my hand, I caused the earth to rise in a wall that would prevent the Nuckelavee from escaping. It thrashed and spun, fighting a foe that it could not possibly defeat as the rain fell unabashed by its challenger. Sensing the opportunity to gain the advantage, I caused the earth to open in a massive pit beneath the Nuckelavee's feet. It fell helplessly, flesh melting away beneath the anathema of rain drops. Undaunted, I called water, both from the ground and from the sky.

Groundwater sprang from the ground, filling the cavity with fresh flowing water. Smoke billowed from its mouth, as the Nuckelavee's skin began to melt from its bones in contact with the water that continued to rise around it. The rain increased in intensity, falling so rapidly that it was nearly impossible to see as it cascaded down my face. The Nuckelavee's guttural screams of pain chilled me to the core, as I blindly moved to find higher ground.

In a matter of moments, the hole was filled. A deformed disintegrating skeleton swirled around its floor. I moved forward toward the abyss, willing the water to cease and move away. Again, it did so immediately. The spring that only seconds before had served as a spout for the water, now served as a drain. The rain stopped falling, leaving the sky dark and cloudy as it waited for its cue to again begin to weep.

By the time I had walked to the edge of the Nuckelavee's doom, I was met with an empty chasm save for the last remains of the Nuckelavee stuck to the muddy floor. As soon as I'd thought it, fire appeared on the skeleton of the beast, licking its bones with an intense affection. It retained none of the Fae resilience, and quickly surrendered its remaining elements to the grave. When not even its ashes remained, I stepped away from the pit's edge, and watched as the earth re-interred all that had ever rested in its cool and dark embrace.

I looked across the clearing to find Bram holding Ayda protectively in his arms. From the look on his face, I could see that somehow, despite it all, she was still alive.

Still feeling strong, I trudged to where the bodies of the Macardles had been so gently placed. I could not understand why a creature such as a Nuckelavee would have paid them such kind regard. The earth was still lush and green under them, despite a slight gray ash that had fallen.

Again, I invoked the earth, and watched on sadly as it tenderly buried the family together within its depths. When there was no evidence of their final resting place, the ground again looking as though it were simply a grass covered meadow dusted with ash, I turned away. I did not wish to leave any more of myself with them than what I had already allowed to be buried along with them. I walked purposefully to where Bram and Ayda were waiting.

Ayda looked terrible; her face a swollen mess of bruises and scrapes, the same being said for the blotchy skin that I could see around her shredded dress. I held my breath when I had to verify from Bram that she was truly alive.

"Just barely," came his quiet response. He cradled his favorite grandchild to his chest, and with his eyes closed, gently rocked her while muttering the spell for healing.

I watched them silently. I was edgy, my senses still heightened from the fight. The slightest patter of rain on the leaves above, or a rustle through the grass, had me whirling to face a new danger.

After a time, it was I who told Bram that we should move away from here, lest any other Fae come to check on their brother who was now dead, as far as I could tell. He readily agreed to the suggestion. Leaving the two of them briefly beside the trees, I walked to the earth that had been touched by the infection of the Nuckelavee, and did the best I could to repair the damage that had been done to her fertile soil.

I then returned and escorted Bram and Ayda to the dock. Bram carried his granddaughter, refusing all of my repeated offers to help. A small boat was still tied to the pier, waiting for to be taken to sea. Quickly, I untied the dingy, and again invoked the wind to carry us away from this place.

We tied up in Dublin. It was now mid-afternoon, and the streets, wharf, and city were in full business swing. Bram had removed his coat to cover Ayda as he carried her directly to a coach that was waiting for hire. We went to "The Rusted Wardrobe" – the very same inn we had visited upon first arriving in Dublin eight years earlier.

When we arrived, Bram went straight inside, pausing only to tell me to call for a doctor. I retained the carriage and went straightway to the closest doctor's home. At first inspection of myself, the doctor seemed disinclined to offer his services to one as bedraggled as I. However, upon producing my purse full of golden coins, and receiving a thorough cursing, he was more than willing to cut his afternoon tea short in order to come to our aid.

I found Bram in the same room we had occupied before, though the tubs had been removed and in their place now laid an opulent bed. In the midst of which was Ayda. She wore a clean shift under the several down blankets which covered her.

At the age of twenty she was in the full blossom of her womanhood, though I had never seen her as more than the pesky twelve year old sibling of the woman that I loved. Obviously, at present, Ayda was not a true representation of herself. Her dark curly hair was a matted and lifeless heap as it clung to her damp face and shoulders. Her skin was pallid, her lips colorless, and her chest rose and fell with labored silent breaths. Her entire body was a mangled mess of swollen and ugly bruises which were only augmented by painful looking cuts, with raw slightly greenish tinted edges. I was sure those could have only come at the hand of the Nuckelavee's ugly taloned fingers.

As I looked over she who was the last of her bloodline and her broken body, I vowed that I would always do everything I could to protect and care for her. I owed her father, mother, and siblings as much – let alone her grandfather.

The doctor took a single look at Ayda, and made an involuntarily audible gasp. He was unprepared for her battered state despite my efforts to thoroughly describe her condition to him as we made our way to the inn. The middle-aged Irish man looked at me quickly, his eyes wide enough to see much of the whites of his eyes. I noticed his hesitation and the way he seemed to have already dismissed his own capacity to help her.

I would have none of it. I gave him a look of menace which had him scurrying off immediately to attend to what he'd been procured to do. After looking over Ayda's many injuries, the doctor shook his head silently and began studiously digging in his medical bag for bought time.

I stood by the door, unsure as to whether I should remain in the room or situate myself elsewhere. The doctor was still shuffling through his possessions and muttering inarticulately when Bram strode across the small room's wooden floor to where I stood leaning against the door.

"Daine," Bram said with a voice so low the doctor would not be able to hear it, "you are free to go. You exhausted much today. I will stay and look over the doctor and Ayda. As you might have already guessed, this is all for the sake of appearances. When you return, please bring with you some cloves and fennel. We will then begin the incantation to begin Ayda's healing." He then left me and hastened to Ayda's bedside.

Being clearly dismissed, I left the room and quietly shut the door behind me. As an added precaution, I hastily laid protective runes about the room's doorway and hallway to provide an added measure of protection while I was away. I then left the inn to find what Bram had requested, something substantial to feed myself, and then a room in a bathhouse in which I could clean the remaining ash and mud off of myself before returning to Bram and Ayda.

None of us needed any further reminders.

The memory of the ruined Macardle home, family, and most especially Brigid, was seared into my mind. It weighed heavily upon my heart and I was sure, would eventually crush me. How merciful Bram had been in giving me a moment to openly mourn in privacy, even if he himself was not aware of his deeply sympathetic gesture.

Chapter Twelve

We remained in Dublin for a little over a month. During which time we heard nothing of alarm from the Druids at Drumcliff. Bram was entirely occupied with tending to Ayda, and this left me with nothing more to occupy myself with than to think.

In those days, my thoughts drifted frequently to the deaths of the Macardle family. I was sure that Maurelle had most assuredly sent the Nuckelavee. After all, she had blatantly warned Bram to keep his family close – a warning that he had failed to heed.

I noticed my first Druidic mark shortly after I had left Bram and Ayda in the inn on that first day. It was a black swirling line on my left shoulder blade, punctuated by traces of red. Druidic marks did not include red, and so I did not mention mine to anyone - despite feeling a sense of pride that I had managed to earn one.

After our initial shock and worry over Ayda, we found that most of her injuries were superficial. However, we took every precaution to ensure her safety. Our ministrations paid off, and it was not long before Ayda began to improve. At one month to the day of her rescue, Bram and I knew that it was time to finally make our way to Strasbourg. And, although I did not like the idea, Bram determined that Ayda would indefinitely be accompanying us there.

As we pushed away from the dock aboard a large steam ship bound for Le Havre, France, I noticed the first signs of anticipation and excitement blossoming in my chest. It had been nearly nine years since I had last seen my parents. The very prospect of returning to my boyhood home and family brought me much comfort in the wake of having lost the opportunity to create one of my own. Brigid had been gone for a month, but I still bore her loss most painfully. Rather than think of her, I tried to focus on caring for what I did have, Bram, Ayda, and my own parents. Not to mention, I had a purpose – to discover how Maurelle had escaped, and to find that damnable Sword of Light.

Bram was terrified that anything might happen to Ayda - something that would remove all traces of Darragh from this world forever. And so he minded her much like a doting new mother. He had no mind or occupation that did not involve her and her happiness, near or distant. Because of this, he left most of the travel arrangements and daily affairs to me; trusting in my inexperience to ensure that everything was attended to in an efficient manner.

"Daine, you are a Master now, and I hardly more then an increasingly old man." He told me one night as we sat beside Ayda's sick bed. He said nothing more, but I knew that he was passing the responsibility of leading the war between humanity and the Fae on to me. I felt burdened, and hoped to God that I would not be left alone in this when I knew so little.

We made the crossing within a few days. I used the same travel template Bram had done when we left France for Dublin. The very moment my foot stepped onto the solid ground of Strasbourg's piers, I knew I was too impatient to wait for our trunks. I gave notice as to where they should be delivered, and procured a coach to take us promptly to my parent's cottage. After a month of confinement and subsequent travel, neither Bram nor Ayda were overly eager to once again remain sedentary – for any length of time. Still, my insistence paid off, and with little coercion needed, they both sat down on the hard seats of the carriage.

Ayda sat across from me, inspecting me with amused bright emerald eyes, "Grandad, I think that Daine might be contemplating racing the horses home." She smiled and sniggered at my fidgeting form as my fingers stopped mid-thrum upon my leg.

I leaned forward, and admitted, "You're right, I am."
Without another word, I leapt out of the carriage and ran directly
across a clearing of wild grasses, the winter wind blowing
through my hair in warm welcome. As soon as the carriage had
passed from my view upon the road, along with the sound of
mirthful laughter within, I used the same welcoming breeze to
carry me to my parent's cottage.

Just ahead, through the trees and the bramble, I could see
my father's shop. It was early January; a light dusting of snow
had frosted the ground and winterized plant life. They crunched
under my feet as I ran. I smiled and chuckled to myself, unable
to contain my relief and joy a moment longer. The trees gave
way to brush and grass, and I pushed easily through the last of it
and into the clearing that held my parent's cottage, my mother's
garden, and my father's barn.

All of it was completely undisturbed. The frozen ground
did not indicate a single footfall had trodden anywhere on the
property. It was pristine, a perfect picture of home and welcome.
I ran to barn, quickly opening the door and peering inside. My
father's shop looked to be in the midst of multiple projects. I
allowed the door to slam behind me as I crossed over to the
house. The door was locked and I knocked quickly, calling for
both my mother and father.

When neither of them answered, I realized that they had
most likely moved into what had once been Bram's house. I
again took off in a run, taking the well worn path that led to

Bram's. I soon came upon the pond where Bram had taught me to fish, smiling again at the memory of the huge fish we had caught. The magic of the moment, despite the fact that Bram had cheated and used Druidry to be able to hook the beast did not matter. I chuckled at the recollection of it all as the pond disappeared behind me.

Finally, the large manor house came into sight. I ran a little faster and did not slow until I reached the house's massive front door. I hardly ceased my momentum as my hand went to the door latch and made to open it. The door never budged, and I crashed into it. I was completely caught off guard by the impact, surprised that the grand return to home that I had been envisioning these long years did not go as planned.

"Hello?" I called out as I knocked on the door.

No one answered, and so I did the same once again. I stepped back and looked to the chimneys for any signs of smoke. There was none. Again, I stepped up to the door and gave it three solid thumps, "Hello? Maman, Papa, are you here? It's Daine. I have come home!" I pressed my ear to the door, listening for anything to indicate that someone was in fact at home.

After waiting and listening intently for what I felt was long enough, I again stepped away from the door. My brow furrowed as I tried to figure out where my parents might be. I jogged quickly to the drawing room windows and peered in. They remained shuttered and I could not see anything. I ran to the other windows, peering into the library, the office, and the dining room, finding that they all had their coverings still in place. I sprinted to the French doors at the back of the house and found that they too were locked.

I turned my back on Bram's home, and invoking the wind, I again ran back to my parent's cottage. The hired coach had come and gone; the frost covered ground was now marred by the horse's footprints and the carriage's wheels. Ayda stood beside the cottage's front door. Her face was white despite the cold winter air, and her eyes scanned the property lines searching for something. Seeing me, she rushed forward, and I slowed to a brisk walking pace. Her hands went straight to my shoulders in an effort to stop me.

"Daine, I . . . I . . ." She looked away from my eyes, her own betraying her fear as they welled with tears. "Just stay here, wait here for Grandad," her lilting voice implored me.

I looked past her to the open door of my parent's stone cottage. A ball of bile hardened in my stomach as I looked down at Ayda's face, she was worrying her bottom lip with her teeth as she stood firmly, doubting that she would be able to hold me where we stood if I chose to ignore her request.

The very fact that Bram was doing something inside of my house that Ayda did not want me to see, sent warning bells sounding off in my head. I told her I was sorry as I brushed past her. I bounded up the stone steps and passed through the front door into a scene of complete destruction. The well used dining table was smashed to pieces, the chairs totally unrecognizable.

My mother's cupboard next to her stove was demolished; her dishes, glasses, and cookware broken and shattered on the floor. Mother's drapes were shredded, the windows behind ruined.

The entire house was shrouded in shadow.

"Daine," Bram called from my parent's bedroom, his voice hoarse but still commanding, "Do not enter any farther. Leave the house immediately, and wait for me outside with Ayda."

Fear coursed through my body as my heart began to hammer in my chest more heavily than I had ever experienced it. I had to fight to swallow what felt like my very soul trying to escape from my body. I needed to know where my parents were. I needed to know it as badly as I needed air to breathe. Bram knew exactly where they were, and the feeling of terror bubbling through my veins promised that I would not like it when I did.

I stepped over and around the broken furniture, my feet, though trying to be careful, crunched pieces of my mother's dishes underneath my feet. The cottage was small and it was only a matter of a few steps before I rounded the stone mantle, and was standing in the doorway of my parent's bedroom.

At first glance, nothing seemed to be amiss. The room was completely untouched. The bed was still made, and everything was in its place – a book that my father had been reading still rested on the foot of the bed where he'd last left it. My mother loved sunlight, and the drapes here were tied back from the windows to let in as much of winter's warmth and light as possible. The only thing out of place was Bram. He stood at the foot of the bed, his face a mask as he considered the wall next to the door where I stood.

His eyes shot directly to me, "Stop!" His voice thundered and bounced off the plaster and stone walls. He attempted to compel me to listen and obey - no matter if my desires were counter to his words.

I closed my eyes, focused on my Druidic training and skill, and with concentration, unraveled the hold the words had gained over my will. Bram's compulsion had not worked, but the fact that he was attempting to use it to deter me, taking charge once again when for the past few months he had refused it, was a terrible prospect.

He marched toward me furiously, and again used a booming voice he charged me, "Damn you, you insanely stubborn boy! Depart immediately - there is nothing that you will want to encounter here!" His face was red with anger, and if possible, his beard seemed to bristle with his agitation.

I regarded him angrily. The waves of ire rolling off of each of us collided explosively in the empty space that existed between us. These were my parents, and of no relation or concern to him. If I wanted to enter any room in their home it was no business of his. I looked down my nose at him, and for the first time in my life, I pushed past him and into the room. Two impossibly strong hands clamped painfully down on my shoulders and threw me physically through the air and across the dining room. I crashed into the stone and plaster wall opposite the entrance to my parent's room. I fell to my knees, and from the floor looked up at Bram. My eyes glowed with hatred. He still barricaded the door; his eyes daring me to defy him again.

"Bram," I shouted at him, "Let me pass. This is of no concern to you, and I do not wish to harm you." I raised myself from the floor, taking the time to dust the bits of plaster that had fallen on my clothes to the floor.

"I will not protect you in this again, Boy. It would do you well to remember that I have advised you twice to leave this house," Bram warned me with an authoritative voice.

I breathed heavily, my chest markedly rising and falling with every breath. "No," I answered him growlingly.

At the sound of my back hitting the wall, Ayda had come to stand at the entry of the house. "Daine, please, do as he says," her soft voice broke, filing the corners of the dark and destroyed room that was my parent's home as well as my mind. I turned my head to once again look at Bram, despite standing like a sentry over the entrance to the room, his face too held the faintest hint of sadness showing through the cracks of the mask his face had become.

I shivered, feeling the winter's cold for the first time. The ashes from the uncleaned fireplace swirled as a breeze drifted into the room.

I knew that they were dead.

"I'm sorry." I looked from Ayda to Bram. "This is something that neither of you can protect me from." I moved forward, once again crossing over the broken furniture and to the doorway of my parent's room. Bram stepped aside with a nod and I entered the room. I knew exactly where I needed to look, and turned my head to the left as I rounded the threshold. I gasped in disgust at what I found.

The reaction was instantaneous, and the tears and sorrow erupted from my broken spirit in choking sobs. I fell to my knees, my hands reaching for but not daring to touch the feet of my parents.

They had been hung on the wall. Their naked arms and legs held fast by crude spikes of metal.

Their feet were streaked by the stain of blood that had coursed down their torn bodies before merging into a puddle on the wooden floor. Their bodies were naked, and utterly mutilated. Both had been eviscerated with surgical precision, their innards dangled freely from their open abdomens. Their eyes, noses, nipples, and finger and toe nails had all been removed. Large tracts of skin had been partially peeled away from their legs and left to hang over their knees and ankles. The same had been done to their faces.

My father's genitals had been removed; my mother too, had been similarly mutilated. Their teeth were gone, their mouths hung widely agape. Both of their throats had been slit, just below the jaw line, and their tongues pulled through to hang in a final gruesome act. My father was completely unrecognizable, and my mother too, save only for her auburn hair that had been left untouched.

I turned, and vomited on the floor.

I remained that way, hunched over with tears clouding my eyes as I attempted to sob between my body's attempts to disgorge itself. I was racked with pain, and could do nothing but become a slave to my body's reaction of the revolting state my parent's had been reduced to. When my stomach stopped spasming, I dragged myself toward my parent's bed, to lean my head against their quilts that hung over its side. I completely succumbed to the interminable sorrow that I seemed unable to escape.

The light began to grow dim. I sat, unable to think or move, smelling the faint scents of my mother's soap and my father's workshop that lingered in their bedding. Who knew how long they had been gone. Who ever had done this had sealed the house, which all but stopped the natural process of decay. All of this could have happened as early as yesterday, or it could have been as late as six months ago. I exhaled, and again inhaled the final scents, reminders, of my always loving parents.

The air in the room shifted slightly, and I felt two small and gentle hands wrap around my chest. Ayda's body embraced me from behind as she crouched to rest her cheek against my own. "Daine," she whispered softly, "let us leave this place. Your parents' remains may be here, but their spirits fly free elsewhere. Remember them for what they were, and allow them to rest from this world."

I lifted my hand to interlace with hers and nodded somberly. She was right, my parents were no longer here. Even though all that was left of them was this macabre shrine, I knew that whatever part of them still existed was not to be found here.

I accepted her help as I slowly began to stand. I had yet to spare a second glance at my parents' bodies, and I did not offer them one as I forsook their room and came into the smashed kitchen and dining room. I stopped by the front door as something caught my eye. I bent down and removed chunks of wood and glass, discovering my father's rifle lying on the floor. It was not loaded.

I stood with the rifle in my hand, scanning the room. Lodged deeply into the wood of the doorframe was a bloody bullet. *At least they'd tried to put up a fight*, I consoled myself. Ayda came to stand beside me. I propped the rifle against the wall, and allowed her to take me outside. My hand trailed over the bullet hole as I left.

I squinted in the sun after spending countless hours within the tomb that had once been a home. When I could see properly, I noticed that Bram was just coming toward us from my father's workshop. "Nothing inside of his shop has been disturbed. Robert's tools still remain where he left them. Perhaps the two of you would do well to wait there while I conclude our business here?"

What he was offering, was to conduct my parents' funeral.

"No Bram, gather whatever information you deem is necessary. After you have, *I* will light their funeral pyre. But, leave them as they are. I do not want them removed from their present state in the house," I informed him very soberly.

He was surprised that I did not want to displace them from where they so cruelly hung. If I could not have what represented a semblance of what they once were, I did not want any kind of false reminder to exist after them. Even if those were their desecrated physical remains – my parents deserved more than that. I could honor them best by my remembering how they'd lived.

Bram left Ayda and me alone as we made our way to the barn, he himself entering what was left of the home that I had grown up in.

Stepping into my father's workshop was like stepping into a place lost in time. As always, large, beautiful pieces of finished furniture waited along the far wall for pick up; others in various states of completion. Tools still remained close to where they'd most recently worked – looking as though they'd just been set down and their handler would return at any moment to take them up again. It made what was left of my heart hurt.

"This is beautiful!" Ayda said, interrupting my heartbreak, as she ran her hand over the dark finish of an intricately carved wardrobe. "They've never made anything like this at home. Now I see why Da always likes to order his furniture from France. I wonder if we have any of your father's work at home."

"It's more than likely that you do. Bram was always saying how much one of his sons would love specific piece of furniture, and that he would cover all the costs to have it shipped to them. There were quite a few things sent, though I don't know exactly where to. There is also a wide array of pieces up at Bram's house. If you see something that you like. . ."

We looked at awkwardly each other. We had both been caught up in the illusion that her home and family still existed, and that my father was still alive creating beautiful works of art through his trade.

Nervously, Ayda looked at the sawdust covered floor, shifting a bit with her foot before adding, "Your father was a master of his craft. I think I would have liked to have met him - and your mother of course. Growing up, I would try to imagine what they must have been like to have produced someone of your likes."

I couldn't help it, I laughed. She must have created quite the image to explain the type of people that had been capable of producing such a selfish and self-absorbed individual as I. "Trust me," I assured her, "they were incredible people and no reflection of me. My mother was the most generous and loving person I have ever encountered. She was extremely intelligent, witty, and I'm sure you'll appreciate this one - defiant. She had this eyebrow that she'd raise when she thought you were being absurd."

"Like you," Ayda added.

I nodded, "She was also fiery," I said as I looked at her. "My father was extremely talented and hard working. He too was genuinely kind, and had an excellent sense of humor. He had this laugh that when you heard it, you couldn't help but laugh yourself. He just laughed all over. And, he was devoted. He loved my mother fiercely, and I always knew he loved me too." I paused, trying to find the right words before I concluded my inadequate description, "They were wonderful. If I can ever become half of what they were, then my life will have been worth it."

I shifted uncomfortably, running absently over the tool that I only now realized was in my hands as I'd recounted their memory. I walked to the back of the barn to the area that my mother had stored all of our old things. I shifted through a few things, old pots containing books that my father did not have room for, trunks of clothes and quilts, and finally wrapped tenderly in what had been my favorite blanket when I was a boy, my fishing pole.

I unwrapped it, and ran my fingers gently over its length.

"What is it?" Ayda asked as she walked up behind me.

"This," I said proudly, "is the world's greatest fishing pole. Your grandfather and I caught the biggest fish that has possibly ever been caught in a fresh water pond with it." I showed it to her flourishingly.

Ayda took it from my hands and swished it back and forth over her shoulder as if testing its ability to cast. "It is light, but strong. I'd bet you caught innumerable fish with this pole."

I had, though I didn't need to tell her that. I just watched her attempting to look legitimate while ridiculously circling the poll in the air around her head. I was taken off guard when she unexpectedly swiped me in the arm with it. She was trying to lighten the gravity of the day and the situation we were currently in. I was grateful for her efforts which had momentarily taken my mind off the fact that my parents had been brutally murdered . . . though, hers had too. As had her siblings, the realization of which made her efforts all the more meaningful.

"Thank you, Ayda. I appreciate the distraction. I should probably tell you that I am always on the look out for someone who will give me a painful welt on my arm, or any other part of my body for that matter. It keeps a man on his toes." I waggled my eyebrows at her.

"Och, you are foul Mr. Dalton," Ayda said with a smile, "Though, I confess that I find the idea of whipping you any time that I think you might be getting out of line, a pleasant one," Ayda teased.

"Pay back no doubt for all the times Gair, Cian, and I excluded you, or mercilessly toyed with you. Considering that I am the only member of that group present, I suppose it is only fair that I take their whippings for them too," I offered chivalrously with a pompous bow.

"So you're playing the gentleman now are you? Or is it whipping boy?" Ayda smacked the fishing poll playfully against her palm.

"I suppose time will tell Miss Macardle." With that I snatched my pole away from her, "Until that time, I will keep my fishing pole for myself," and I swatted her lightly on her backside.

"Ooooh, Daine, I might just have to tell Grandad on you for that one." Her emerald eyes shone with intended retaliation.

"Good, maybe it will give him a distraction as well."

Bram returned to the barn just then, clearly consumed by thoughts that I didn't want to think about. Instead, I looked at Ayda with raised eyebrows, my pole tapping lightly against my palm, questioning if she was going to make good on her threat. Her pink lips pursed in an effort not to smile, and she slightly shook her head in the negative.

"I've attended to everything that I needed to," Bram informed us sadly. His words had brought the reality of the situation blaringly to mind. The momentary easing of the sorrow I felt while bantering with Ayda had left me now. I felt entirely overwhelmed by what we had discovered here, as well as by the enormity of what still needed to be done.

Entirely sober once again, I stepped toward Bram, handing my fishing pole over to Ayda for safe keeping, before speaking generally to them both, "I do not think it is necessary that we wait any longer, if you do not have any issues with lighting the pyre now, I will attend to it immediately."

Neither said a word, and I moved soundlessly out of the barn and for the cottage. The sun was now beginning to sink, and the last streaks of bright orange shone upon the layers of untampered frost. The potential beauty of the moment was lost to me.

I stopped perhaps thirty feet from the cottage and directed fire to consume what was left of my childhood home. The dry old wood throughout the cottage's construction provided an excellent accelerant for burning. The flames needed little coercing before the entire structure was aflame. It was not enough though, and I encouraged the fire to grow larger and to burn hotter.

I turned to the barn. Ayda and Bram now stood outside, standing a few feet away from me. "Is this really necessary?" Ayda asked a little dubiously. "We should salvage the last of your father's work."

I did not give her an answer. I simply strode past the both of them, and allowed the fire that was already with me, to have the freedom it wanted to frolic over and throughout the old barn. It too took to flame quickly, and we all had to step back from the intense heat. The blaze was enormous as it reached into the sky. But all of that was fine with me, the hotter it burned, the more assurance I had that there would be absolutely nothing left.

"I think it would be best if all of us took to rest for the duration of the evening. My home is heavily warded, and by my guess, still untouched. Am I correct in that presumption?' Bram looked at me and I nodded in response. "Well in that case, it would do well for us all to move on immediately; lest we run into local citizens coming to worry over the unexpected conflagration."

He set off knowingly toward the well known path that led to his house. Neither Bram nor I needed light to know every bend and turn of the trail. Ayda however, could do nothing but stumble blindly between us in the dark. I reached for her arm, twisting her around to face me, and then I lifted and carried her over my shoulder the remainder of the way. My pole thumped against my side as she held it, falling into an even tempo with my footsteps.

Bram's house was indeed warded exceptionally well. I doubt anyone, Druid or not, would be able to enter the home with his wards in place except himself and those whom he wished to welcome in. We entered the freezing foyer, our breath clouding before our faces. Bram moved to the study, used the conveniently placed wood beside the fireplace that had been laid in wait eight years before, and started a fire that almost immediately began to warm the room.

Ayda went to stand before it, her dainty hands stretched out before its warmth.

"Keep it burning, will you Lass?" Bram asked as he moved from the study to the other rooms in the house to do as he'd just done in this room.

I went to work removing dust covered sheets from the furniture and wall hangings. With them out of the way, the room took on a completely different feeling, one of comfort, warmth, and life. Promptly, I went in search of the other rooms in which Bram had left the fires burning to clear them also of their dusty shrouds. It did not take long for both Bram and I to complete the tasks we'd given ourselves to perform. With nothing more to attend to, I made my way back to the study.

"Daine, I have something for you," Bram said as he entered.

I stared blankly at a pair of shuttered windows, while sitting ungentlemanly in one of the room's many upholstered chairs.

"Ayda," he asked, "will you be able to manage here for a moment by yourself?" Ayda gave him a tight nod, her dark curls catching the fire's light as she moved.

Bram then walked away, and I got up and followed. He went up the stairs and to the room that I had used occasionally when I was his student.

"You'll find a night shirt laid out on the bed for you," he said as he indicated to the bed with his head.

I went to the bed, quickly stripped my clothes off, and put the nightshirt on. Out of habit I went to the washbasin to wash my neck and face before going to bed, and was pleasantly surprised to find that Bram had already filled the pitcher for my use. Grateful, I went to work washing myself vigorously in an effort to rid myself of the day's memories. When I had finished, I walked blearily toward the bed.

Bram stood patiently beside it. I was exhausted. As I drew closer, I saw that Bram held a cup in his hand. He held it out to me with the simple command, "Drink this. All of it, please."

I did not have the will, or strength to question him. I was emotionally rent, and not to mention physically exhausted from using so much energy to create such a large and quickly burning fire at my parent's cottage. However, mentally, I was alert and miserable. I could not stop thinking about what I saw and how my parents must have suffered. I was so consumed by their pain that I was completely unaware of my own.

I took the cup and drank whatever it was that Bram had given me. I felt heavy and even dizzy. I vaguely recall Bram helping me into bed, as I fell into a blissfully dreamless unconsciousness.

Chapter Thirteen

I awoke three days later, completely starved and dehydrated. Someone had been anticipating my awakening and had left a plate of still warm meat, bread, cheese, winter vegetables, a large dram of whiskey, and what appeared to a sizable mug of milk waiting for me on the bedside table. I ate voraciously, feeling as though my stomach was a bottomless pit. My clothes had also been cleaned, and now lay in wait a top a chair that rested beside the wardrobe. My father had made both.

I did not want the memory of either, but found the clothes much easier to manage. I tossed them into the fire and went to the wardrobe, feeling burned myself to even touch it. I found all of my clothes from the trunks that had accompanied us to Strasbourg, hanging inside. I dressed, combed my hair away from my face, and went to the heavily draped window to discover if it was night or day.

It was night, though there was no moon so I could not tell if the night had only just begun, was in its fullness, or was quickly fleeing before the dawn. It didn't matter, I was restless. I took a woolen coat that was draped across the back of a chair, and went directly downstairs to the rooms where Ayda and Bram might be found – if they were still awake.

It was 2:24 in the morning, and neither was to be found. Truthfully, I was relieved to be alone. I opened the front door, feeling the wards shiver as I crossed the threshold they protected, and stepped out into the freezing January night air.

It was both invigorating and calming to walk through the well known and loved places of my childhood under the cover of winter and darkness. I wandered aimlessly, not thinking much of where I was going. However, I soon realized that I was on the path that led back to what had been my parents' home. I stopped abruptly. My fist pumped lightly as I thought about where I had been unconsciously going – home.

I looked around me, searching for another option. I froze entirely when I noticed that I was precisely at the fork that would either take me toward the remnants of my childhood home, or to the stream where Maurelle had tempted. Neither was a good, but having no desire to ever again see where I had grown up, or what was left of it for that matter, I cautiously began to walk down to the stream.

I didn't know what I'd find, though I wasn't sure if I expected to actually find anything. The trees that marked the edge of her confinement were quickly in view as the ground began to slope dramatically downward toward the river's cut course. All too soon, I was standing before what had once been the perimeter line of Maurelle's territory.

The runes glowed with an eerie blue hue when I revealed them. They were all still active and in place. I couldn't begin to fathom how a Fae Royal had ever managed to escape, especially when I was now looking at ancient containment runes that I did not even know existed. They were intricately intertwined with those that I knew were completely unbreakable. Suspicious that there may have been a breach at some point along the border, I began to walk the tree line. I circled the entire perimeter, and not anywhere could I find any signs of tampering or weakness.

I walked back to where the river path was intersected by the barrier wards. I kicked some dirt away from my feet in frustration, feeling as though the idea of even being able to begin attempting to figure out this whole mess was an impossibility. I stared down the path, watching as it disappeared into the dark. I was no closer to learning anything standing outside of the wards, and seeing no reason not to proceed, I entered Maurelle's prison.

I was consumed by a wide barrage of thoughts as I moved forward. Nothing about this situation made any sense. Maurelle should have never been able to escape her confines - unless Bram himself had allowed her to go. But he had not been anywhere near France in the past eight years.

A whisper being carried on the wind stopped dead in my tracks. A winter fog had accumulated and hovered lazily about the ground. The gentle stream provided the perfect amount of moisture to allow such a phenomenon to happen on its own. The night was clear. The stars shone brightly in the sky as I spied them through the tangle of bare branches overhead as I searched for what had startled me. There was nothing. Unnerved, I again began to descend toward the stream. I hadn't gone more than a few paces, when again, I heard what I can best describe as a whisper sliding through the trees.

I whirled around, searching for its source. My senses heightened and flexed out in an effort to locate whatever it was that I was obviously hearing. It started out as nothing, a slight change in the winter's air and darkness. But no matter how insignificant, I knew for certain that I was not alone. I moved to stand beside a large oak, readying myself for what, I couldn't know.

Soon I came to notice a faint … almost flickering in the mist. Ever so slowly, it seemed to be building upon itself, seeming to take great quantities of energy and strength to do so. As I watched, a figure clearly began to take form using the mist as its medium.

I scanned the area with my Druid's heightened senses, searching for another presence that might reveal this merely as a trick of sight. When I was unable to sense anyone present but myself, my guard was heightened. Wary, I searched more thoroughly. No draws of power were being taken from the elements in order to fuel this being's formation.

I watched defensively as something that had began to resemble a human form, now made to define itself. A dress took shape, hugging a feminine figure. Strong and lithe hands formed, complete with definition that would lead one to assume that they were middle aged. I gasped when the transformation was complete. A full head of long waving hair framed what was the perfect face of my mother.

I was horrified. I was unclear if this … this thing hovering so innocuously before me was a creation of the Fae made to distract me from some ulterior purpose that was presently unfolding, or if it was purely, a ghost. I watched, my mouth pursed tightly in preparation for whatever this creature should decide to do. The figure that was my mother did nothing, but remained lightly where she had formed. Swirls of mist curled and wisped around where her immaterial feet met the ground. I shivered as her mouth moved, and the wind carried my mother's whisper of my name to me.

It was her voice, there was no other voice that had ever existed that was quite like hers. I closed my eyes and swallowed heavily before opening them again. My heart hammered almost painfully in my chest. I braced myself for the possibility that this was a very cruel distraction, and hoped against everything, that I would not have to do battle with this creature that was such a perfect replica of my mother. I would in no way survive it.

Almost imperceptibly, she began to move forward. It startled me back to the reality of this situation. I thought quickly, and concluded that wind might provide the best defense against something that seemed to be immaterial. I stepped forward to meet its advancing form, threatening the warmly smiling face with my own menacing promise. "Do not move any closer, or I will have no choice but to destroy you."

She ceased advancing and raised her hands in a gesture of peace. I stalked forward, claiming the slightly higher ground to my advantage as I approached. All the while, she remained perfectly still and motionless. Even when I circled around her, she did not turn her head to watch me as I passed. I circled in closer, never once letting down my guard.

"Who are you?" I demanded.

She did not say anything, instead one of her hands moved slowly from the motion of peace that she had maintained, to tap her throat. She then sadly shook her head.

I understood her meaning, but still sought the verification, "You cannot speak?"

In answer, one of her brows raised as she smiled at me with the exact face that my mother would have made. Again, my heart wrung itself over their similarities.

"Who are you, and what do you want?" I knew it could not speak, but I asked it anyway. She was going to have to convince me that she did not want a fight between us.

The being seemed to take a deep breath and slightly shake her head in exasperation before motioning for me to follow her as she began to recede and turn, moving down the path toward the stream.

I stood there. Just what was it that I was up against? When I had made the decision to turn and go the other way, the wind again carried my name to me. I shivered with chill. Against my better judgment, I found my feet following the smoky apparition ahead. To what end, I had yet to find out. I grew even more skeptical that I would be pleased with whatever it was when I did.

We moved slowly, the ghostly figure that had chosen to take form as my mother in the lead and myself trailing about fifteen feet behind her. Aside from the fact that I was following a ghost, nothing else seemed out of the ordinary. In fact, everything was silent and hushed as if it did not wish to disturb either of us as we passed. Even the trees seemed almost reverent of our passing.

She stopped before a large tree. I moved closer and allowed myself to stand relatively close the being. Remarkably, this brought a pleased smile to her face. I ignored this, and instead focused on what it had led me to. It was the mistletoe covered oak.   The figure of my mother motioned toward the tree, but indicated that I remain where I was. I was more than happy to be a silent observer to whatever it was that I was meant to be party to.

She moved toward the tree, looking through the barren winter branches to the moon above. She again smiled, revealing the shadow of teeth when she saw that the sky was clear and that the moon was able to shine brightly through the bracken to the frost covered ground where we now stood.

She excitedly pointed to the moon, and then to the massive oak tree that was before us. With a nod she indicated that I look at the tree. Without a word, I did so. I was curious to see what had made this apparition so visibly excited. Despite my curiosity, I retained my skepticism of the ghost's intent, and stared at the section of the massive oak with my senses flared to warn me of any potential danger.

It was gradual, almost so scarce that I could hardly notice it. It was like one of those tricks of the eye in which you'd swear something was there, but when you looked at it face forward, you couldn't see it. So, I resisted the urge to focus, and allowed it to grow. The tree was shimmering or flickering, as though the bark of the tree was readjusting or re-aligning itself to the moonlight. I extended my hand, and saw that the area around my palm too began to shimmer.

I looked at the image of my mother. She smiled at me encouragingly, so sure that I would soon come to understand what she couldn't articulate herself. The realization struck me like lightening. I knew what I was standing before. A Silver, a Silver was hidden on the surface of the tree. This explained why the introduction of a new dynamic, such as moonlight or the palm of my hand, had caused the tree's bark to readjust itself. It had to in order to continue its perfect illusion.

"There's a Silver in this tree!" I said wonderingly for her benefit. I glanced at my mother, for the first time allowing myself to believe that it was really her that was here with me. Her eyes were crinkled with happiness as she began to nod wildly to confirm my thoughts. She smiled broadly, and I offered her a warm smile in return.

She mouthed my name as she moved forward. I held entirely still, and allowed her hand to tenderly cup my face, feeling like it was nothing more than a cool breeze. I closed my eyes, relishing the sensation of experiencing my mother again. When I opened them, it was to find that her eyes held a hint of sadness despite the overwhelming smile she still held upon her face.

"What is it Maman?" I asked her worriedly.

She shook her head dismissively. Stepping away, she looked me up and down appreciatively. Her lips formed the word "handsome" when she had finished. I felt a sense of pride at having my mother approve my adult form; she had never beheld it with her mortal eyes. I watched with humor as she began to mime the action of eating. I couldn't help but laugh at the irony that even in death, a mother would still worry if her child was eating enough.

I hated to ruin this moment of blissful reunion, however, she seemed urgent despite our happiness. Seeing it, I felt a sense of duty awaken inside of me. I needed to find out what had happened to her. If it was as I had suspected, then I had no choice but to avenge my parent's murder.

"Maman," I asked her softly, "did someone named Maurelle kill you?" She nodded her head. I'd had the sneaking suspicion of such, but having it confirmed by my mother's sad nod was devastating.

"Oh, I am so sorry, Maman," I said as I instinctively reached my hand out to comfort her. Unfortunately, my hand went right through her in a swirl of haze as the fact that she was immaterial was tragically reaffirmed. Instead of redefining herself, she was simply what could be best described as smudged where my hand had passed through.

"I will avenge you, Maman. I will make sure that Maurelle feels every pain that she gave to you."

I was surprised when my mother shook her hand vehemently in the contrary. She then bent down, and began writing in the dirt. "We are more than that," was all she said. With the same defiant nature that she'd had in life, she looked up at me with just as much conviction in death.

I nodded simply, unhappy that she had so easily rebuffed my willingness to honor her. But, she was right. I was more than that. To become as merciless as the Fae would be a dishonor to whom I was now, and to everything that had once had been.

My mother's eyes shifted uneasily, searching around her. Her hand gestured to me and then the ground, indicating that I stay right where I was. I felt it then, a change in the air. Again, it was something that I couldn't quite communicate, but knew for certain was there.

Then the ground seemed to vibrate and hum, like a stampede that could be felt growing in the distance. I glanced around wildly, uncertain of what I should do, or even if I would be able to do anything. I looked at my mother as the rumbling suddenly stopped, replaced by the sound of trumpets blaring loudly in the distance. Immediately after the horns had sounded, the ground resumed its wild growl.

I turned my back on my mother, spreading my arms wide in an effort to shield whatever was left of her from whatever it was that might be coming. With my back cool from her presence, we backed away toward the stream. My feet crunched over the frosted ground as my breath came in quick puffs when I exhaled.

The rumbling grew into what I could feel as a literal physical shaking. I could hear what sounded almost like the baying of hounds, mixed with the wild cacophony of horns at various pitches being sounded as everything seemed to draw closer. The thunder of many hooves could be heard as the Wild Hunt drew dangerously near.

Suddenly, everything stopped. No longer did the earth tremble, nor could any bugles or hounds be heard. The only sound was of my heart beating deafeningly in my ears. Fear took hold of me. This was an enemy that no one could escape unless they were allowed to.

I felt a cool pressure on my right arm, and I turned my head briefly from where the noise had stopped just as it threatened to crest the wooded hill before us.   My mother's face was serene and resigned as she stared bravely into my eyes. Her eyes eagerly regarded my face as her hand came up to once again cup my face in a cool but loving caress. Within a blink of an eye, my mother was nothing more than a quickly moving mist that was moving away from me and up the hill toward the where I knew the Wild Hunt was waiting.

I raced after her, calling for her to stop. The fog still hovered over the ground, and I tripped as I ran, slowing and falling behind her. As I continued to run, I watched as a pair of pointed ears grew into a massive black horse with glowing red eyes as it appeared in silhouette on the crest of the hill above me. A cloaked figure sat astride the horse's back, staring down at me from where I stood in the tangle of bracken. The horse stomped its hooves menacingly, promising death if I dared to move even a single step forward.

The mist that was my mother glided toward the cloaked figure on the horse. She materialized once she reached the side of what I knew could only be the Wild Huntsman. He reached down for her hand, and effortlessly lifted her to sit upon the horse behind him. More solid than she had been before, entirely corporeal, she looked at me reassuringly from her place behind him. Not once did she take her eyes off me as the Huntsman turned his wild steed away from the hill, and took off at a gallop toward the undeterminable location of his waiting hunting party.

A single horn sounded, loud and echoing in the silent winter night. The single note lingered in the vale, dying away gradually as it dissolved into nothing. Once it could no longer be heard, only then did I hear the hounds and the rumble of hooves. Soon, I only felt them as they departed – running toward a never ending hunt in a location that I didn't know.

I waited in dark winter's freeze, scarcely daring to breathe as the silence began to grow oppressive . . . listening for anything that would break the deafening silence. My mind was racing, trying to discover a way in which I might be able to make it away from here alive.

Those, whom the Hunt perceived to be against them, were not taken to kindly. The purpose of the Hunt was not entirely known, though it was guaranteed that if you were found to be guilty of delaying the Huntsman and his band of riders and hounds, your life and soul were theirs. In what capacity, I was not sure. But, the idea of being hunted by an undaunted foe, was one that I did not feel up to avoiding.

I scrambled most ungraciously through the woods, becoming tangled in brush, grass, and branches as I moved as quickly as I could manage, looking over my shoulder for fear that I was being pursued. Ahead I could clearly see Bram's wards glowing reassuringly marking the barrier of this strange containment. I ran through them feeling the distinctive shiver as I passed. Immediately, I called the wind to aid me in my flight across the now relatively obstacle free terrain that lay between myself and Bram's house. Bram's wards had done nothing to either keep the Wild Hunt out, or inside, of the confines clearly lain out to be Maurelle's prison. Perhaps there were things in this world to which the ancient arts did not apply.

Bram's house came into view. It was still deep into the night, though I lacked the reserve to be discreet and quiet in my haste to reach the house. Without slowing much from my aided flight, I managed to both open and close the door behind me with a massive gust of wind following behind me. The papers in the study and library rustled with the unexpected presence of the wind, and the fires in their hearths whooshed, popped, and cracked as the wind sought to exit from their flues.

I had not taken many steps in crossing the large entry foyer before I was crashed into and held in a frantic embrace. The ancient Druid inside of me prepared to fight, and then subsided contentedly as I looked down upon wild ebony curls. It was Ayda, her cheek pressed firmly against my chest.

"Daine! Ye've been gone for four days!" Her wild emerald eyes looked up into my own. Within them I could see the ferocious mix of anger and worry. I hoped that affection was hidden in there somewhere too, it might temper her mood.

I shrugged my arms from Ayda's hold and held her close. I had not realized until I held her, that I was deeply worried that I would return to Bram's home to find them missing – fallen prey to the Wild Hunt in my absence.

217

"No, it can't have been that long. I was asleep with Bram's tonic for quite sometime, but I have not been gone more than," I looked up at the clock, it marked 4:01 and considering it was still dark outside it was most definitely in the morning, "two hours."

Ayda stayed locked against my chest, her own head noting the negative in my statement as I said it. Her face pulled away to look up at me, "No, ye've been gone for four days. Ye slept for three, but then ye just up and disappeared one morning, and Grandad and I've not been able to find any sign of ye for the past four days. Where the devil have ye been, Daine? I was worrit sick." She again laid her head on my chest and held me tighter still. Her accent was always thickest when she was emotional.

I let her hold me as I realized that I had been lost in some sort, or part, of Fae. I had not even been aware that it happened. In people's past dealings with the Sidhe, in my case the Wild Hunt and possibly even my mother, time passed by much differently. There is an account of a man who had happened upon a feast in the forest upon his way home. As he passed the gathering, he was asked to join in. Thinking that no harm could | come from so simple a request, he joined in a happy jig. Soon, his friends came round, and pulled him away, much to his frustration. Their faces were in complete shock as they informed him that he'd been nearly gone a year. All the while, he was sure he'd not even finished his first dance.

A full week had passed without my knowing since I had arrived in Strasbourg. I pushed Ayda away, holding her at arms length while I crouched to look levelly into her eyes. "Ayda, by chance did you hear any trumpets, bugling, or anything that sounded like a hunting party while I was away?"

She looked at me with concern, "No, I dinna hear anything of the sort."

"Not at any time?"

"No, not at any time that ye were gone. Nor have I heard anything like it at any time that we've been here for that matter. Why do you ask?" she questioned.

I breathed a sigh of relief. The hunting party had not passed by here. I needed to speak with Bram immediately.

"I'll tell you about it later. Where is your grandfather?" I asked her hurriedly.

Her eyes were still large and worried as she looked me rapidly over. "He's in his study. He has not left it since he went in search of you after we'd discovered that you were gone. That was three days ago," She responded matter-of-a-factly.

I moved to leave, and her hand shot out quickly to reach for my own. Bravely, she confessed, "Daine, please do not do that again. I would have died myself if I had lost you too." She looked down at the floor. Her bravado had disappeared with the admission as she strove to hide whatever it was that she did not want me to see.

I waited for her to lift her eyes when she was ready. When she did, it was under the cover of her long lashes. "Ayda, do not worry yourself over me. I cannot promise that I will not leave again, or that my life will not be in danger. But, know that I will not be dying anytime soon. I've got too much left to do, and two people who are all that are left to me to take care of." I gave her a reassuring smile before slipping my hands away from hers. My boots fell heavily upon the wooden floorboards as I passed the staircase and entered the long hallway that led to the kitchen, dining room, and Bram's small personal study.

I found him in a state of agitation as he studied masses of scrolls, papers, and books that had come to clutter his entire office. He had not heard me approach and so I lightly tapped the door frame before I entered. He looked up, his eyes were red and weary. "Ah, Daine!" He came around the heavy desk to embrace me. "I am relieved to see you. I knew that you would reappear - I just had no way of knowing the when or where of it. I am most pleased to see that it was sooner rather than later. Despite my reassurances, Ayda was quite convinced to the contrary and no amount of stating otherwise could console her. Needless to say, it has been a long few days for the both of us."

I took a seat in his study, Ayda following just behind me, and began my recounting of everything that had happened. Our discussion, though lively at first, fizzled to a point of impassé. There were too many, and at the same time, very few options for us to take.

By the end of it, I was spent. I went to my chambers and fell into a deep, but haunted sleep.

My dreams were dark. No matter where I went or what I did, every move I made was checked by a cloaked figure astride a dark and terrible horse. The ghost of my mother clung fiercely to the rider as she sat behind him upon the horse's back, her eyes filled with love and wonder - not for me, but for the rider himself. My heart raced as I recognized that I knew I would be seeing him again.

I awoke with a start. My mother's clearly spoken words, "We are more than that" echoed loudly in my mind. It reaffirmed what I needed to do.

Ayda and Bram were found sleeping in the library. Ayda was on the couch that faced the warmly burning fire, and Bram sat in a high wing-backed chair that was half of a conversation pair facing a window. Seeing them so clearly at peace, I turned away in an effort to leave them undisturbed. But, Bram's voice, cracking and deepened from sleep, stopped me before I could slip away unnoticed.

I turned back, and crossed the expensively carpeted floor quietly, noting the sleeping Ayda comfortably tucked away as I did. I sat in the chair to Bram's left, shifting uncomfortably. I was resolved to action and confining my mind and body to that large chair was a battle.

"Do you know what you must do?"

I nodded, "Yes. I will be entering the Silver - alone." I looked at him until he understood very clearly that I would be doing just that.

"You do understand that that is an exceedingly dangerous course of action to take?" His brows lifted and his fingers drummed on the chair's armrest before adding, "No one enters a Silver willingly, and we know very little of how they operate. I am unsure if you would be able to again open it once you were inside," Bram expressed to me.

Silvers were tricky, even for the best of us. They were known to open, usually just as the sun was setting or rising, to allow unsuspecting humans fall or be pulled through. Those poor people were never to be seen or heard from again.

"Yes, I am well aware of the dangers. However, I do not see any other options left to us. I wish to do all in my power to find the Sword, and if that means stepping into the unknown, then so be it." Regardless of having Bram's approval or not, I would do what must be done.

Bram remained quiet; his fingers were again steepled before his mouth as they tended to do whenever he was deep in thought. "I am loathe to not stand in your way," his green eyes looked up into my own, "it would mean sending you into the indefinite, without my aid." His eyes again returned to staring at an unknown spot on the floor, his mouth resting against his still pointed fingers.

Motion seen out of the corner of my eye drew my attention away from Bram and to the couch before the fireplace. A pair of large emerald eyes found mine briefly before sinking to hide themselves behind the back of the couch. That fraud. The corners of my mouth turned up at her attempt to be discreet against the likes of myself and Bram. It just wasn't possible. I returned my eyes to him. He too looked at me, his own eyes indicating with mirth that he had known for quite some time that Ayda was not truly asleep.

Bram began to nod, his face mirroring the resolve that I felt, "Aye, I will not stand in your way. When were you expecting to be leaving us?" He was earnest, and though as determined as I, I could see that he was worried for me.

"There is no better time than the present. I will be attempting to pass through at twilight." My own fingers fiddled with my sapphire ring as I waited for Bram to process what I had said. Again my eyes were drawn to the couch where Ayda no longer bothered to hide, her head shaking adamantly as her mouth wordlessly framed the word, "No."

I looked down at the floor, there was nothing for me to say.

Seeing that she was having little effect on the course of action about to be taken, Ayda had stopped worrying her head and rushed to where we sat, falling to her knees before her grandfather, "Grandad, No. You cannot let Daine do it." Her eyes implored him, and threatened to begin to weep.

Bram regarded her affectionately. It was clear that he himself did not wish to bring her pain. His eyes left hers to find my own. In them I found the same emotions she was able to openly express reflected. He did not wish me to go, but he also knew that I would be going anyway.

Ayda's gaze looked between Bram and I. Bram lowered one of his hands to stroke her wildly curled head, "I am sorry, Love . . ."

But his words had no effect. She scrambled on her knees to stop just before me, her hands clasping together as she pleaded with me, "Please Daine, there has to be another way. I cannot bear to lose you too." Her tears now fell freely, and she hung her head upon my knee and began to sob.

Bram reached forward, gathering her easily to him. "My dear, do not weep," he whispered to her gently, as he held her fastly against his chest.

I could not stand her tears. The sight of a woman crying always undid me. I stood, and with a single look back at Bram and Ayda, left the room.

I went immediately outside, strolling reminiscently about Bram's property. I was lucky in that there were only a few hours left before dusk, and that I was able to spend those in relative peace. I tried not to think about the potential difficulties with what I was about to do, because they were never-ending. I ended up at Bram's pond, watching as the fish began to jump as the day drew closer to its end. Soon, the shadows and slightly orange hued light indicated that it was time that I set off.

I had everything that I needed with me - my daggers, my torque, armbands and ring, and a pouch of gold coins well inside of my pocket. I walked back to the house, where I hoped I might be able to tell Ayda and Bram good-bye. They had not left the library. Ayda sat in the seat I had occupied earlier dreamily staring out of the window and Bram in his chair, his nose in a book.

As I approached, Bram lowered the book that he'd been reading, "I've been searching the texts for any mention of what you might encounter on the other side of the Silver." He moved a worn hand up to his eyes and rubbed them before continuing to speak, clearly annoyed, "I am sorry to say that I have not uncovered anything that might be of an aid to you." He shifted in his chair, he too was restless.

I spared a glance for Ayda, but she was too distant to notice. She was avoiding eye contact with both her grandfather and I. I rolled my eyes and returned my glance to Bram, "Thank you, Bram. I appreciate your efforts whether they'd proved to be fruitful or not. I am well aware that this will accompany unforeseen consequences. However, I find the risks to be outweighed by the potential of discovering Maurelle, and the undoubtable prospect of broadening our knowledge of the Sidhe. If I can learn anything that might help us defeat them, then this is worth it."

I could tell that he did not agree with me, and the slight pucker of Ayda's face indicated that she did not either. It did not matter. "Thank you again, Bram," I said with a slight bow as began backing away from them.

"Just a minute Lad, you will not be without a proper farewell. If you will but wait a moment, I will to see you to the Silver."

I nodded briefly as Bram stood and made to precede me out the door. I paused, allowing Ayda one last chance for farewell, but she still refused to glance my way. I couldn't help but chuckle as I saw the evidence of the same pesky little girl she had always been, still alive and well in her adult form. My hand slapped the wooden door frame twice in parting, and I followed Bram from the house.

We walked toward the Silver in silence. There were no words that needed to be said, nor was there a need for false reassurance to be uttered. We took in the quickly falling night, measuring the descent of the sun so as to correspond with the cadence of our step.

"Did you know that it was here, Bram?" I asked when we stood before the Silver.

He shifted a bit before turning his face in my direction, "No. It was not here when you and I left for Ireland. I find its presence now to be entirely unnerving. I have not been able to learn anything concerning the particulars of the moving and placement of Silvers, so I have no way to explain it. There simply has not been anything created that would enlighten us. Perhaps you'll remedy that."

I nodded grimly, my lips pursed in less than hopeful agreement. I studied the tree. It looked as though it were an entirely normal tree. Though, now that I knew what I was looking for, I was able to discern the faint glimmer as the Silver easily. I took a few deep breaths as I attempted to center myself. I did not know what I would face on the other side. It could be that I was stepping into a world void of oxygen, an environment of nothing but smoldering fire, or quite possibly somewhere under water.

With the now sun setting, the Silver would be open. It was as good a time as any. "Bram," I hesitated, unsure of what exactly I should say, "I . . . well, I . . ." I swallowed forcefully and cleared my dry throat. "Look after yourself, and, Ayda too. I know she won't believe you, but tell her that I will be coming back." I could not look at him, my nerves were scattered enough without having to see his troubled face.

The snap of a stick had both Bram and I whirling defensively around. Ayda stepped clumsily through the brush, muttering something under her breath as she tugged her skirts free from the undergrowth. I watched her suspiciously as she came forward to stand close to her grandfather.

She looked at the old oak, seeing nothing. She turned to me, glowering. Her head tipped in the slightest inclination of a greeting, but she remained wordless despite her unannounced appearance. She annoyed me beyond comprehension.

I again turned to the tree, took a deep breath, and after letting it slowly out, stepped forward with my hand stretched out before me. The Silver responded immediately. I had halfway hoped it would remain closed to my intrusion. But, before my eyes, my hand seemed to be absorbed, becoming invisible as it passed through and to the other side. Positioned such, I made some vague notes of the other world beyond. This Silver did not open into water, fire, or anything else that I could tell only by touch was adverse. In fact, I swished my hand and became fairly certain that there was a cool atmosphere on the opposite side. Whether it was breathable or not was something I would only be able to find out the hard way.

I pulled my hand out gradually, marveling at this strange, magical, means of transportation created by an alien race.

"Daine," Bram's voice came from behind me, "mind yourself vigilantly at all times. There could be Sidhe waiting for you." Bram's words were less than comforting.

I swallowed hard and nodded curtly. The sun had now set entirely, and there was nothing more for me to do then step through. I outstretched my hand and allowed it to lead me through the Silver. I couldn't help but breathe a little quicker as I allowed my arm to gradually disappear inch by slow inch.

I paused just before my face was to go through, only long enough to fill my lungs with air. Just as I was to again begin moving through the Silver, I heard Ayda scream as something slammed into my back, and I recklessly stumbled forward.

Chapter Fourteen

My elbows and knees fell painfully onto what felt like a cold stone floor. The air was cool and stagnant, but breathable. I tried to orient myself in this completely lightless world, but found it impossible. A mass of arms and legs had entangled itself with me on the floor. No words were spoken, as only the sharp intake of breath escaped from us as we struggled against each other in the dark. I managed to get myself behind its human like form, locking its arms against it in a vice like hold. I placed my hand over its mouth.

The two of us panted heavily. Despite a concerted effort on my part to be as quiet as possible, our exhales rattled loudly around us. My captive now held submissively in my arms, I strained to hear anything outside of our breathing. There was nothing but myself and whomever it was that I held. I felt a smile break beneath my hand, and before I could react, teeth clamped down on to one of my fingers.

I pulled my hand away, shaking it to dampen the fleeting pain. Contrary to what it had possibly intended by the action, my arm tightened even more firmly around its waist, making movement and further inhalation far more difficult.

"Do not attempt anything like that again," I growled menacingly beside its ear.

I felt wild hair brush against my cheek as its head moved up and down in affirmation to my words. This close I could smell vanilla and spice in her hair, like the scent of something sweet baking in the kitchen. Recognition crashed over me.

"Ayda?" I whispered tentatively in her ear.

Again, her head nodded, but this time it was hesitant and slow.

I did not loosen my grip, unconvinced that it was her I held imprisoned in my arms. "Say something," I instructed her dispassionately.

"Let me breathe a bit, will ye?" came her breathy voice. It was her. I loosened my grip, but did not release her entirely.

Right against her ear I whispered angrily, "You are truly a fool. Don't you know what you've done? Stay beside me, silent, and avoid making this any more difficult than it already is, hmmm?" I then released her. To her credit, she remained motionless.

Still on my knees beside her, I risked a bit of light in this cold place. I called fire, small and dim, and squinted as it formed in my palm. I looked down at Ayda, and was met by her radiant face full of defiance. I smirked inwardly, without a doubt it was most definitely her.

We huddled together upon a dirty cobblestone floor, the grayish dirt fine but heavy where it collected in the cracks. Nothing stirred in reaction to the light. I willed the fire to grow brighter and was taken aback to discover that we were in a room made entirely of stone. The ceiling and walls were the same as the grey cobblestone floor. A shiver ran down my spine. It was like a tomb.

"Where are we?" Ayda's voice whispered shakily.

"I am not sure yet." I stood for a more advantageous look around the room. Opposite of us was an entirely blackened doorway; our light was not bright enough to breach its shadows. Cautiously, I moved to the wall where I thought the Silver we had come through was. My hand was met only by the cold touch of stone. The wall was entirely solid. I ran my hands over the wall, hoping I'd find the Silver and send Ayda back through it to her grandfather. But, there was no sign of it.

I moved to the opposite wall and again began to search for any trick of light or sensation that might indicate where the Silver was placed. I then searched the floor, ceiling, and three of the four walls of the room, avoiding the doorway for fear of my light would alert any others that we too were wherever this was.

My search was all in a vain. There was nothing here but us, rocks, and dirt. I left my fire burning on the floor.

I walked back to Ayda, who still sat on the cool floor, all the while keeping my eyes focused on the doorway. "Ayda," I said to her with all of the annoyance I felt obvious in my voice, "why would you jump through the Silver? You were completely thoughtless. You should have stayed with Bram, he would have kept you safe." I raised a hand and ran it through my hair in frustration. "And now, not only do I have to worry about my own neck, but I have to worry about yours. And I don't even know what we're up against!" I dropped my hand. My hair stood wildly on end from where I had worried it. "Why did you do it?"

She didn't answer. I made my way back to the wall where I thought we had come through, and allowed my hands to continue searching for the means to send her back. When I was again met with nothing, I punched the wall for good measure. It felt so good, that I continued to hit it until my knuckles were split and bleeding. Even then I couldn't bear to look at the idiotic girl who had followed me so blindly into the unknown. I was angry, but if I were being honest, I was proud that she'd done it, and that made me angrier all the more.

I leaned my head against the cold stone and breathed rhythmically, sorting through my thoughts that had scattered so inconsiderately in my mind. I watched the blood well up on my knuckles.

It gave me an idea. I grabbed the dagger from where it hung at my belt, and slowly drew the blade across my palm. The cut was not deep, but just enough that blood began to collect in my cupped hand. I allowed it to pool. When I had enough, I used my other hand to draw the same runes Bram had used to reveal the Silver on Ben Bulben. I stepped back expectantly.

Nothing shimmered or even flickered in recognition.

"Finished?" I heard Ayda ask me.

I turned to find that she was no longer on the floor, but stood against the wall opposite of me. Her arms were crossed over her chest and her eyes watched me with anger. What did she have to be mad about? I had hoped that she would find the sense to realize the gravity of the situation we had landed in. I did not know if we were still on the earth, or more likely, if we now found ourselves in the vast and unfamiliar lands of Faery. If the second were true, there would be a host of beings who would not take to our intrusion kindly.

Fury once again flooded my mind at her unbelievable stupidity. Instead of taking it out again on the wall, I crossed the floor in ten easy steps and stood directly before her seething. My eyes bore into hers. "Ayda, let's lay some ground rules, shall we. At no time are you to speak unless I directly ask you a question - and even then, it will never be in more than a hushed whisper. Secondly, you will not do anything to further endanger yourself. . . or for that matter, me." Her mouth quirked up in amusement, a trait that only served to aggravate me further.

"Furthermore," I ground out through my teeth, "you will do as you are told - always. And, you will remain close to me unless I specify otherwise." I shifted my weight, again running my hand through my already untamed hair.

Her still amused mouth was driving me to the edge of my control. I was seriously contemplating throttling her, and didn't see any real reason not to.

"Daine, I am fully capable of taking care of myself," Ayda said with this look that seemed to indicate she knew exactly what I was thinking, and dared me to try it.

"And you did a rather fine job of that now, didn't you."

She was nonplussed, "Of course I did. I am still breathing, am I not? I knew full well the risk I was taking in coming with you. I couldn't stand the thought of not knowing if you were alive or dead, and so, I followed you to make sure that you do not become the latter." She huffed, gauging me loftily.

"Oh, really?" I asked her pertly. "For all we know, we could be trapped here forever. But you already knew that, didn't you. What then, was your glorious plan to guarantee that I continue living?" My eyebrow quirked up at her in question.

Her brows narrowed as her hands balled into fists. Her voice a mix of passion and determination, "I do not know, but I will make sure it happens." She then pushed me away lightly, dismissing me from such a close proximity to her.

I watched her closely as she took her turn in running her hands over the cold cobblestones that made up the walls of this room. In total the room we were in was roughly ten by fourteen feet and little was required to make one's way around the room.

She made a few rounds, pausing here and there to inspect cracks and crevices. She exhaled her frustration. She turned her attention back to me, "Should, perhaps, we explore wherever this leads?" she said from where she had stopped a few feet away from the blackened doorway.

I indicating that we would with a slight nod. I raised my finger to my mouth reminding her of the need for silence. She nodded once, and stepped in beside me. I stepped to the opening, but stopped when her hand took mine as if wanting to hold me in place. I raised my questioning eyebrow, searching for what gave her pause.

She gave a small smile as gently, she took the hand that I cut with my dagger moments before. I had forgotten all about it. She released it, expecting me to leave my palm upturned. She bent down, ruffling under her skirts, and tore a clean strip of fabric from her petticoat. Her bottom lip was caught up in her teeth as deftly, she wrapped my palm, her hands working with precision as she tied off the bandage tightly. Satisfied, she offered me another familiar smile as she stretched her hand out in invitation toward the door. Now we could proceed.

We left the room cautiously, finding that our doorway was just one of many that opened into a long hallway - the ends of which our light didn't touch. There was nothing to entice us to go either left or right, so we blindly went right. As we left, Ayda allowed the last bit of her torn petticoat to fall on the ground as a mark of where we began.

For the most part we found nothing, though some of the rooms contained random relics, indicating, at some point, humans had been in these very rooms. However, there was no way for us to determine how long it had been since these walls had last seen mortals. From the amount of dirt, and the general untouched state of everything, it had clearly been quite some time since humanity had last breathed this stale air.

The tunnel ended at a rock wall with a small cellar like room on the left, and a larger cavernous room on the right. We explored each, finding that neither contained anything more than cobblestone walls, floors, and ceilings. I was unsure if I felt relieved or disappointed at not having found anything. With Ayda still pressed close behind me, we moved back the way we had come to explore the other end of the corridor. Once again, our search revealed nothing. We were trapped. There was absolutely no visible way out of whatever this place was.

With no where else to go, we went back to the room where we had started, viewing our only possibility of escape as the Silver we had come through. We sat together, our backs against the wall opposite of the Silver, studying for any chance that it might be opening. Of course, there was never anything more than stones and mortar. For the longest time, neither of us said a word as we allowed the silence consume us.

At some point, Ayda retrieved two hard rolls from the satchel under her cloak. We ate, grateful for something to do other than stare at the lifeless wall before us. Soon after, Ayda leaned against my shoulder with a sigh. Instinctively, I wrapped my arm around her and drew her close, whispering for her to sleep. It was not long before her steady breathing indicated that she was.

Our predicament was not a good one, and the old comfort of not being alone did not lend me much consolation. If anything it made it worse. I could handle being trapped alone much more easily than I could feeling responsible for someone else who was in the same terrible mess with me. I didn't know how I was ever going to find us an exit out of this cobblestoned prison. I let out a long and steady breath and listened as it seemed to echo off of the walls around us. Ayda, still sleeping, leaned more deeply into my chest. I looked down as I held her, tucking a few stray curls that had fallen onto her face behind her ear, before I resumed staring at the wall.

I must have drifted to sleep as well, because a sudden quickening of my heartbeat roused me into an awareness of my surroundings. I had allowed the fire that I had called to go out, and everything had returned to being impenetrably dark. With Ayda still held tightly in my arms, I listened hungrily in the complete darkness for just what it was that had put my Druid on guard.

There it was, a faint scratching coming from somewhere down the corridor of endless doorways and nothingness. I straightened myself a bit, and strained to hear anything more. It started out as almost nothing, but then turned into the definite humming of voices. They sounded musical and lovely, though I could not understand a single word that they were saying. My heart thumped even faster. Finally, the Sidhe were coming.

The light that they carried was adding just the vaguest sense of visibility to the nothingness. There was no where for us to hide. I placed my hand over Ayda's mouth as I nudged her awake. The light had grown to be enough that we could see each other's features. Wordlessly I indicated with my head to the door. Her eyes grew wide as she heard the voices drawing nearer.

We moved quickly, putting ourselves against the wall that contained the doorway. My body was closest to the door, and I pressed Ayda as far as I could into the corner behind me. I extended my hand over her, wishing I could hide her well away. The light built, and I heard as their feet lithely stepped upon the dirty cobblestones in the hall. The light paused beside our door.

We held our breath as we pressed more deeply into the shadows. This corner offered the only place for concealment as their light burst through the entryway and lit the rest of the room. Nearly human fingers reached down, delicately clasping the small piece of Ayda's petticoat from the floor. It disappeared as the Fae brought it into hallway for closer inspection.

239

I readied myself, drawing as much energy as I dared from the light and air around us in preparation of the fight I was sure was about to ensue.

Words in a pleasant, but still unknown language broke the profound silence; followed by laughter that was distinctly lewd in tone. The faintest view of the strip of petticoat appeared in my vision as it was discarded onto the floor. The Sidhe resumed moving toward whatever it was they knew to how find here. I was just glad it was not found in here.

Once the light had nearly disappeared, Ayda and I took our first tentative breaths.

"Ayda," I whispered against her ear as quietly as I could manage, "we need to follow them. If there is a way out of here, they will know where it is." Despite her fear, her hand squeezed my own in agreement.

I stood, helping her to find her feet. Placing my hand against the wall, I felt my way to the door and thereafter down the passageway. Blindly, we followed the faintest of lights and only the slightest possibility of escape.

We moved quickly, but for all of our haste, remained well within the shadows. Their light veered to the left as they entered a room. I braved a quick peek, there were three of them.

As individuals, they resembled human men entirely; with the exception of possessing more beauty that a human, male or female, could ever possess. They were well muscled but lean, and they each dressed in clothes the most common of men might be found wearing. Though not one of them had any imperfections to ruin their perfect features, their clothes were worn and dirty. It was a pairing entirely at odds with the other.

They stood facing a wall that was just the same as every other within this place. I watched as one stepped forward with his hand extended, speaking words of command in his own tongue. Those words I ran over and over in my mind in an effort to memorize them perfectly.

Instantly, a Silver revealed itself. Its view was of a dense and green forest with pines, leafed trees, shrubs, and vines . . . all competing for dominance in a landscape where it didn't appear that any could win.

This must be what it is like for the Fae as they use the Silvers, they can see exactly where it is they're going, and who and what is directly on the other side. I turned quickly to Ayda, and with the slightest of glances indicated that this was our chance. My hand found hers just before we charged into the room. All three of them had already passed through the Silver, and we made it through just before it closed behind us.

Ayda and I collided onto the leaf cluttered floor. The sound of water could be heard, as could the voices of men speaking drawling English. I threw Ayda behind me, and stood at once to face the three Fae who watched us with unreadable expressions. They had chosen to lose the last of their otherworldly beauty, and now resembled only very handsome men. They regarded me steadily and impassively, their lack of

241

blinking now the only trait that would give any indication that they were not human.

Ayda stood slowly, and hid herself behind me. Neither of us moved.

It was the Fae who spoke first.

The words came slowly, spoken as though he found the sound of our language on his tongue to be distasteful. "Caradoc, it is a pleasure to be finally met with your acquaintance. We have heard much of you." He gave me a slight but still perceptible bow. "I am Anwyn. These are Welk and Morgan."

I inclined my head slightly to them. I could play cordial. "I assure you, the pleasure is all mine. I hope you'll forgive me for my insensitivity, but might I inquire where it is that one so lowly as I, has had the honor of meeting three such as yourselves?" Flattery was our best option. If I could delay them, I might have time to think of something that would allow us to get away. With no weapon to me, aside from two limited iron daggers, time was all I had going for me.

Anwyn responded warmly, "Ah, yes, it is unsurprising that you are so greatly disoriented from your time in the vaults. Let us see, how long was it that you were there . . ." he paused, making a very human gesture of stroking his bristled chin while appearing to spend a moment deep in thought. His eyes had been averted from my own, but he returned his gaze as he spoke, "It must have seemed only one day and one night," I nodded, which he registered before continuing, "yes, how strangely time passes for you mortals. . . "

I knew where this was going. I only hoped Ayda was prepared for what was about to be revealed.

Anwyn leveled the blow with brevity, "Twelve mortal years have passed since you first entered the Silver." Ayda gasped from where she hid behind me. Anwyn enjoyed her discomfort and grinned evilly as he continued. "I am sure you find that to be greatly disturbing. Therefore, I must do nothing else but strive to orient you to what is now the present."

I nodded my head appreciatively of his unnecessary courtesy. I needed to learn every thing that I could from them.

"The human year is 1877. You will find yourselves in what you will know as America, in a place that has been titled Mississippi. The name of the closest settlement is insignificant, and I shall leave you to discover it on your own at a later time. The barriers the Druids strove vainly to fortify, have been eliminated. We now move freely amongst your human race, and enjoy the finest of all pleasures that your kind have to offer us." His eyes left mine to find those of Ayda behind me, doing nothing to hide his lust for her from his gaze.

"Where are the vaults you mentioned located?" I asked quickly to bring their attention back to myself.

Anwyn gaze turned into a glare. He was clearly annoyed that I had interrupted the amusement he and his companions were about to have at Ayda's expense. "Scotland," he said without a single note of inflection, "Edinburgh, to be precise."

I was baffled. How had time managed to pass so quickly and so uncharacteristically if we had remained in our own world? Since our companions seemed to be in such a giving mood, I decided to press my luck and ask them for more information. "I hope you'll again forgive the simplicity of my own feeble mind, but how is it that time was able to pass so differently if we were not more than twenty-four hours within these vaults, and them being on earth?"

"Yes, you are forgiven," Anwyn replied. "The design came from no other than our very own Maurelle. I do believe that you have already been most fortunate in meeting her," he was probing for reaction, and I did not offer him one. "It was she who was instrumental in, how shall I say this, grafting portions of the Tylwyth to your mortal sphere - interweaving them, more or less. Now, all of our Silvers are active, regardless of the cycles of your mortal day, and we are free to travel betwixt our worlds with the utmost of convenience."

"For this, we have you to thank, Caradoc. And so, on behalf of all of the Tylwyth Teg, I give you our most sincere proclamations of gratitude. It is not my place to reveal the minutiae of your service - that I will most humbly leave for the orchestrator. But, allow me to say, that the ability to collectively house our all of our Silvers in your mortal sphere, has made our integration so much more tolerable. Now we may partake of the joys of mortality, but continue to reside in Tylwyth at will." At this, he finally blinked, and although I had not noticed it before, to also breathe. The illusion was complete, and there was no longer any clear division between our species.

Welk stepped forward, taking his place at their lead instead of back. His voice full of the proper inflection and tone that made his disguise of humanity entire, finished by a smooth southern drawl, "You will find that your numbers have been reduced; both in the membership of your organization, as well as the global population. Perhaps it will console you to know, that we made every concession to dispose of your fellow humans as painlessly as possible."

I shivered involuntarily at his admission. Any death at the hand of the Fae was sure to be horrific. The image of the remains of Brigid and rest of the Darragh Macardle family, shriveled and burned, flashed violently into my mind and left me with a sick pit in its wake. "I appreciate your consideration," I said heartlessly.

Welk made no mention of my agitation. "You are more than welcome. I suspect it will also be of a great relief to you to learn that the elder Macardle is still counted among your living."

The sweetest of mercies. "Yes, it is. Again, I thank you." I took a step away as an indication to them that I wished to be leaving, "In light the new understanding of our current situation, I would think it most gracious if we were permitted to excuse ourselves from your presence in order to reorient ourselves."

Welk, who appeared to be the actual leader of the group, nodded his head. "Of course. However, before you take your leave, I wish to advise you that our courtesy will not extend into our next meeting. Should our paths cross again, we shall experience no reservations about dispatching of you by whatever means we deem equal to the intrusion."

I let them see that I understood, and delicately began to herd Ayda away from them. Never once did I take my eyes off of them, until they too had turned and walked away in the opposite direction, and the birds again began to call out in the trees overhead.

I whirled around quickly once I was relatively confident that we were safe. I looked Ayda over. Finding no visible injuries from our tumble out of the Silver, I tipped her face up to mine, and searched her eyes deeply; seeking for any indication that something was wrong within their depths. She equally searched me, our breath coming out labored and ragged. We must have sensed the same need in the other, because without warning, we fell into one another's arms.

My cheek rested against the top of her head, as she shook in my arms. I had thought to find tears when I drew away, but found instead that she was shaking with fury.

Her emerald eyes flamed, resembling her grandfather's almost identically, "What the hell are they doing here!? Do they think they can just waltz in, and use whomever, whenever they fancy? If I ever see them again, I'll give them something to fancy!" She was the embodiment of pure defiant fury, and I found that I was entirely smitten.

She then turned her anger on me, "And you! You are one fine piece of work. Why would you waste an ounce of respect on creatures too vile to deserve it? I'd be ashamed if I were you! I am ashamed of you!" Her manner indicated that there was a real possibility I'd soon be receiving spit, a slap, or both on my face. I was steeling myself for all of them.

"Ayda, you have no idea what you are…"

"Yes! I do!" she cut me off furiously. "I know exactly what I am talking about. You are supposed to be a defender. Brimming with the desire to destroy every Fae that you see, and even those you cannot. But, but there you were cowering like . . . like . . . a coward!" Her normally creamy skin had flushed in her anger, her hair wild and standing on end giving her the appearance of what I assumed a Ban Sidhe, or Banshee, would probably resemble.

I pulled away from her entirely, and stood more upright. "A coward? Is that how you think of me?" My voice was calm, but everything else about me was murderous. Her face fell and she averted her glance to the floor. "Need I remind you, that had I fought them, there would have not been much of a fight in the first place? They would have killed me, Ayda, and easily. That would have left you to be the object to 'strike their fancy.' I couldn't let that happen to you. So it was for you, that I was a coward. Think of me how you like, it will not affect me further.

However, I would ask you to remember that without the Sword of Light, there is nothing, even with all the help from the earth that you, I, or anyone, could possibly do to leave them with more than the slightest of bruises."

Ayda shifted uncomfortably averting her eyes away from me.

Feeling an awkward silence growing a divide between us, I exhaled loudly through my mouth. In my heart I knew I couldn't let things stay this way. I swallowed my pride. "I suppose a positive note to all of this, is that I owe you some expression of gratitude. True to your desire and self-proclaimed purpose, you made sure that I stayed alive. Thank you."

Her eyes danced to mine, vibrant and joyful as a radiant smile broke across her face. "See, I told you that I would do it!" She jumped to her toes, lightly planting a kiss upon my cheek before she turned away and resumed walking away from where we had left the Faery royals.

I rolled my eyes and followed her. I did not know where we were going, but it was bound to be better than what we would find in the opposite direction.

Chapter Fifteen

About an hour after stepping through the Silver, we stumbled onto well used gravel road. Wagons loaded with lumber moved down the roadway ahead of us. We followed them cautiously in to what we discovered was a town named Kamarina.

Kamarina was small, but by many respects busy, due to its relatively close location to the Mississippi River and being the region's only railway stop. Here, the trees were thick and green, and flowers bordered the many lushly lawned areas. Women with children in tow bustled in and out of shops; and men, though present, were highly focused upon completing the wide array of the day's tasks. In many ways, it reminded me of Strasbourg, only much smaller in scale, trade, and capacity.

"Ayda," I held her elbow as I pointed with my other hand to a sign that overhung the walkway, "perhaps we should collect ourselves for a bit?"

She nodded emphatically. Though she was still beautiful with tendrils raven hair falling loose from where she had pinned it before following me into the Silver, her emerald eyes were weary and her porcelain skin was smudged with dirt. I held my arm out to her, and graciously she took it, allowing me to lead her into the inn.

Our host, assuming us married, gave us many wishes for a long and happy marriage as he handed me the key to his last available room. It was tiny, slightly dingy, and ill-equipped. Having looked over the room's meager furnishings, I turned to Ayda. She stood at the one of the room's two windows, taking in the view. I spoke, hoping that I might relieve some of the disdain that now furrowed her brow. "I know it's not what you are used to, but it is only for the night. Just until I can figure out what we should do next." I removed my winter coat, relieved to have its extra burden removed from my shoulders in the warm spring air.

"After that, I will see to it that you are accommodated more comfortably."   I sat down gingerly on the side of the bed. It was wonderful to sit on something soft, as opposed to unyielding cobblestones. Ayda looked uncomfortable as she stood properly, alternating glances between me sitting so comfortably on the bed to just outside the window.

"Ayda, for Pete's sake, forget propriety for a moment will you. It's not like I haven't known you for over two decades now." Even though I'd said it, I still found the idea that we had been in the vaults of Edinburgh for twelve years extremely disturbing. "Besides, according to the landlord, we've just been married. So, come ma belle, sit, relax yourself for a moment. Shortly, I'll see to finding us both a change of clothes. Once I've returned, we'll go and find ourselves something to eat."

Her shoulders slumped, and I heard as much saw her exhale slowly. "It's not about the room or propriety, Daine," her bright eyes danced to my own, "it's about the fact that the world has moved on for twelve years, and we had no idea of its passing. We were just forgotten and left behind. We must to send word to Grandad. I am sure he has been worried sick, and has most likely given up hope that either of us will ever be returning." She flumped onto her back on the other side of the bed.

I reached out, and took her hand, rubbing my thumb across her knuckles, "I'll see what I can do about that too. In the mean time, why don't you rest? I'll be back soon and then we need to eat, I'm starved." I admitted with a smile.

She gave me a tight smile and nodded.

I then stood and moved to the door. Before closing it behind me, I instructed her to lock the door and not to open it for anyone but me. I closed the door gently behind me, waiting on the other side for the click of the door's lock turning in place. I warded the door to discourage anyone from wanting to enter, and left in search of clothing for the both of us.

When I returned I wore a new set of clothing and carried three new fashionable dresses for Ayda, complete with coordinating gloves and hats. I had also sent a telegram to Washington DC, where it would then be transcribed and sent by steamer to France - where I hoped Bram was still to be found waiting for us. Though, just to be sure that he learned of our whereabouts, I'd sent another to Drumcliff Castle as well.

I found my wards unbroken and left them in place as I entered our room. Ayda lay sleeping in the same position I had left her in upon the bed. She breathed softly and looked so peaceful. I envied her this moment. I lay her dresses upon the bed, and set my dirty clothes bundle upon a chair. Rather than wake her, quietly, I lay down on the bed beside her, pausing only to lightly dust a stray lock of hair away from her face. As I lay listening to her smooth and even breathing, soon, I too was asleep.

I awoke with a start, the new day having already begun without me. I looked around, disoriented. I found Ayda already awake and dressed in one of her new dresses. Once again, she was staring out of the window into the forest beyond. I cleared my throat, my voice low and gruff from sleep, "Good morning."

She turned her head to me, her face bright and smiling. She too seemed to be greatly refreshed by the night's rest. "Good morning. I trust you slept well?" I inclined my head and she continued, "It is beautiful here. It reminds me somewhat of Ireland, but warmer, and not entirely the same either. But, everything is green, not cold and grey or brown, and for that I am happy." She was referencing the muted and lifeless colors of the catacombs.

I raised myself up slowly, taking my time to stretch. She watched me tenderly as I made my way to the washbasin intending to arrange myself into some sort of presentability. I looked into the old mirror, marveling at my wild and unkempt appearance. I turned aside to give Ayda a wolfish grin, "I hope you find my morning's best attractive – I would guess that you'll be seeing it for quite some time," I chortled at her rueful expression.

"By the time we'd entered this room yesterday afternoon, our host had already begun to spread word around town that he had a young French man and his exceedingly lovely bride staying in his rooms." I looked back into the mirror, moving closer to get a better look in its tarnished surface, "I might have managed to get a shave while I was about yesterday." Then louder, "Beard and all, I'm afraid you're stuck with me, ma chère."

Ayda just laughed amusedly, "I suppose there are worse things than being wed to a caveman," her eyes teased, while she did her best to look down her haughty nose at me, "though, at present I'm not able to think of any."

I chuckled myself, and made quick work of smoothing my hair and clothing under her watchful gaze. When I had finished, I turned to her with my hand extended, "Shall we, my dear?"

She nodded and immediately took my hand and allowed me to place it upon my arm. I escorted her out of the room, down the stairs, and promptly seated us within the first dining establishment we came to.

After we had stuffed ourselves on grits, pork chops, and biscuits with butter and sorghum syrup, it was then that I confided to her that I had sent word to her grandfather. I elaborated that I didn't know where to find him, nor how long the message might take to reach him, but despite these reservations, I felt a great sense of satisfaction spreading in my chest as I watched the tension worrying her brow vanish immediately upon hearing of it.

Little discussion was needed for us to determine that we should stay. Not only did we need to discover why the Fae had chosen such an odd place for a Silver, but this was also where Bram might soon learn to find us. We would continue in our assumed roles, I as her husband, and she, my ever lovely wife.

Immediately, we set about creating a life for ourselves there in that small southern town. Both of us were eager to create something tangible, infused with the feeling of permanency, after having so much time inexplicably pass us by. I had not been the only one to consider the need for financial resources before leaving Strasbourg. Ayda had also brought with her a large purse of gold. Our combined wealth and interest in a depressed economy worked to our advantage. We were able to purchase a small single bedroom home just a few blocks from the town square, two horses, and a milk cow. After all of this, we still had a large reserve that we kept hidden away.

To all of the town's folk, we were simply immigrant newlyweds – a single couple out of many. This assumption allowed for a seamless integration in to Kamarina society. I joined a logging crew, and while working, continually searched for the intent and whereabouts of the Fae.

Ayda played the ever dutiful housewife, and minded our home and property thoroughly. It was not long before she had our small home well manicured and trimmed, and had managed to change the overall feeling from old and worn, to cozy and quaint.

I'd even purchased her a gold wedding band to finish the ruse. Everything about the lives we'd chosen to portray was exact - with the single exception that instead of sharing her bed, I slept on a pallet on the sitting room's wooden floor. But, the town was none the wiser of that.

We quickly established friendships, helped our neighbors wherever we could, and attended the predominant Christian religion's Sunday services. The more we became involved, the more we found a fondness for Kamarina that we did not expect to find. For the both of us, it had become home. And, as a surprise to me, I discovered that the lie we were living allowed us both to be happier than either of us had been in a very long while.

But, for all of our contentment, our enthusiasm was tainted. Three months after our arrival through the Silver, we still had not yet managed to determine the reason the Fae were here. However, our lack of understanding did nothing to cease their continual arrival and assimilation into Kamarina. The consistent influx of Fae did nothing to ease our trouble minds. If that were not frustrating enough, we also had not heard anything from Bram indicating that he had learned of our presence here. And so it was, that we lived our relatively enjoyable days under the constant shadow of apprehension.

It was around this same point in time, when the evenings presented the coolest time of the day for pleasant socialization, that Ayda and I accepted the invitation to a community dance and gathering in celebration of the first fruits of summer. I greatly looked forward to any event in which I got to be actively involved with Ayda. In my eyes, she had yet to cease growing lovelier with every passing moment.

Tonight she wore a dress of mint green, which complemented her fair skin, dark hair, and green eyes perfectly. I dismounted my horse, and moved to her side where she still sat upon hers. I reached up, holding firmly to her waist as I lowered her gently to the ground. There was no one else around, and the sky was deepening, casting everything about her into shadows of velvet. I couldn't resist the impulse as I held her body close to mine. I stared longingly into her eyes and began to lower my face to hers.

Even though we had been living together for the past three months, as soon as I had recognized an undeniable attraction between us, and that I did not want to ignore it, I had endeavored to court her properly. Living together made the temptation of doing things improperly... difficult, at best. I had kept my expressions of affection, chaste and seldom – probably for my own sake more than it was for hers.

"Ayda," I whispered to her. Her breath had quickened as I had lowered my face to hers, "You look beautiful tonight. Positively breathtaking, Ma Belle."

We gazed into one another, both of us breathing heavily. Finally, I closed the few inches that separated us and brushed my lips softly against hers. I heard her sharp intake of breath, and felt as my desire for her immediately blossomed inside of me.

"Ayda," I again whispered her name, and then for the first time, I kissed her more deeply. She was completely willing and pliant as I held her, matching my almost reverent fervor as she pulled me closer.

Unwillingly, I pulled away as I heard another group of party-goers approaching. My thumb came up gently under her chin, tilting her head so that she could look up into my face. "Ma Coeur, I do not think you know what you do to me."

"Nor you to me," she said and embarrassedly looked to the ground.

My hand still was held under her chin, and slowly I again raised her face to mine, "Never be afraid to tell me how you feel.

I want no one else but you." At this, her face lit up, and my heart began to swell to the point that I feared it might explode.

"Daine, what are you and your Missus doing over here?" came the direct, and unwelcome, interruption to our private moment. "The music has started, and no party can start without the two of you. Come on. Nita is desperate for someone besides myself talk to, and she'll be sorely disappointed if I don't bring you back with me. Well, at least you Mrs. Dalton. As for that rascal, I'm sure she would be just as happy without him." Matthew, a fellow laborer who had become what I would consider a friend, joked as he approached us.

Nita was his wife, and was expected to be delivering their first child any day, or moment, now. Nita and Ayda had struck a chord fused by their passion for life. Where one was, it was generally expected that the other would also be.

Ayda chuckled, looking up at me a bit exasperatedly from under her long eyelashes, "Just a moment Matthew. Daine, would you mind getting my basket for me?"

I moved past her, and undid the leather belt that had been wrapped around a large lidded basket that held our picnic dinner.

"Thank you, Love," she said in her beautifully lilting voice. She strolled forward to take the arm of Matthew, and then asked to be taken directly to his wife.

I followed behind them, rooting around in the basket for a biscuit and then eating it as we walked across the eaten down pasture toward the gathering of people. I set our things down

near the trees and away from the crowd, watching as Ayda
hurried off to Nita.

As for myself, I sat back on the blanket, savoring the rest
of my biscuit, and enjoying the atmosphere. Mostly I watched
Ayda, the way she moved and laughed, and how perfectly kind
and considerate she was of everyone. They all adored her, and it
was easy to see why. I felt a momentary pang of regret whenever
I thought about how long it had taken me to realize it myself.
But, it was better late than never.

Matthew came over after having just received some
chiding from his wife, and sat down roughly on the blanket next
to me. He accepted the biscuit I handed him gladly. "Hey
Matthew, how are you holding up?" I asked him as I motioned
toward his very pregnant wife.

"All I can say is that at this point, I am lucky to still be
alive." His face twisted into one of mock terror, and we both
burst into laughter. "I'm just happy that she doesn't want to
dance. I can't imagine how I'd even be able to get my arm
around her in her present state, and my inability to do so would
most assuredly bring down the wrath of something terrible and
mighty upon me."

"It'll all be over soon my friend," I said as I clapped him
affectionately on the back.

Our conversation was light and easy as the evening
progressed. Ayda eventually decided to join me on the blanket,
and Matthew quickly took his leave to rejoin his own wife. We

both snacked on the picnic dinner she'd packed, my personal favorite being the early raspberry pie that she'd made solely because she knew I loved them.

I stood, and with a regal bow as I extended my hand down to her, asking her for her hand in as many dances as she'd allow me. She accepted gladly. How long we danced, I do not know. The night, the music, and everyone else faded away until there remained only her. Her skin was dewy from prolonged dancing in the summer's heat. Her vivacity had become a thing I craved.

Without warning, I felt that well known tingle blossoming across my skin. It felt like an unexpected shiver on an exceedingly hot night. Immediately, awareness returned to me. "Ayda," I said, my tone making her eyes grow wide with worry. I did not need to say anything more. I clasped her elbow firmly and escorted her from the dance floor, hustling to our picnic area, collecting our things, and then moving her into the thicket of trees that had been at our backs. Hidden inside the tangle of branches, I placed Ayda behind me.

I scanned the crowd wildly. They approached the gathering from where the horses and carriages were waiting. Four very handsome men, all holding a mortal woman on their arms, walked happily toward the scene. These were not the same Fae that Ayda and I had encountered at the Silver, but were four that I had never observed in Kamarina before. My fist clenched in fury. I watched, ever silent from our place within the trees.

Easily, they integrated with their dancing partners into the soiree, melting into the carouselling medley of townspeople as they joined in the dance. Their movements were graceful, gliding as they moved with their stumbling companions to the fiddled music

Ayda began to tug on my sleeve, pointing toward the horses' area once more. Three more approached. Again, I had not seen these before either. Together, we pressed a little deeper into the darkness, silently aware of the intrusion that no one else noticed. Ayda was anxious to be away, but I could not risk the chance that we met more Fae as they approached on their horses. I needed to know that we could make it away safely before I was willing to risk trying it.

In time, their mortal partners grew weary. All seven of the men moved to stand in the area where our blanket had not long before lay. I crept forward, leaving Ayda hidden behind, and ever so carefully got myself into a place where I could hear their conversation.

The male Fae discussed nothing more than their sexual exploits with the women they had come to the gathering with, as well as innumerable others. I had almost believed my desire to overhear their conversation was to prove fruitless, when without words leading to his rapid change of subject, one said, "The son of Caradoc is here."

His words made my hair stand on end. I scrutinized him, watching his every expression.

His long elegant fingers began to tap the glass of iced tea that he held. "I grow anxious with his presence remaining so near. We are close to finding the Sword, but I suggest we increase in our haste."

"He does not know of our purposes here," another chimed in. After that, they were all silently left in thought.

"Have you seen the Macardle woman? He is a fool for not having claimed her." A third had now entered the chorus and broke their silence. "I intend to bed her. Hot tempered virgins have always been my weakness."

This comment brought many rumbles of agreement from the assembled Fae.

"Gaelan, I think you will need to beat me to her first," the second to speak chimed in.

"Oh, have no doubt about it, my brother. I will get to her first. But, content yourself knowing that I will be gentle enough to ensure that there is something left for you when I have finished. Though, I cannot promise what state she shall be left in after I am through," Gaelan wiggled his perfectly manicured brows suggestively.

"Enough, both of you," interjected the first, before Gaelan and his companion could resume their banter over who would get to ravage Ayda first. "We have our commands to find the Sword, and that will be our first priority. As agreed, we will meet at the farmer Jackson's home to begin searching the watered areas near him."

Gaelan spoke for the whole, "Theon, forgive us our momentary poor memory of purpose."

Theon looked each member of his assembled party in the eye, nodding solemnly when each of their faces showed the amount of resolve he expected from his own. "All is forgiven. We are one in our resolve. However, that does not mean that there is not room for abundant experiences whilst we are performing our investigation. Be off my brothers, enjoy yourselves. The night is still young and the women are plenty. Though, it would do you all well to leave the Macardle woman to me!" Theon chuckled whole heartedly, as he and his companions dispersed to once again capture the individual attention of the women they had arrived with, as well as many more that they had not.

I went straight to where Ayda hid in wait. I tucked her into the shelter of my arm as I squired her quickly to our horses. She did not say a word as we rode away, and for that I was grateful. I did not trust myself to be able to be discrete when I'd just overheard the Fae's lust for her. *My* Ayda. I called the rain, asking it to fall upon us. I was hoping that it would mask our trail as we rode directly to our home. Leading the horses to their stable, we unsaddled them in expectant quiet.

The very moment we had finished, I brutishly took Ayda's hand and practically dragged her into the house. The ward's tingled comfortingly as we crossed the threshold. Closing the door solidly behind us, I dug deeply into my inner Druid who was bristling, keen, and alert. I lay runes across the doors and windows that I did not recognize, nor did I know the purpose of. They glowed a deep crimson red, a stark contrast to the cool glowing blue of those that had already been placed. The protective wards surged with power.

Smugly content, I turned to go to Ayda who was standing helplessly in the center of our seating room floor. Water dripped from her hair and face, drizzled from her skirts and creating a puddle on the floor beneath her. My eyes were full of promise and emotion. Whether she saw the anger or the passion I felt, I didn't know, I couldn't discern between the two myself. For everything that surged through me, I reached down gently, and took each of her hands into my own. I raised them both to my lips, and pressed a kiss against the palm of each.

Ayda ducked her head in an attempt to meet my eyes questioningly as I looked into her hands - willing that somehow my lips had left visible brands of possession upon them. I met her eyes, and withdrew my hand from holding hers to cup my palm against her cheek. Her eyes closed as my thumb slowly traced the curve of her cheekbone. When her eyes reopened, they glittered a shade of peacock green. Longing blossomed across her face, leaving the exposed skin of her collarbones and cheeks flushed.

I couldn't help but mirror her desire. "Ayda," I said, my voice rough, as I again lowered my hand from her face to clasp her hands in mine. I looked down, amused by the wedding band

I'd given her. I'd yet to see a time in which she did not invariably wear it. I paused, unsure of how to say what needed to be said.

"What is it?" Ayda asked soft and concerned. She searched my face for clues.

I steeled myself and began brusquely, "Marry me. Now, Ayda. I cannot bear the thought of not having you truly as my wife a moment longer."

Worry seemed to vanish from her face, her mouth breaking into a surprised smile. "Is that all, Daine Dalton? I thought you were going to tell me that our home was about to be stormed." She shook her head with mocked exasperation. "Just tell me, how exactly would you have me marry you, when I've supposedly already done it? I do not think either of the priests would condescend to marrying us again." Her right hand left my own to rake through my sodden hair playfully. In response, my thumb began to rub over the gold band on her left.

I closed my eyes, savoring her touch. "Handsfast, ma chère. Marry me by handsfast."

"With no priest, Druid, or anyone to witness it?" she asked facetiously.

I smiled at her jest, "It only takes two to make a promise. We do not need any more witness than that of our own." Her hand had fallen from my hair and was now draped around my neck, where her fingers toyed at my nape.

I stood a moment looking into her teasing eyes, thinking her the most enchanting creature to have ever graced the earth. "What say you?" I asked her.

Her mouth had remained a constant, radiant, smile. It did not falter when she warmly answered, "Yes."

I wrapped my arms around her and dropped my head to hers, kissing her until I could nearly no longer breathe. I pulled away, and slid my iron and rune laced dagger from my belt. Holding it tightly, I strode with purpose as I went into her bedroom to find a white handkerchief. I made a complete mess of the linens in her drawers before I found one. I returned at once to the sitting room. I met Ayda every bit in the same excited and happy state that I had left her in, still dripping wet and with a greatly expanded puddle at her feet, but not caring enough to notice. As I moved to stand before her, I opened the neck of my shirt, exposing the runed iron torque at my neck.

"Are you ready? And, I guess more importantly, are you sure you want to do this?" I asked, knowing that I did not need to. Her face left no room for doubt.

"Oh, just quit your stalling. I'm ready. I've been ready since the moment I first met you in Killiney." She said hastily, closing the scant distance between us as her soaked skirts made a swashing noise across the floor. Calmly, she extended her wrist out to me, her veins exposed.

"Last chance," I told her calmly.

Her extended hand moved quickly to push me coyly in the shoulder. Just as swiftly her wrist was again held out toward me with her tender veins upright.

I handed her the white handkerchief, which she took with her free hand and held it casually at her side in wait. I took a deep breath as I went to hold her proffered wrist. Quickly, so as not to make her wait for what she knew was coming, I drew my dagger across it, watching for any signs of her discomfort. Instead, her entire demeanor and face radiated her delight.

Without delay her blood welled and flowed from the wound my knife had left. Her features were filled with awe as she reached up to touch her bleeding wrist to the runes at my torque. They glowed with acceptance. She lowered her wrist, her cut held upward as the blood dripped onto our wooden floorboards.

Competently, I slid the same dagger across my own wrist, watching as the blood eagerly flowed into freedom. I extended my cut wrist to hers, our wounds held firmly to one another's, and together we bound the white handkerchief around them. Holding her wrist tightly in my hand, and feeling her solid grip as she held mine, I looked lovingly into her eyes. I loved her. I hoped that if nothing else, in that moment she could absolutely know that.

"Blood of my Blood, flesh of my flesh, I give myself wholly to you, under heaven, upon the earth, and forever throughout eternity. I am yours, as you are mine. Wherever I may be, there you will also be found. I take you as my wife, my heart, and very soul. I claim you always as my own." I said the binding vows solemnly, expressing the sincerity of the promises that I had just made.

Ayda, her face still bright though genuine, began spoke her vows ardently. "Blood of my Blood, flesh of my flesh, I give myself wholly to you, under heaven, upon the earth, and forever throughout eternity. I am yours, as you are mine. Wherever I may be, there will you also be found. I take you as my husband, my heart, and very soul. I claim you always as my own."

Our vows spoken, we were now married, as legitimately as any other ceremony could have performed. No longer would it be a façade in the face of those we associated with. I leaned down and kissed her sweetly. I rested my forehead against hers, my free hand pressing her lower back so her body was flush against me. "I love you," I told her honestly, amazed at the emotion in my voice as I said so.

"And, I love you Daine," her voice devout.

I kissed her again.

Slowly, I pulled away from her kiss, and began to work the knot that had bound our wrists together. I held her wrist near my lips as I whispered an incantation to begin her healing. Without delay her body responded, her wound closed and the process began. I did the same to my own, caring not if it healed, as I only had thought for Ayda.

"Are you scared?" I asked her as I tenderly held her, her head resting against my chest.

She did not immediately respond, and I concernedly drew away so as to see her.

Upon meeting my eyes, she gave a reassuring smile. "No," she said gently, "I am not afraid. I am elated."

I swallowed, nodding at her word. I took her hand that had not recently been injured, and with certainty led her away from the sitting room and toward our home's single bedroom. After she entered, I shut the door behind her. She stood with her back to me, bravely facing the bed.

"I will be gentle," I promised her as I approached her to stand behind. My hand moved to trail up the delicate skin on her neck, noting the way her breath hitched at my touch. I went up to the pins that held her dark hair off her back, and began to loose them. Her raven hair fell upon her shoulders in dark, wet waves. She smelled of vanilla, and honeysuckle.

I placed the pins upon her dressing table and turned her body around to face my own. She was warm, her skin blushed. The rain continued to fall outside, making our room that was lit only by dampened moonlight, intimate.

Then in the shadows I heard her whisper, "Do not overly concern yourself with my comfort. I do not intend to be gentle with you."

I took her face in my hands, and kissed her feverishly. Vaguely, I remember her wet clothing falling to the floor, mine following immediately behind, as I carried her to our marriage bed.

Chapter Sixteen

I lay awake, morning sunlight shining through the rain-kissed leaves and into our room. It was Saturday, and although there was work for me with the lumber crew, I had no desire to leave my bride alone. The Fae had expressed an interest in her, and I would not leave her so soon unprotected with myself being so far away. But, it was more than that. I couldn't find the strength of will to leave our bed, when Ayda was sleeping so peacefully beside me. Her naked body was pressed against my side as her head lay on my shoulder. Work could wait - this moment, and this day, would not.

And so, I lay in bed for what seemed hours. Listening to Ayda's quiet breathing, holding her close, and trying to figure out where I should begin looking for the Sword. I resolved that the best option I had was to continue with the lumber company. The nature of the job necessitated continual movement

271

throughout the forests that surrounded Kamarina, and under their employment, I would be able to move about their ranks without drawing any undue attention to myself.

It would mean leaving Ayda alone, but I hadn't really much choice. If I wanted to protect her indefinitely, I needed to find that Sword. And, I realized heavily, if she were now with child, I had all the more reason to find it.

Ayda stirred beside me. I held her tightly and kissed her head, "Good morning, ma femme."

"Good morning yourself," and she stretched languorously up to plant a kiss on my lips. "What do you have planned for today?"

I looked at her and smiled, "Rien, ma chèrie, nothing my darling. I intend to spend this day with you. How would you feel about taking the horses out later?"

Her face momentarily grimaced and flushed as she looked down at the bed linens and said, "I think that does not sound like a very pleasant idea at all."

Embarrassed myself, I chuckled at her candor. "Well, what would you prefer to do?"

"I don't think I have any intention of letting you or myself out of this bed at any time, with the exception of attending to the necessities," she said casually.

Necessity.

What an interesting choice of word.

Necessity demanded that I go out immediately and begin attempting to find the Sword, or in the very least narrow in on an area in which I should begin my search. I could not go anywhere near Jackson's farm. And, as the Fae had mentioned, they were concentrating their search around water which meant that I needed to do the same. But, what was I looking for, and how would I know it when I found it? I was willing to look, but I would be going about it blindly.

There were so many questions. So many things that had obviously happened in the twelve years that Ayda and I had been in the Silver, and I had no idea of their passing. Not for the first time, I wished that Bram were here.

Ayda had grown silent as she watched my face mulling over the obstacles that were before me. "Daine," she said tentatively, "what did you overhear the Sidhe discussing?"

Did I tell her that they were discussing who would get the first chance at her, or did I skip over that part and focus on their mention of the Sword? She would be terrified if she knew that they had even mentioned her.

"Ayda, we are all that each other have, and we've just created the opportunity to make something of our very own. Although I will endeavor to always do my best by you, there will be times that I will undoubtedly fall short. There will be times where I chose to keep things from you. Not to hurt you, but to protect you." She then moved and rested her head on the pillow so that we were face to face. "However, I will always be honest

273

with you, and I ask that you do the same for me. If there is something you'd rather keep to yourself, please just tell me so."

She nodded her head in agreement. "Does this mean that you are not going to tell me what you heard the Sidhe say?" She began to worry her bottom lip with her teeth.

I raised my hand, rubbing the re-growth of beard that had come in since I had shaven the morning before. I stared up at the ceiling above us. I blew my breath slowly from my lips. I turned toward Ayda, propping my head up with my hand. "Ayda, all you need to know is what you already do know. The Fae have a proclivity of using humans for their lustful satisfaction. Please, just always be careful. If ever you are afraid and I am not here, run into the house, shut and lock the door behind you, and do not open it until I return. As long as you are within the wards, you will be safe." I raised my hand to brush her wanton waves behind her ear. She nodded solemnly. "You must promise me, you will always keep yourself safe."

She nodded again.

"That is not good enough," I told her, "I want to hear you say it."

"Yes, I will do what I must to keep myself safe," she said a bit begrudgingly. I gave her a look, indicating that I knew that she could be reckless and impulsive. To which I earned an earnest, "I promise," from her lips.

"Good." I told her. "Make sure that you do. The Sidhe are dangerous. Never underestimate them." I lowered my head on the pillow, rearranging it so that it held my head up more comfortably. "They mentioned the Sword. It's what they're here for. They believe that it is here in Kamarina, near water. I do not know if this means that it could be around the River, a pond, or simply a manmade fountain. I don't know anything. All that I do know is they are here, and that is why."

Ayda was silent, thinking herself over the possibility of them finding the Sword before we did. If they found it, she knew as well as I did, that there would be no stopping them. "Looks like we'll be taking the horses out after all," was all she said as she then moved to get out of bed.

So much for hopes of spending the entire day in bed with my wife, I thought completely disappointed as I followed her lead and found dry clothes to wear.

We rode north of Kamarina. Jackson's farm was on the west near the Mississippi River. There were a few ponds and streams this way, but nothing of note that I could think of as being a pulling or drawing feature. It was just trees, marsh, and more trees. It was hot, and the close confines of the swamp grass and trees made it feel almost claustrophobic. I felt terrible for even allowing Ayda to come this far with me.

"Do you know what we're looking for?" Ayda asked as she walked through ankle deep mud. She'd raised her skirts to help with her mobility, but unfortunately it did not seem to be helping. Gnats hovered in clouds everywhere, and biting flies did their best to taste us. It was miserable.

"No, I'm sorry ma amour, I do not know what we are looking for. I highly doubt we'll find a sword just lying in the open. I wish I knew what clues the Fae had to go by, it would make our search just a little easier," I said exasperatedly. I was beyond frustrated, and the flying pests that seemed intent on eating me alive did not help the situation.

"Gah!" Ayda vented as she struggled to remove her foot from where it had been sucked down into the mud.

I moved quickly to catch her as she was about to stumble. "I suppose we should go back into town, we are not doing any one any good out here." I took her arm and began helping her move through the muddy bog.

"Grandad will come, Daine. If there is anyone or anything that can help us, it will be him," Ayda told me reassuringly.

I knew that she was right, I just hoped he made it before the Sidhe found the Sword.

It was slow going, but eventually we made it back to the firm ground where we had left our horses. We drank thirstily from our canteens. The sun and heat seemed to suck one's strength almost immediately out here. I helped Ayda mount her horse, and then easily made it on to my own. Leisurely we moved the horses along at a slow walk.

"Remind me why we like this place again," I joked while we lumbered along underneath the thick canopy of leaves overhead.

"Oh, I don't think I can recall that at this moment. But, maybe," she said as she closed her eyes feigning mental effort, "I think it might have something to do with the beautiful spring weather and the kind people."

I smiled as I reached up using the back of my hand to wipe the sweat from my brow. "Yes, maybe it was that. I just can't be sure. At present, nothing sounds better than a cool Irish summer."

"Agreed. Entirely. Wholeheartedly. Absolutely. Agreed."

We continued to meander, not in any rush, nor feeling any need to push our horses in this heat. The poor beasts had to be miserable enough as it was. Ahead I saw someone walking toward us along the path.

I reined up my horse vigorously, and shot out a hand to hold Ayda back. She too was pulling on the reins as her horse nervously began to erratically step backward, fighting to get it back under control. Both of our horses were panicked and moved fitfully, proving difficult to restrain from throwing us both, and then bolting away.

The warning on my skin grew to a steady hum as the person walked closer. As he drew near, I noticed that he was entirely unaffected by the humidity and heat. Furthermore, he possessed that unearthly gait of grace when he walked, composed of the elegant features and beauty that were indicative of the Fae.

"Good Afternoon," Theon greeted us with a bow. His skin was goldenly tanned, his eyes a piercing blue and hair that was bittersweet chocolate and loose, his jaw square and strong, showing the finest hint of stubble. "Daine Caradoc and Miss Macardle, what a pleasant surprise to have found the two of you here. I am Theon. It is a pleasure to make your acquaintance." His accent dripped of southern honey as he spoke.

I said nothing, but stared at him comfortably, waiting for him to state his purpose.

"I am appalled. I was told that you were both to be found possessed of only the finest of manners. Apparently, your civility does not extend to me. Though, I confess to be entirely at a loss as to why I have earned such hostile regard." Seeing that his words had little effect upon our moods, he continued. "It is a shame that I have stumbled upon you. Despite my best efforts, I had hoped to avoid you and thereby avert your untimely deaths. However, seeing as how I am under the order of our most esteemed king and queen to dispatch of you, I can in no way disobey." His body seemed to radiate sorrow, but his words reeked of his joy at the task he had been given.

Five of his companions seemed to materialize from nothing as they came into view, sifting in from where they had been hidden somewhere behind the trees. They sauntered forward until they stood beside Theon.

Theon began to stroll forward, his eyes trained solely upon Ayda. She and her horse backed away to shield themselves behind me and mine. "It is also a great tragedy that one so delicate, beautiful, and spirited should have to die with having never known what it is like to be touched by the Tylwyth Teg. I can assure you child, you will have never experienced anything quite like it in your virtuous state." Desire radiated off of him, as well as his companions. The air was filling with a scent I'm sure they thought was appealing.

Ayda was about to respond, when I cut her off by warning, "Ayda, stay behind me."

We both fought the urge to turn our horses and run. But the fear of what might happen should we turn our backs on them stopped that from happening. Just because they were dampened and had chosen to take on a more humanesque appearance, did not mean that they did not possess all of their alien powers as Fae royals. They could thereby do any number of things to us the exact moment that they chose to do so. Their diminished state was why Ayda was able to look at them without her eyes beginning to bleed; as well as resist them. All they had to do was look at her as the Sidhe, and she would have been their willing slave.

I would do what I had to in order to stop them.

"I warn you Caradoc, should you stand in our way, we will have no choice but to restrain you and force you to watch as we have our way with her over, and over again. Come, step aside, and let us dispatch of you quickly," Theon said as casually as one might discuss the weather.

"Prepare yourself Theon, for I do not intend to give her up to you, or anyone else. She is mine." My voice echoed with power as malice dripped from my words with pure threat. I may not have the Sword, but I would prevent them from harming her, even if it cost me my life.

"Suit yourself," Theon said. A blast of invisible energy slammed into my chest and knocked me clean off my horse and into the nearby tree. My eyes had a difficult time focusing as I fuzzily saw Ayda scream and quickly dismount to crouch beside me.

"Ayda, get on your horse, and run," I implored her between ragged gasping breaths. My ribs were broken, the Sidhe were going to make quick work of me. But, perhaps I could create enough of a distraction to give her time to get away. Tears fell down her cheeks, she defiantly shook her head.

"You promised," I reminded her coughing and choking on what I was sure was blood filing the inside of my lungs.

"No. I'll not leave you." She stood abruptly, and squared her shoulders to face them. "You may have me if you so wish, but know, I am not a virgin."

This divulgence was met with grumbles and clear annoyance by all of the Sidhe present. She'd just ruined half of their game.

"It was that Caradoc, wasn't it." Theon said as he stabbed the air with his finger, pointing to me angrily.

Ayda was unperturbed by his outburst. She looked down her perfect nose at him, "Yes. He is my husband, so naturally it would have been him." She glared at them haughtily.

I was doing my best to stand, to get beside her, but every move I made my vision swim and go dark, threatening to lose consciousness if I did not move more slowly.

I called the wind, while the Fae clamored amongst themselves about Ayda's lack of maidenhood, forcing it to move in and out of my lungs as I rapidly breathed the incantation for healing. Focusing, I drew energy from the earth. She was all too willing to give me whatever was asked in aid if it meant removing these creatures from her face. My vision began to clear and breathing was made easier as I felt my ribs moving and fusing into place. I drew more, feeling the water coming to my aid, and fire only a request away.

As I healed, I came to the barrier I had erected inside myself. The thing that kept this unknown thing that I feared contained and in control. I knew that to remove it was to delve into things and places, a genetic memory of my lineage that I didn't know if I was ready for. At least, I hadn't been until now.

I eradicated my shaky hold and plunged into my powerful druidic bloodline, all of its secrets, powers, memory, and knowledge, sinking into everything that had been capped and hidden deep away inside of me. I was flooded by capacity and ability, more than I had ever known existed. Everything the earth could give, as well as thousands of years of honed skill, talent,

281

and power from my line of descent was available, and eagerly waiting at my fingertips. I began to resonate, and felt the earth reverberate in joy and hope that her chosen champion had finally come into his own.

"Then he will pay most dearly for taking something that we had so greatly looked forward to taking," Theon seethed.

"You'll have to make it past me first. Though I warn you, I will not make it easy for you," Ayda boldly stepped in front of me.

I felt something strange then, a draw from the earth who readily gave as a player she believed to be forfeit once again joined her team.

The Sidhe, completely unaware of what was happening began to move, fanning out around us. "As you wish, my child," Theon said as he gave a slight tilt of his head toward us.

Color exploded as Ayda had called a massive gale of wind and directed it toward Theon, meeting his invisible attack just feet before us. Ayda hadn't waited to see what would happen, and had also called for massive bursts of fire to shoot up through the ground where the Fae had stood. They were caught off guard by this attack, yelping as they felt the heat of her called fire instantly begin to singe them.

At once, all of them sifted, reappearing just before and beside her. They took hold of her arms and again sifted her as one. They reappeared nearly fifty feet away from where I was maniacally fighting to heal. I tapped into my Druidic bloodline and found an incantation that would cause almost complete and instantaneous healing.

They held Ayda on her back, as Theon was pushing her skirts up her wildly fighting legs. She caught him in the jaw, and he laughed wickedly. "Yes, fight me my child. I always enjoy it so much more when they fight," Theon sneered as he continued to ruck her skirts up her bare thighs.

Ayda warred between moments of stillness and savage fighting, unsure whether to fight and give him the satisfaction he'd just declared he'd have, or willingly submit and deprive him of what he favored.

It did not matter, they would not get that far. I stood, my hazel eyes streaked with flame, feeling power like I had never known coursing through me like life's blood. "Stop!" my voice boomed off the trees, echoing as thunder rolling.

This caught their attention.

"Step away from her this instant, and do not dare to lay so much as a finger on her." Again my voice built and rolled through them as it surged forward.

"Ah, Daine, I see that you have learned Compulsion. How delightful. Unfortunately, I am occupied at the moment and cannot presently devote the time needed to develop your talents properly." Theon then went back to ripping away the last of Ayda's clothing to reveal his goal.

I drew upon something that had always been present, but I never recognized and I didn't quite know how to define. It surged at them, and with a crack it threw them all into the air and away from Ayda, where they landed with a violent thud upon their backs and sides. It was only a fraction of what I could have called.

Ayda wasted no time in stealing a moment for freedom. Immediately she drew herself up and ran as quickly as she could to my side.

I spared her only the briefest of glances, reassuring myself that she was not hurt, and just as quickly returned my attention to the Sidhe who were now beginning to stand amidst moans of discomfort.

"You'll pay for that. Both of you," Theon growled as he raised himself. Soon all of his companions had stood as well, and sifted to stand around us in a large circle.

I kept my hand on Ayda, seeking to always keep her protectively behind me. I moved us against a large pine, and kept her between its trunk and my body. I looked around frantically, unsure of where the attack would come from. Every member of the Fae party seethed with anger, and it was impossible to discern who would attack first.

Seeing as how Theon had been the leader thus far, I assumed it would be him, and I was right. I saw his hands move toward us and did not wait to throw a thick wall of earth up to shield us. Rock and dirt flew every where, raining down upon us. The concussion resembled the impact of a bomb.

Theon grunted in frustration. I did not have more time; every moment wasted gave them a chance to strike us down before I did them. At my will, it began to rain. Thunder rumbled in a definite warning to beings who wrote it off as nothing.

Theon began to laugh, "You're going to have to better than a little rain, human." His companions laughed loudly in chorus.

I looked at them with eyes I knew were glowing a hot hazel fire, eyes that could only be possessed by something ancient and knowing. I allowed the wall of dirt to fall, looking up to the sky as rain fell cool upon my face. I glared at Theon, giving him a smile that belonged to none other than the Reaper. Six bolts of lightning shot down from the sky, and charred their bodies to inarticulate ash.

Behind me came Ayda's gasp of shock, followed only by her quick breaths and pounding heartbeats that were the only sounds in the silence that permeated everything around us.

Still acting as a shield to my wife, I called fire, hotter than any I had ever called before, and scorched what was left of the ash until nothing remained on the ground but six fierce black marks upon the earth. I felt the earth sigh in relief, and relished as the rain continued to fall, washing everything clean.

I cocked my head left and right, looking for signs that would indicate their reappearing. I could not sense anything myself, and so I turned to the earth and knelt down, placing my hand upon her now damp soil. The earth could not sense the Fae anywhere near, nor could she feel them collecting and reconfiguring themselves anywhere upon her face.

I breathed deeply with a sense of relief. I turned to Ayda. I saw her eyes grow wide in terror as she pushed her self against the tree trunk. I heard her heartbeat quicken, her breathing grow sharp. She was afraid of me.

"No, ma belle femme, you will never have anything to fear of me." Slowly, I reached my hand out to cup her cheek.

She tensed at my touch, shutting her eyes to me.

"Ayda, please, look at me. Tell me what you see."

She swallowed heavily, her eyes still tightly held fast, and I could not hear a slowing of her heart beat.

I dropped my hand, sadly, and backed away.

Only then did her eyes begin to open. "No, Daine . . ." her hand extended toward me and gestured for me to approach her.

I stopped a foot away from her, smelling her scent of sweet vanilla and honeysuckle, and sought to fill my lungs with nothing else. It soothed me even as she regarded me carefully.

Though she was putting on a brave face, I knew that in this moment, she feared me greatly. Her hands were clenched tightly at her sides. "You look like a man possessed. Your eyes are aflame. I've never seen anything like it. Grandad's occasionally seem to glow when he's upset, but yours . . . yours positively burn. I think that if I were to look into them too long I might be consumed."

She paused a moment, scrutinizing me further, "And your face looks hard and cold, not soft and tender like I am used to. But," she finally closed the distance between us, stepping into my arms easily as she looked up into my eyes, "it is still you." She laid her head against my chest, feeling it rise and fall with breath and hearing the steady beat of my heart.

I stroked her dark hair, grateful for her strength. I tipped her face up to my own and kissed her soundly. Again, her heart and breathing quickened. I felt mine speed up to match hers. I had nearly watched her raped, and had something inside of myself not come into sharp focus, I most assuredly would have done so. The idea of it only enraged me again, making me demanding of her. She took it, feeding my passion with her fright.

I pulled away forcibly and stared down into her seemingly innocent face. "Ayda, you're a Druid." Had I not seen what she had just done I would have not believed it. "Does anyone know about this? You should have been in Drumcliff with me."

I watched her as she shifted uneasily, "That is not something I'd like to get into just now," she offered quietly.

I nodded my assent. I understood, and I wasn't going to force her to speak of something that she didn't want to. I had promised her that I wouldn't.

She then looked up into my eyes, worry plain on her face, "Suffice it to say that no one, except for you, knows about me."

"If that is how you'd like to keep it, no one else ever will," I said as I kissed her head. "Tell me, have you known long? You were incredible."

She replied easily, "I have known for years, since about the time that you first arrived with granddad at Killiney. Part of my reasoning for wanting to follow you, Gair, and Cian, was simply because I wanted to learn. I dabbled here and there, but never fully embraced it. Fact is, I decided to ignore it – that is, until now. Love is quite the motivator," she grew quiet as she reflected over some unknown past.

When she again chose to speak, it was excitedly, "As for being incredible, that was you. I didn't know it was possible for anyone to be able to summon and control lightning. Are you sure you're not a descendant of Thor?"

I allowed the joke to slip by, focusing on the facts instead. "It's not possible, or at least shouldn't be. Lightning is not an element. I have ever heard of a Druid possessing that power. I do not know how I did it, but I know that if I ever wanted to do it again, I could . . . and, easily at that." I then lowered myself a bit so I could look levelly into her eyes, "Ayda, it would probably be best if we kept this between us. I do not know what has happened to the Druidic order since we stepped into the Silver, and I do not know how any of the others would respond to it if they found out what I just did. I am not the thunder god, but that wouldn't stop them from thinking so, and there could be grave consequences if they did."

"Of course," she nodded agreeably and smiled.

That night when we were once again in the safety of our home we found that another Druid mark had appeared, this one on the opposite side of my chest, originating under my arm and swirling around on the skin of my pectoral.

We also discovered Ayda had developed her first mark, a small little ring of thorns on the side of her left ribcage. Ayda immediately began to fret over it, upset and ashamed that it had appeared at all. I kissed it gingerly, proud that she had warred against her decision to ignore her Druidic gifts, and had gone to battle for me.

Chapter Seventeen

I did not stop scouring the area for the Sword after Ayda and I's run in with Theon. Many Fae still came and went from Kamarina, and I took it as a sign that they had yet to find the Sword either. Hostile words were exchanged between us whenever our paths crossed, but it never amounted to anything more.

One night, I came home late. It was now October, and the perfect weather provided a comfortable environment for extra work and pay. The windows of our small home were lit by the warm glow of oil lamps from within as I came up the drive. My stomach rumbled as I smelled something wonderful wafting its way from the house. I hurried to tend to the horses before striding quickly into the house through the back door.

I stopped mid-step. Bram sat at our small dining table, looking older and frailer than I had ever seen him before. For the first time, he truly appeared to be nearly as old as he claimed. His back was bent, his beard long and scraggily, his skin thin and nearly translucent. I couldn't help but gape.

"Hello, my lad!" He stood slowly with Ayda rushing from the kitchen stove to help him to his feet.

"Hello, Bram!" I swiftly caught him in my arms for a long embrace.

He stood back from me, his hands lacking the strength they had always had as they feebly held my shoulders. "My, my, why look at you, Daine. I swear you have not changed a bit. Are you well?"

I smiled warmly at him, "Yes, I am, very much so. And, if it were possible, all the more so now that you've finally joined us."

"That I have. I am sorry it took so much longer than I had hoped." He clapped my shoulder a few times and then inched back to again find his seat.

He watched as Ayda came to my side, and I put my arm around her waist and drew her in for a quick kiss.

"Sit," she said to me her eyes full of love, "supper will be ready shortly. Please occupy Grandad so I that can attend to the gravy without burning it." I nodded, and watched as she seemed to sashay coyly to the stove.

I took my seat across from Bram. He stared at me with his eyes wide and eyebrows raised, nodding his head as if to invite obvious conversation. I must have been a complete dolt, because it was not until he blatantly looked between Ayda and myself that I was finally able to understand what it was he was wanting to discuss.

"Oh." I looked at the table momentarily, and then to Ayda who was silent, biting her lip in an effort not to smile. I see she'd saved revealing our marriage for me. "Bram, I'd like to ask your permission to . . . to . . . to remain married to your granddaughter?"

He laughed, a sound that was so much more enjoyable than I had remembered it to be.

"I highly doubt you ever thought you needed it," he said through his chuckles. "But, you have my most sincere blessing nonetheless. Words are not able to express the joy I find in knowing that you have married my dearest granddaughter. I always considered you a son, and now that is concrete." I smiled widely at him. "Tell me," he asked, "how long have you two been married?"

"It has been a week over two months, Grandad," Ayda answered proudly as she stirred the beginnings of our gravy in her heavy cast iron pot.

"I wish I had been present to join the celebration. You both look to be in the highest of spirits, and I can honestly say that marriage suits you well." Ayda and I looked at each other with bashful smiles, before looking away as if we had been caught red-handed

We ate the supper Ayda had so wonderfully prepared, enjoying one another's company greatly. And then, Bram sat back in his chair. His face lost its mirth and grew somber. His tone was serious. "Daine, I am very sorry, but I must speak to you of something grave, it cannot keep any longer."

I nodded my head, wishing him to proceed.

"You and I are all that remains of the Druidic order," he said with finality.

Ayda gasped, "Grandad, does that mean that . . . my uncles and cousins too, have . . . ?" Tears flooded her eyes.

He did not have the heart to speak, his head nodded most grievously in the affirmative.

I looked down at my hands. My sapphire ring was still solid and sure on my hand, an iron bracelet was firmly clasped around my wrist, and the heavy torque, a constant weight, were reminders of who I was. Without the order, I would have been lost. I mourned them all.

In time, Bram cleared his throat. "It was sudden," he said. "We were entirely caught off guard – even with our defenses being heightened. Upon our departure from Drumcliff, Daine, the Council had convinced Braesal that every man, woman, and child should be gathered within the Castle's wards."

"The Sidhe, as you have noticed, have found it within them to diminish their glamour until they are indistinguishable from humans. It is offensive to them to resemble a human, but they are doing it nonetheless. As the Druidic families came to the castle, the Sidhe had intermixed themselves within our numbers. We had not the faintest warning that they were not the siblings, or children of the Druids with which they entered. Our wards prevented any Fae from entering – but when they so dampened themselves, we had nothing to keep them out."

"And then, it was too late. The Sidhe forced the wards to be removed, and then watched idly as a vast horde of their creatures wrought havoc upon our poor people. It was a massacre. When I stopped receiving communication from Drumcliff, I knew that something terrible had happened. I left Strasbourg, and made my way for Ireland in all haste."

"Drumcliff was in ruins. The Castle burned and beyond repair. The crops and fields were nothing more than dried wastelands. The homes that had once held growing families were desecrated tombs. All that remained of the once proud walls was a single jagged scar of piled stone, blackened unrecognizably from flame and smoke."

"I called upon the earth, and watched heartbrokenly as the ruins began to sink below the soil. When it was finished, not even a single stone remained behind." He swallowed hard, fighting emotion. "Forgive me, I find it hard to recall how much we have lost." His voice wavered, "How little we have left."

I was about to console him, but he did not allow it. "I left, taking my hired horse and riding hard to the Bulben Guard. My heart froze, when after scouring everywhere, not a single member could be found." Bram sighed, now leaning forward with his elbows placed upon the table, his hands clasped together in support of his chin. His face was intense as he proceeded, "I searched everywhere, carefully investigating the location of every posted Group in Ireland - nothing was left. I went to my sons' homes and found them ransacked and ruined."

"I sent word immediately to members of our order in England, Scotland, Denmark, France, and Germany. The only response I received was from our German branch. I rushed to join them. Alas, by the time I had arrived, they too had been destroyed. I had hoped to find survivors, but I do not think any remain."

"It was with an exceedingly heavy heart that I returned to Strasbourg. It was the only place that I knew wherever you were, you would know to find me. I cultivated my library - all that we have left of the Druid texts are there. I was left in peace for five years." Bram then took his glass of wine, and drank heartily from it. He gave us both a disconsolate smile and looked down at his exceedingly worn hands. Ayda and I shared a brief look that spoke volumes - the prevailing sentiments being both worry and dread.

After a cursory break, Bram began again. But this time he spoke very slowly, as if he was hesitant to share what he needed to. "Five years, and then I received my first uninvited guest. Maurelle." He gazed at us with abject seriousness, "I first met Maurelle many, many years ago, when I was naught but a sixty-four year old man. A beautiful female, with open arms and body

- I took to her unquestioningly. I knew what she was, and fool that I am I still kept her in my arms. She gave me of ambrosia to drink, and it left me perpetually in my sixty-four year old state. It was thus that I have remained, until recently."

"When in exchange for her gift of eternal life she asked only for my ring in return, I adamantly refused her. I would not give up something akin to my very life's blood. At my refusal, Maurelle became incensed. So much so, that she could no longer maintain her lessened appearance and withdrew from me."

"I did not see Maurelle again until I realized that it was she who was so intently watching your parents in France. She was there for you, Daine. To prevent the words of O'Carroll's prophesy from coming true – that you would hold the Sword anew and prevent the Fae from ever being able to claim the earth for their prize and plunder."

I felt Ayda's hand squeeze mine, but I remained silent as Bram continues with his story.

He looked at the floor, and then over the tidily minded house that Ayda so painstakingly created. "There are things for which I am not proud of having done. The foremost of these has been that I ever allowed Maurelle into my life at all. As a Druid, I knew better, but I allowed my emotions and shortcomings to blind me to the consequences."

Bram reached for Ayda's hand, seeking a grounding source and security as he began to relate the final portion of his tale, "Seven years ago, Maurelle arrived at my doorstep. She did something to me, I . . . I don't know what it was, but I lost consciousness of all time and events. I did not regain awareness until it was to a bucket of freezing water being thrown into my face. I had been chained and manacled to the wall of my wood shed. Maurelle was no where to be found, and I was left to the hand of a Sidhe named Theon, who took great joy in my struggles and suffering."

"After hours of torturous treatment, Maurelle finally re-appeared. With nothing more than a look, the manacles that had held me fell away, revealing my raw and bleeding flesh. I fell to my knees. The brief reprieve was not to last. With only a motion, she caused my arms to stretch out into to the air in the same position they had been held in by the manacles for hours. With my arms extended, I was raised a taunting eight inches above the ground. She had not said a word, but I needed none to see the gleam of joy that brightly shone from her eyes. Heavy metal spikes materialized in the air. I paled knowing what I was about to endure."

"They shot forward and drove into my flesh and bone with such force that they pinned me to the wall. Thus secured, Maurelle and her companion vanished, hilarious laughter filled their wake. With them went the power she had used to raise my body into the air and drive in my lances. It was then that I felt the true agony of their sentence. My body weight hung excruciatingly upon the seventeen spikes that impaled me. I bled profusely, bleeding until I lost all consciousness, only to regain it again and find that I had lost all the more."

"For two and a half days they left me, and then my fastenings fell away, and I to the floor. I dragged myself into the safety of my warded home. Calling upon the absolute dregs of my strength, I used the incantation for healing to take hold and repair my broken body. Gratefully, I traded my awareness of pain for the mercy of darkness and oblivion. When I came to, I was much improved, but was in the state you currently find me in."

"But . . . but I thought that you couldn't age, or die, Grandad," Ayda blurted out.

At her hurried word, Bram's face changed from stark fury as he recollected his condition, softening until it was gentle and considerate. He regarded her tenderly. When he spoke, it was quiet. "Ah, my dear, I can do both. The catch is that I cannot die, nor grow ever older until I reach its cold embrace, unless it is at the hand of one I love."

Ashamed, he looked away, as realization for the continued depth of his feeling for Maurelle washed over us. Ayda was rendered entirely speechless, and for a brief moment so too was I. I tried to begin to speak, but nothing came of it. I tried yet again with another question, and was unable to formulate the words in order to make it audible. I looked at Ayda, who was blandly staring at the myriad of dishes sitting on the table before us, and I returned my attention to Bram, finding his gaze still averted.

He spoke in a hushed voice, "I admit I was a bit disoriented when I realized what had become of my physical state. Initially, I seemed unable to adjust to the lack of youthful vigor, and the great reduction of my human adroitness. As I was shuffling about, I happened to notice that this had been nearly pushed under the kitchen doors." Bram then reached into his coat pocket and withdrew an envelope. He placed it on the table and slid it over to me. I withdrew my hand from under the table where I had been holding Ayda's, and took it, using both of my hands to open it so that I could peek inside.

There was a single sheet of neatly folded vellum. Ayda leaned close in an effort to see. I tilted the open envelope toward her allowing her to see its plain contents. I pulled out the carefully folded paper and straightened it, adjusting it so that I could see it clearly.

In a large, elaborately scrolling hand the following was written:

The Sword of Light will be found once more,
Where the forgotten of old is found in the new.
Where the fountain springs amid les fleurs d'or -
Flowing forth from a lion's mouth it will come to spew.

My heart seized, as I read over the words again, looking at the formation of the words more than I was their meaning. This had been written by my mother's hand. I put the recognition out of my mind and read the words again, trying to derive their suggestion.

"Bram," I said, unable to hide the excitement in my voice, "is this what I think it is? Is this telling us where to look for the Sword? 'Where the forgotten of old is found in the new. Where the fountain springs amid flowers of gold.'"

"I believe it is." Bram answered matter-of-factly, a faint glimmer showing in his own eyes. "I did some research once I learned of your location. Apparently, Kamarina was the name of a now long forgotten city in Sicily – once found in the old world, but now found in the new…" he let it hang to add weight to his words, "The most difficult task will be finding the exact location of the Sword now that we are here. I've no doubt there are probably hundreds of thousands of golden flowers near a water source. But, at least we have something to go by, and perhaps we now possess the same information the Sidhe have been using to direct their search."

"One can hope Bram, and in this case we will carry only that with us as we move forward." I said positively. I then looked at Ayda, smiling the first real smile I had managed since Bram had begun his tragic history. Bram nodded, and then attempted to stifle a yawn.

"It's getting late. Perhaps we should all get some rest." Ayda said sweetly, her eyes were full of compassion for her grandfather's clearly wearied state. "Grandad, surely you will stay with us?" She waited politely for his answer.

"That is sweet of you Lass, but I would not wish to be a burden to ones so newly married as yourselves. I have arranged a room with an inn in town." Bram said logically.

"Och, Grandad, I'll not hear of it. I know we do not have much, but we do have more than enough for you to remain here with us. I'll just be a moment, and then I'll have you a most comfortable bed made just here upon the sofa. Really Grandad, I cannot believe you'd think that either Daine or I would permit you be anywhere else but here - especially since we have been so long apart." Bram opened his mouth to protest, but Ayda cut him off sharply, her eyes wicked with amusement, "No, I'll not hear another word about it." With that Ayda stood from the table and went directly to our room where the extra blankets and pillows were kept.

I raised myself from the table, and began to stack the dishes and carry them into the kitchen. Bram raised himself in order to help, but I insisted that he sit. Ayda was not the only one concerned about his appearance, he looked absolutely exhausted. "Bram, how long have you been traveling to make your way to us?" I inquired, truly interested.

He thought a moment before answering, "I left Strasbourg just after I received your telegram. So, it would have been five months that I have been in a constant effort to get here. I tell you Lad, it would not have taken me longer had I been asked to travel to the farthest reaches of Africa. You've landed yourself in quite the difficult place to find," his eyes seemed to twinkle as he joked. It was so wonderful to see him like this once again.

"That said," He continued, "I find that this 'Kamarina' we find ourselves in has potential. Perhaps if I am to be staying with you, we should find ourselves a bit of a larger humble abode?" his eyebrow quirked in question as he offered me a smile.

"You'll have to discuss that with Ayda," I said with a chuckle. I knew that she would not necessarily mind being able to offer her old grandfather more than a couch to sleep on, but I also knew that she had dedicatedly slaved in order to get our home into its current condition. For all its shortcomings, she loved this place. Though, she did love her grandfather more.

Ayda returned just then, brandishing a wide array of thick quilts to stave any potential of chill from Bram's thin frame. "Here you go, Grandad," she said brightly, clearly overjoyed to be caring for the old man, "I'll have this fixed up in no time and then we'll be out of your way." She walked past us, going straight for the sofa and immediately proceeded to layer it in comfort.

"I suppose I'll wait until morning then," Bram said to me, amused by his granddaughter's fervor for making a bed.

"Morning for what?" Ayda asked absently as she placed another newly fluffed pillow upon the makeshift bed.

"Ah, it's nothing Lass. Don't pay it another thought. If neither of you mind, I think I'll be off to bed." Slowly, and with apparent effort, Bram stood from the table and pushed his chair away. Ayda and I watched as he shuffled toward his bed, and sitting on its side, removed his shoes and overcoat. Without another word lay back upon the bed with a loud sigh of relief. "Ayda, thank you. I know for the first time in years that I shall rest well tonight."

"You're very welcome, Grandad," Ayda said humbly. She took my hand and began to lead me to our room, turning down the oil lamps as she went. The only light left in the house came from the dimly burning lamp in our room.

"Good night, Bram," I spoke into the darkness quietly. I heard his soft breathing, already indicating sleep, answer in reply. I smiled fondly, and closed the door to our room gently behind us.

"Can you believe all that?" I asked Ayda rhetorically as I undressed. "We are all that is left." Ayda was quiet lost in her thoughts, wearing only a night gown as she stood before the window removing the pins from her hair. I moved to her and wrapped my arms around her waist, kissing her neck softly. "It doesn't matter," I consoled, "we have him back, and we are together, alive and well."

"Aye, it is good. He looks so worn, and old. I scarcely recognized him when he came to the door," she admitted in a whisper, afraid that her voice would be heard and wake him.

I simply held my wife, resting my chin on her shoulder, breathing her in, as I reflected over everything that we'd just been told. It was a lot to take in.

"It will be good that he's here. For all of us," she turned in my arms suddenly glowing. "Now, I won't have to worry if he'll be here to meet his first great-grandchild." She smiled the most amazing smile I'd ever seen.

My eyes went wide as I realized what she'd just implied, "What?!" I whispered excitedly, bending away to look at her still flat belly that was covered by her nightgown.

Ayda just nodded excitedly, unable to remove the smile of joy from her face. "I think it will be sometime in May."

I held her face in my hands, and crushed my lips against hers. That night I slept holding the wonderful promise of a bright future in my arms, secure in the all abiding peace that we were a family once again.

Chapter Eighteen

The following May we welcomed a son, Robert Darragh Dalton.

I had not known what it was to feel helpless, terrified, and entirely unworthy, until I reverently held my newborn son in my arms. I marveled as his tiny fist fiercely clutched my finger. *So this is what it is to be a father* I thought, completely in awe of his tiny perfection. As I paced the floor, I realized that I had been incomplete until he was born.

In the following three years, we welcomed as many children. Two additional boys and a perfectly precocious daughter named Charlotte. Bram and I simply adored her, with her curling auburn hair and bright blue eyes. We let her get away with practically murder - much to Ayda's chagrin. And, true to his desire, Bram had purchased and moved us into a large plantation home within a few weeks of his arrival without so much as a words of protest issued from Ayda's lips.

Despite the exceedingly lively nature of three boys, and one very spoiled girl, Bram insisted on personally educating each one of them. Ayda and I were given no choice in the matter. And so it was that we watched, sometimes with winces of discomfort, as our elderly grandfather did his best to turn our little brood into model citizens. Surprisingly, it seemed to do him more good than it did them. Little by little, he was returning to the man we recognized.

We maintained our pursuit of the Sword. Bram, in the little free time he had when not schooling, mapped and researched, focusing in on possibilities where the Sword might be hidden. I would then go and thoroughly search his proposed targets.

The Sidhe were also still searching for it as well.

For ten years we were happy in Kamarina. I was now 36, Ayda, 31, and Bram, well, I still wasn't sure exactly how old he was. Our four children were 10, 9, 8, and 7. Those ten years were good years – the best I have ever known. The Fae were quiet, keeping to themselves, and we, amid the monotony and chaos of a growing family, were happy.

I cherish those years above all else.

Chapter Nineteen

I awoke from bed with a start, sitting upright and breathing heavily with the bedsheet draped about my waist and damp from a cold sweat. The night was dark and heavy, oppressive even. I looked around the room searching for something, anything, but there was nothing that should have caused me to wake so abruptly. But, despite not knowing why, I was filled with an unshakable feeling of panic.

I looked over my shoulder at Ayda. She was still sleeping peacefully. I slid out of bed quietly, pulling my pants on agilely before leaving to check on my children, Bram, and if necessary the rest of the house. I was relieved to find that everyone was undisturbed. Going downstairs, I checked the wards at all of the many doors and windows.

Everything was protected and as it should be. I dropped into a large upholstered chair, rattled. I rubbed my weary eyes. It must have been a nightmare. I leaned my head against the back of the chair and closed my eyes, fighting to remember my dreaming thoughts. I dozed.

It was dark, objects that should have been distinct were blurred. I had no recognition of where I was. A breeze blew gently across my bare chest. Waves crashed somewhere not far from where I now stood. The ground was covered in a short grass underneath my bare feet. I inhaled deeply, the air was cool.

The night began to grow faintly in light, as the stars and moon above in the sky lost their obscurity. Not a cloud marred the inky canvas. Slowly, everything returned to focus.

I stood in the middle of a clearing that I now saw was perched on the top of a hill. Around me the trees and brush were thick and vital, feeling as though they were sentient beings. I shivered, as much from the cool breeze as the idea of being watched so keenly. Just inside of the trees, I could make out the ridged edges of standing stones. The hill sloped down dramatically to my left, sheering off into a cliff that fell away to the sea below. I closed my eyes, reaching with my Druidic senses to discover more than I could see.

I whirled around abruptly, finding myself a few feet away from a cloaked figure. I drew from the earth, preparing for a fight, but was met with nothing. It was as if the Druid were gone to me. I went for the dagger at my hip, but found it was gone. I had not put it there when I left my room and here, I wore only what I had come with – my pants.

The breeze blew my dark hair across my eyes. The wind had no effect on my mysterious companion's cloak. It did not move at all. Surely, this was a dream. I reached out to touch the figure, to understand the meaning of his presence. I had only moved a few inches, when a voice boomed from the cloak. It was deep, raw, and definitely male, "Do not touch me, lest you die in flame."

I drew my hand away, feeling as if I had already been burnt.

"Who are you?" I queried, my voice insignificant and weak in comparison to the one that had preceded.

The cloaked figure did not reply.

I studied him intently. If he were regarding me as well I could have no way of knowing with his face hidden well within the shadow of his hood. Strangely, despite a menacing appearance, I did not feel as though whoever he was wished me any harm.

The silence between us stretched, filled with the sounds of the ocean and wind, bringing with them a feeling of control and security, much like being at home with my loving father. I began to relax, and against my better judgment, to enjoy the moment.

Finally, the figure spoke. "I am one who has come before, the one who wore your ring in the beginning. I am Máedóc Dalatún." The moonlight caught his cloak, and I saw that it was not the black I had initially thought, but a deep forest green with golden threaded ancient runes throughout.

"I am honored," I said humbly, offering him a slight bow of recognition. If this were true, his blood ran in my veins.

He circled me slowly. He then chose to speak. "You have grown well, Daine Dalatún, Son of Caradoc. Your energy is strong. Though, not as it should be after the attainment of so many years. You have become weak and complacent. You have not been exercising and exploring the Druid within. Despite a pressing threat from the Sidhe, you have chosen to be content with mediocrity. Perhaps, it would be best if the Druid was removed from you, and given to another who would more greatly value its worth?" His words hung cloyingly in the air, pressing down on me with the weight of all that such a warning would entail.

I paled, struggling to set my self right. I knew his threat was not idle. He could remove this gift and burden from me. I desperately did not want that. I spoke, choosing my words wisely, "I humbly ask your forgiveness. Teach me how I may improve. Please, that I may be worthy of the Druid."

Máedóc appraised me in the silence that followed my words. My heart prayed that it was enough. "I commend Bramwyll for his instruction, he has taught you well. He is unquestionably adept, though he does not possess the same talents and strengths as your own. And yet, despite his subordinate abilities, he has been in open rebellion against the Sidhe on more occasions than yourself. You were to be the world's champion, yet you have cowered. How could you have allowed such remiss?"

My heart sank at having obviously been found lacking. There was not much I could say by way of explanation. He was right. I exhaled slowly, speaking steadily despite feeling as though my world were in danger of being thrown off axis. "I have not ceased to search for the Sword. That is all that matters."

White hands removed the hood from Máedóc's face. He was regal in bearing an appearance. A thin and stately nose centered his face that was both handsome and noble. His square chin was cleft, and his hair was of the same shade and wild nature as my own. But, it was his eyes that caught me off guard. They were identical to my father's. The very same shape and bottomless brown that bordered on black – eyes that were so deep you could swim in them, my mother used to say. They too were kind, and as I gazed upon them, I felt an instant pang of longing for my father.

"Daine," the voice was no longer as thunder but sincere, "there is no time left with which I could further instruct you. You must persevere with what you have thus far managed to acquire. The Sidhe draw perilously close to finding the Sword, within a day, all efforts to circumvent them will be too late. Search yourself. Inside of you lies the knowledge necessary to find the Sword. The ring will show you the way," Máedóc smiled encouragingly.

A red dawn showed signs of breaking along the horizon of the sea.

I did not understand. I opened my mouth to voice as much, but was met with Máedóc's own words, "You will. The knowledge is inside of you," he addressed to my unspoken thoughts. His face grew sad, "I must leave you with a warning, one that pains me to convey. Beware of your grief. If you allow it to, it will destroy you. Find strength wherever you may, and anchor yourself there. No matter how large the storm that rages against you is, you must hold firm." This time he did not smile, but remained grim as his hands returned his hood up to again shadow his face. With a slight bow of his own, he righted himself and began to back away. Once outside of the standing stones, he was gone.

Without a moments delay, I was whisked out of the peaceful place and flung back into an abrupt awareness of my body. I was still sitting comfortably in the upholstered chair. I shook my head in an effort to shake my frantic thoughts back together. I was slightly disoriented, and the panic that I had felt after the first dream, now seemed to grow until it threatened to choke me.

The Fae were about to find the Sword.

I stood up too quickly, momentarily dizzy and forced to steady myself against the chair until the room ceased to spin. I walked to the window and raised my hand to the moonlight. The sapphire gleamed with promise. I went into my study, drawing the doors closed tightly behind me. If the answer was inside of me, and I had been blatantly chided for not fully exploring the inner Druid, that was exactly where I needed to begin.

It was as though my mind knew exactly where to go, skipping over inapplicable knowledge. I supposed it should, given that my subconscious would have known no boundaries in exploring every part, hidden away or no, that was of me. Having found what I was looking for, a memory came.

It was faint, ancient, but still clear enough to see and understand.

Four men stood within a grassy clearing upon a hill. Standing stones circled its crest, and lush trees and foliage served as a barrier to protect its guests from unwanted eyes. To the left, the hill fell away sharply down to the sea. The men were all dressed in heavy leathers and furs, iron swords and torques hung about their necks. They were large, with bodies that were accustomed to hard and heavy labor merely to survive. Three had long beards and wild, braided long hair. The fourth, Máedóc, was the only one who wore his hair short, with his face cleanly shaven. Instantly, I received an answer to the question that my mind had wondered, *it reduces the chance of lice and fleas.*

A stone altar stood between them. Upon its surface lay a beautiful sword, with a blade that shone like the most finely polished silver. The hilt was decorated by large sapphires and runes. The largest sapphire of all served as the pommel. Quickly, the men worked, randomly looking over their shoulders as if afraid of being discovered. Words were spoken in the Fae tongue, as runes were laid meticulously upon the diminutive area where the grip met the pommel. With the last rune in place and the last of the Fae words hovering in the air, blinding white light erupted from the Sword. The men turned away attempting to cover their eyes from the light that would surely blind them.

A loud crack was heard, sounding out like a stone being broken.

At once the light was gone. The most ragged of them all, Aiulos, was the first to turn his face to the altar. He lifted the large sapphire that had broken cleanly away from the hilt into the air in triumph. He set it down intently upon the stone platform, which I now knew had cracked as well. Nimbly, he crashed a massive stone hammer upon the sapphire. All men huddled in more closely, anxious to discover what had happened. The gem had split into four equal pieces.

Rings were made, with hidden binding runes placed into the iron that had been overlaid with silver, forging the precious stone and the metal of the ring to be bound as one. The men had successfully been able to steal and divide some of the Sidhe's magic. Máedóc took the Sword and his ring.

They split up, fearing that remaining together would make them easier targets of the Fae's malevolence. The barriers between Faery and the earth were secure, but they had reason to fear.

Maurelle.

Suddenly the scene switched. Maurelle had found Máedóc, and stood beguiling him to return the Sword that he had stolen. His eyes bled, as her alien pheromones caused his brain to overload. She smiled wickedly, promising him heaven if he would return the Sword.

He did not have it, he lamented. He'd lost it, thrown it away and into the sea when he feared she would find him. Disgusted, she cast him away. When Máedóc had recovered himself, he began to laugh with sheer joy. She had underestimated him.

Máedóc had discovered a rune that would bind two things irrevocably together. He had placed it on the Sword and its match upon his ring. Being each a piece of the other, they would forever know where the other was to be found. Speaking the words of passage, the sapphire called to its other half.

I burst from the memory. Silently, I sent a word of gratitude to Máedóc, hoping desperately that he heard it. Miming what he had done, I held my ring near to my heart and spoke in his ancient tongue.

It was as if a current had connected my mind directly to the sapphire of the ring. I could see exactly where the Sword was located and the proximity of all life forms to it.

Máedóc was right, soon it would be too late.

Chapter Twenty

It was the quiet time just before the dawn when I rushed into Bram's room, waking him roughly in the dark.

"What is it, Boy?" he said worriedly as he sat up in bed and worked his way toward its edge.

"I've found the Sword. Hurry, Bram," urgency was thick in my voice. Bram sensed it as he dressed quickly, taking his own daggers from the small table beside his bed. Together we strode swiftly, but soundlessly, from the room.

"Where is it?" he asked as we hastened to the stables.

I was not in the mood for talking, time was of the essence. "There is no time to explain, stay close to me, it will not be far." I swung myself up to my favorite horse's bare back, feeling so pressed that I did not know if I had moment enough to saddle him. Bram followed suit.

We kicked our horses into a gallop, flying toward Kamarina. I did not slow as we drew close to town, but kept at it, taking the road that jutted away from Main Street just before the town grew clustered. This road curved, making a large arc before leading back again toward Kamarina. When we drew near, I slowed my horse to a steady trot. I couldn't help but look for the Sidhe that I knew were about.

We were here.

I abruptly slowed my horse and jumped off, running into a thicket of brambles. Bram muttered curses behind me as he did his best to catch up. The sun had risen, and the birds sang sweetly in the trees overhead. Before long, the thick forest and undergrowth cleared, revealing a meadow, sun filtering through the leafy boughs overhead to shine down upon a sprawling field of golden flowers.

I couldn't hide my smile as I moved into the clearing. Ahead, a natural rock wall rose about fifteen feet above the flowered covered floor where we now stood. There would be a deep pool of clear water beside the wall, the water springing forth from the rock's face before cascading into the pool of water six or seven feet below.

I knew this place. I had brought my children here many times over the summers to swim in the pool's cool and clean water. Now that I was here, I wondered if I had not been drawn to this place by my ring all along.

I stopped at the water's edge. I was looking for a granite boulder that was wedged between the meadow's floor and the wall's edge. There it was. Exactly as I had seen it in my mind's eye.

I went to stand before it, and without waiting to see if Bram had followed, I opened the earth, revealing a sword hidden deeply inside of the wall. It had not tarnished, but still shone like highly polished silver in the morning's light. Sapphires sparkled from where they had been carefully laid into the hilt.

I reached out, and took it in my hand, marveling that it seemed entirely weightless. A feeling of rightness began to resonate from within in me, growing in strength until it had flowed and washed over my entire body. I could not be sure, but in that moment, I felt as though I too shone as brightly as the Sword itself. I closed the earth, and turned to finding Bram just behind me.

His eyes were wide, going from the Sword to mine as his face was absolutely elated. He nodded; this was the Sword of Light. I motioned for him to follow me. I knew that the Sidhe would be close, and I did not want to risk meeting them just yet.

"Hello, Daine. It has been too long since last we met. I find myself more than pleasantly surprised at the effect the years have had upon you. You've matured into the most handsome of men."

A shiver ran down my spine as my every molecule became attuned to the bearer of that voice. I turned around slowly, holding the Sword out in front of me. I would not hesitate to see if it lived up to its claim of being able to kill the Fae should she so much as blink in a way I did not like.

Maurelle stood ten steps away, and though she paced, she never drew nearer. It was clear, even without having used it myself, that Maurelle believed that the Sword I now possessed was fully capable of ending her.

"Bram," I said evenly, "get behind me."

From the corner of my eye, I saw my old friend taking shelter behind my back, though I did not take my eyes off of her for a moment. I allowed the Druid free rein, and awed as everything was brought into acute clarity. I could hear Bram's steady heartbeat sounding behind me, as well as the speeding hearts of the birds from where they now cowered in the trees.

She continued to smile warmly, a fact that only seemed to put me more on edge. "I hope you are not still so adamant about refusing our undeniable chemistry. We could be explosive together." She waited to see if I would react. Her bottom lip protruded as she mocked pouting, "Pity, I have always had an appetite for older men," she winked at Bram. I felt him inwardly wince as her dart had found its target. She gave a small, mirthful chuckle in response.

"Daine, I see that you have found something that is mine. It has been lost to me for quite some time. I would be most rewarding and appreciative if you would but return it to me." She smiled, using the smile that could rob me of myself.

Instead of complying, I laughed cruelly in her face. I possessed the Sword, my Druid ran free - she no longer had any effect upon me aside from the faint tingling of my nerves as I noticed her pheromones being released. She smelled good, I'd give her that, but that was all.

Bram's sudden tensing behind me made me aware of what must have been his plight.

"Bram," I hushedly spoke, "close your eyes. Fight the temptation to look at her. Cover your ears, and resist. I'll not leave you alone, but I expect the same of you." Bram instantly obeyed. It was imperative that I face Maurelle without expending too much concern elsewhere.

"Oh Daine, you do so amuse me. You will give me the Sword, and I would be the most grateful beneficiary should you chose to do so without a fight." Her voice oozed of rancid honey. Her sweet voice masked the venom that coursed through her veins.

"No," I sneered, "The answer will always be no."

She walked back and forth at the same careful distance, feigning that she was sulking. Her eyes were calculating, "Do not be so sure of that." She smiled a smile that was pure poison, and sifted away.

I could not sense her anywhere near, and neither could the earth. I turned to Bram, gently removing his hands from where he held them firmly against his ears. His eyes remained firmly shut. Blood that had begun to fall in tears marred his skin, beard, and clothing. I removed the handkerchief from my back pocket, and swiftly went to work on his face.

He refused to look at me, so determined was he to abstain from looking at Maurelle and become a pawn of her will ever again. "Bram, it's all right. She has gone. Come, let us not waste any more time, and do just the same." His eyes popped open, and he nodded his definite agreement.

We pushed through the thick undergrowth, finding our horses chewing sweet summer grass not far from where we had left them. In much better spirits, we mounted our horses, and turned them around to begin the journey home. I'd had piece of mind enough to bring an old table cloth with me before I'd woken Bram. I wrapped the Sword in it now, and lay it solidly against my legs, feeling it shift from the left to the right as my horse walked.

Just before mid-morning we turned onto the long drive that led to our home. We allowed the horses to move past the house, they were anxious to get to their stalls and oats and water. We tended to them, taking our time to make sure that we had done it well. I took the Sword from where I had kept it always at an arm's length, and removed it from its covering. It was beautiful as it glinted in the sun.

I was anxious to show Ayda. Our children would now always be safe from any threat. I breathed a sigh of relief, finally allowing myself to feel the joy I had been too afraid to acknowledge until now.

As we mounted the stairs, I began to feel uneasy. My disquietude seemed to increase with every step we made toward the house.

Bram stopped walking and looked at me curiously, "What is it Daine?"

I extended my hand, rapidly moving it in an indication to cease his inquiry. I closed my eyes, listening - the house was silent. The house was never this quiet with the children around. Perhaps they had gone into town? I allowed my senses to fan, noting that the breeze had ceased to blow, the birds to chirp, and even the insects to hum. I inhaled deeply, and smelled blood ever so faintly.

My eyes shot open, as I grabbed Bram's hand and pulled him forward. I felt him charging, as he too began to feel the terrible wrongness that had veiled our home. We stormed up the large curving stair for the upper floors where the bedrooms lay. We dashed into the children's bedrooms, entirely dismayed at having found them all empty. My room too was deserted.

"Do you think they went into town?" I voiced, strained and grasping for threads of hope that were hurriedly slipping away.

Bram pursed his lips, his head only barely moving to indicate that he did not.

My heart contracted, terror exploded inside of me. I raced back through each of the bedrooms, searching them all again. I felt a calm hand firmly squeeze my forearm as I blindly stared at my daughter Charlotte's made bed, tears blurring my eyesight as they refused to fall.

"She took them." Bram's voice brought me to sharp attention where he stood. "Come, she will have taken them into the shelter of the woods."

I needed no further coaxing and rushed from Charlotte's room, down the stairs, and out the back door. I ran with the wind as my aid, making it as swiftly as I could to what had been my boys' favorite place to play. A massive log that had had its interior partially rotted out served as their dungeon, castle, fort, and keep. I knew instinctively that this was where they would be.

The sun continued to shine brightly, breaking through in patches to the forest floor where it had found its way through the heavy canopy. The heat was interminable. There was no relief to my suffering in sight.

I broke through the trees, finding the area where my children played to be entirely empty. I heard Bram coming to a stop just beside me, and set my jaw to mask my dismay at having not immediately found them happily at play. It was Bram who then closed his eyes, taking a deep breath to steel himself, he motioned to the far side of the tree. The roots had come free of the ground and made a perfect shield to our eyes of the other side.

With trepidation, I made my way around. Bram followed a mere step behind.

Both of us were ready for the fight that Maurelle was sure to give. I raised the Sword, and moved quicker than the eye could catch to the other side of the upturned roots.

I froze, the Sword nearly dropping from my hand as I lost the strength to hold it up.

My three sons lay dead, torn and bloody. Their bodies were flayed to ribbons in some places, as they lay unfamiliarly upon the forest floor. The ground around them had collectively dampened with their merged blood.

I fell upon my knees, my heart truly broken and rendered almost entirely useless as I stared up into Ayda's eyes.

She held my daughter fiercely with unnatural clawed hands. She had one poised and ready at my silently crying daughter's throat.

"Ayda. Please. You do not have to do this." I swallowed heavily. Was there even air to breathe here?

Ayda laughed evilly, a sound that I had never heard cross her lips. Her clothing resembled the tattered rags that had hung from her after her encounter with the Nuckelavee. Her hair was a wild, unkempt mess, her eyes glowed an unearthly flat blue. She was everything that would have rebelled against the well groomed woman with lively eyes of emerald green that I knew and loved.

Then she smiled, revealing teeth that had been broken and turned into crude fangs. It was the voice of my wife that then spoke, "Ah, but I do. And what's more, I want to. Have you any idea how disappointing it was to have born children with no hint of the Fae?" Her eyebrow rose, making a parody of the woman that I loved.

"Why would our children have carried traits of the Fae, Ayda?" I asked roughly, confused. I looked at Charlotte, and longed for nothing more than to hold her.

Ayda looked blatantly at me as she ran a claw down our daughter's neck, causing her to begin to openly weep. I watched with wide-eyed horror as blood trickled down her neck and onto her dress. "Because, you fool, that was the deal that I made with Maurelle. If I were to help her, in any way that she asked, then I would be made into one of the Fae."

It was my turn to laugh, and I did so mockingly, "I, the fool. Oh Ayda, when have you not learned that deals with the Sidhe never work out as promised?"

"Apparently, you must be blind. Are I not now similar to them in power and capacity?" Her hand flexed above my daughter's throat.

In response, my own hand tensed. I could not kill her with lightning, that would undoubtedly kill my precious girl too. There was nothing I could do but try and convince Ayda to let her go.

"Ayda," Bram's voice sounded out as he came to stand beside me, "it is not the Fae that you have been changed into, but nothing more than a *Ban Sidhe*. You have become their puppet, and slave, and willing traded your own soul to do so."

"Pot calling the kettle black, aren't we, Grandad?" She began to sharpen her claws against one another; the hand that held our daughter now pierced the delicate skin on Charlotte's chest. Charlotte cried out, and Ayda leaned down to whisper something into her ear, something that had her simpering in a massive show of will to stop crying. Having succeeded, Ayda stroked our daughter's cheek with her claws almost tenderly.

I cringed.

"Tell me, when did you so lightly trade your humanity? Was it when you could no longer do anything to thwart Brigid from marrying Daine? Or was it when your father refused to allow you to move to Drumcliff to pursue your Druid training and conquest of possessing Daine as your own?" Ayda raised herself and regarded both Bram and I squarely, Bram's questions had surprised her.

"So, you knew about all of that then?" Ayda said rhetorically.

In unnecessary response, Bram gave but the faintest inclination of his head.

Straightening herself, concernedly regarding her claws as if they were painted and chipped, she answered coldly, "I met Maurelle sometime before that. I was a young girl, hopelessly in love with a boy who didn't even notice that I existed." Her gaze tore away from her claws to give me a blatantly murderous look. Then she demurely returned to inspecting her elongated fingers and nails.

"When I found that I possessed the Druid, possibilities blossomed within me. Perhaps now I could join my love in Drumcliff, and win his affection all for my own. When I revealed my Druidic capacity to Father, he refused to send me to Drumcliff. He was spiteful, choosing to instead instruct me personally and keep the knowledge of my gifts to himself. Apparently, he did not truly do that, now did he Grandad." She looked up to regard Bram suspiciously.

"And so you killed them." There was no question in Bram's voice.

"Yes. Maurelle appeared and made me an offer: to live forever as the Fae in exchange for my willingness to help. I eagerly accepted. If I could live as the Fae, with their beautiful men as dutiful companions, then it did not matter that I was rejected and scorned by the only human who ever made me burn with desire. She sent the Nuckelavee, and I helped him kill them all. All, that is, except for Brigid. She knew of my feelings for you," she pinned me with her lifeless blue eyes, "and stood in my way. For that, I killed her myself."

"I watched as the Nuckelavee used her, and then in amusement as his semen burned and began to consume her from the inside out. Only then, as she writhed in pain, did I pour the lamp oil upon her body. I called fire, and sent the flames to gently lap at her skin. I delighted as she was burned slowly alive, the fire held back from ending her quickly by my very own hand." Ayda beam with pride at us.

"And now," she continued, "Maurelle has asked that I retrieve the Sword. I have already killed the three," she gestured callously toward the broken bodies of our sons that lay upon the ground, "and should you refuse, I will kill the girl too."

My jaw tightened visibly as I bit down, feeling my teeth ache in the effort.

"Quite the conundrum, isn't it, Daine?" She drummed her hand upon the auburn curls of my daughter's head, "Save your daughter, or retain only the merest possibility of saving humanity. Whatever will you choose?" She laughed giddily.

"Ayda, you have. . ." Bram was not able to finish before Ayda had called the wind and had him blown forcibly into a tree behind her. The tree groaned upon impact, and although his body was hidden behind the massive root system, I heard his body strike the ground with a sickening thud.

"Why, Ayda? Did I not love you enough? I gave you everything, everything that I am. There was never a second thought for Brigid, I only dreamed of you," I said desperately.

Ayda stuck out her bottom lip, twisting her face into a mask of sadness. "Oh, my poor baby." She then smiled, revealing her broken and jagged teeth, her lifeless blue eyes ghastly. "Come now, you're stalling. Choose. Your precious Charlotte, or the Sword?" Her hand moved to fondle the throat of my daughter with her claws.

I allowed my eyes to fall away from Ayda's, dropping until they found the terrified eyes of my daughter. I choked on the sob that had begun to rise in my throat. My voice ragged and breaking, somehow I managed to tell her, "It'll be alright, Pumpkin."

I had barely gotten it out, seeing the hope blossom in my daughter's eyes, before Ayda's claws slashed down and tore out Charlotte's throat. Ayda cruelly let her fall to the ground, stepping away with blatant hatred.

I fled forward, uncaring of the consequences. I watched helplessly as Charlotte's tiny hands went up to mangled throat in an effort to stop the torrent of blood that was spurting out. My hands incapably covered her own. There was nothing I could do to save her as she began to choke on her blood. Her lips turned a deathly shade of blue as her skin waxed sickly pale. I leaned over her, speaking the words for instantaneous healing against the exposed muscle and tissue of her neck.

Her body convulsed in a series of spasms, and I watched as the light and life forever disappeared from her beautiful eyes.

"You should have given me the Sword, Daine," Ayda said idly from somewhere not afar.

I rocked the now lifeless body of my daughter, blood soaking into my clothing as I spat in response, "You would have killed her anyway." A swelling rage took control of my mind and body. I turned my head, seeing her start as she encountered eyes that burned with living fire.

Ayda quickly regained the air of indifference, admitting simply "Yes, you are right about that. She had quite the likeness to Brigid, don't you agree? I almost couldn't bear to look at her without feeling like I needed to immediately kill her too – and I did. So, I suppose it all worked out for me in the end."

I couldn't believe what I was hearing. I felt nothing but revulsion as I looked at her. She deserved to die, and I would personally see to it that she did.

I lay Charlotte gently upon the forest floor. My clothing was saturated by her blood. I raised the Sword in my hand menacingly toward Ayda, my daughter's blood blotting its blade. I was beyond being able to speak words. I stood in a bloody field, surrounded by the lifeless bodies of my massacred children. I was capable of only one thought, revenge.

I stepped forward, Ayda's pulse quickened at her neck. I watched her like a focused predator as she began to back away fearfully.

"I warn you husband, Maurelle will be most unhappy if you damage me," Ayda warned desperately.

"Doubtful," I growled lowly. I stalked closer, my eyes focused intently on hers. She did not mistake my intention.

She began to side step away and I matched her, caught in a dance where only one of us would walk away. She and I both knew that it would be me. I would not use Druidry to kill her - that would be over too quickly. I wanted to feel her die as I avenged my fallen children with my bare hands.

"I will fight you Daine, and it will not be pretty. I am more powerful than you can ever imagine." She called fire, causing it to shoot up in a pillar around me. I was untouched. I used her own fire against her, wielding it as though it were my own, manipulating it into a warm and protective cocoon before I stepped through it entirely unscathed.

Her face paled, her eyes wide, "That's not possible!" Her foot stomped on the ground in a tantrum. She huffed as she thought of her next attack.

"Do not even try it. I will remain unharmed no matter the Druidry you use. The world bends its self and its devices only to me," I said to her pitilessly, my voice a thing of ultimate authority.

Her claws seemed to lengthen even farther, her face twisting into an ugly amused glare. "It does not matter, you will be easy enough to dispose of without the use of something as menial as Druidry."

Bram's face appeared behind her, his arms snaking around to hold her arms pinned down at her sides. He was using all the strength he had left to hold her, forcing his body into one final purpose. "Throw the Sword, Daine, end this!" His eyes though fierce pleaded with my own.

"No! I would kill her myself!" I roared at him. I prowled closer to them.

"Do not stoop to their level, be true Daine," Bram countered, grunting in pain as Ayda fought rabidly against his hold. His voice was soft and even, but somehow it managed to break through the rage that sheltered me.

"But you'll die," I said, my voice faltering.

Ayda must have mistaken my tone for indecision, she began to laugh hideously. Her voice was breathy from Bram restricting her movements and lungs, "Poor Daine, always having to choose between the lesser of evils," she mocked. "He'll choose life, Old Man. You'll live to fight another day, mark my word." Her eyes rocked to mine, taunting as she smiled with a mouth full of obscene teeth.

I could not stand to look at her a moment longer. She was a sick, twisted illness that had been masquerading as a devoted wife and mother. Bile rose into my mouth, and I sneered as I tasted it.

"Throw the Sword Daine! I cannot hold her much longer. It is too late for me, I will not recover from these wounds. Let me die honorably, allow me this final act of vindication." His green eyes, the same shade that Ayda's had once been, were resolute. He wanted this. He wanted redemption as much as he wanted to redress what had been done to his family.

"Finish it! Now!" His face was strained with the effort to contain something that would soon overpower and kill him.

I drew my arm back and threw the Sword with all my might.

It flipped end over end as it flew through the air.

Ayda let out a scream, and Bram, despite holding a raging and wild beast in his arms, managed to express a silent, and final, appearance of absolute gratitude.

The Sword struck true, piercing them both through their chests. They toppled to the ground, their blood seeping out to tangle and intertwine, becoming indiscernibly one.

I stood as a statue. Breathing ragged breaths that threatened to rip apart my chest. I fell to my knees as the pain of my inconceivable loss washed over me, drowning everything in darkness.

I heaved, sick with what had been done, my tear filled eyes darting to the fallen bodies of my children, and to Bram who had died protecting me, just as he always had. I sobbed, guttural sobs that seemed to originate from the farthest reaches of my soul.

The Druid receded, lost in our shared grief. It wasn't long before I realized that I had just died too.

Chapter Twenty-one

I burned Ayda's remains, not wanting to befoul the earth with something as malign as she. When it was done there was nothing left, and for that I was afforded some peace.

At night fall, I loaded the carefully wrapped and prepared bodies of my children and mentor, tenderly placing each in the back of our wagon. I rode alone, a solitarily mourned funeral procession of one.

I did not feel. I was dead inside. However, no matter how much I willed it, I could not stanch the flow of tears that refused to cease falling from my eyes. Slowly, the horses pulled the wagon forward. I did not want to bruise my most precious cargo.

Too soon, I arrived at the spring where I found the Sword.

I wanted to lay them to rest in a place that held only good memories of us together. A meadow adorned with golden flowers was the least that I could give them. It seemed as if it had been years since I was last here.

The horses stopped.

I don't know how, but I climbed down from the wagon's buckboard, and stood unblinkingly before the five delicately wrapped bundles. I bent and picked up the first.

I cradled each of my children to me. Holding all that was left of them as tightly as I could, as if by so doing they would feel and know that I was there. That I was with them even in death.

I stumbled and shuffled forward as I pressed my weeping face against them. There were moments would I could do nothing but collapse to the ground and sob.

I carried Bram, reverently, laying him down beside them. He would guard and protect them in death just as fiercely as he had in life.

I opened the earth of the wall just below the spring, deep and dark, aligning stones to make their tomb. The water fell tranquilly over the opening. I ceased its flow. Then, with agony, I stooped to carefully lift my children, stifling my heartbroken lamenting against their burial shrouds. Lovingly I placed each into their final place of protection and rest.

I lay Bram down last. I placed my hand upon his gently chest and whispered a pious plea, "Please keep them safe."

Taking one last glance to assure myself that they were all well, I allowed the earth to close, to blanket and shield them forever.

The spring had issued forth from a large stone that jutted out from the rest of the rock wall. I went back the wagon and returned with a hammer and chisel. I worked, tirelessly, thankfully losing myself to the task before me. Ever so gradually, the stone was transformed into the head of a lion.

It was frozen mid-roar, its mouth wide with teeth bared. I could think of no better emblem to protect my family as they rested peacefully behind. When I had finished, it was once again day. After standing back to survey my work, I released my hold on the spring. It cascaded from the lion's mouth, falling loudly into the clear pool below.

The words my mother had written on the parchment had finally all come to pass.

I memorized the place, the smells, the feel, the sounds, and wished with everything that I had that I could join my family forever here.

A young family appeared, the picture of pure happiness. Their daughter, who was perhaps five, charged the cool water of the pond, giggling with joy as its coolness met her warm skin. She was followed by a fat and jolly little brother of perhaps two years, who squealed with his own delight. Their parents greeted me, undetecting of the way my insides rent as I heard the children's laughter.

I closed my eyes, knowing that my own children would never again be joining in the fun. I moved most painfully toward my wagon, feeling pieces of myself being irretrievably left behind.

Chapter Twenty-two

The memories the house held were too painful. My mind continually deceived me. I'd swear that I heard children laughing, and then expected my own to run through the front door and into my office at every moment. I suppose that is what grief is, the time that it takes for our minds to accept that someone is really gone. Until that point, we're lost in the belief that they are not truly gone at all, simply away and will shortly reappear.

The idea of waiting and hoping to see their ghosts haunted me.

After carving the lion's head, I made my way to the house. I was numb, in shock and unthinking. I think I went there purely out of habit. I stared at the house, silent and dark, and after putting my horses away, went inside.

I smirked bitterly as I felt the wards tingle on my skin as I crossed the doorway, *can't keep the wolf out when he's masquerading as one of your own,* I chastised myself.

I passed by the liquor cabinet, grabbing Bram's newly opened bottle of Irish whiskey and took it with me into my study. I drew the curtains closed, casting the room into darkness. I sat in my chair, sinking unfeelingly into its familiar curve, and brought the bottle to my lips. I drank heavily, not caring for how it burned. I found the discomfort an incentive to drink all the more.

Contrary to Máedóc's warning, I nursed my grief, wallowed in it, and reveled as it grew.

I drank myself into a stupor every night for weeks. I couldn't stand my waking hours, they were too painful to bear. The house that had always been loud and lively was now constantly enveloped in silence and stillness.

If the days were bad, the nights were worse. In the darkness I allowed my mind to hope that maybe my misery would qualify me lucky enough to be haunted by the ghost of one of my children. They never came, and the disappointment was nearly maddening.

Rather than endure more than I was capable of surviving, I found it much easier to simply drink until I could no longer remember.

Two weeks into my drunken mourning, I had once again drifted off into the unconsciousness that I so craved. The wind picked up, rattling the shutters against the house. The rattling escalated into a forceful banging. Loud enough, to wake me from the drug induced sleep. I lifted my head slowly from where it had lain heavily upon my desk, feeling my neck knot and tighten from having rested at such and awkward angle.

The first thing I saw was the Sword, unmoved since I had let it lay beside my head upon the desk. I looked around groggily, my head swam and I felt as though I might be sick. The sound of the shutter slamming against the house vibrated dully around in my skull. I was going to have one devil of a headache in the morning. I stood gingerly, holding my hand to my head in an attempt to steady myself as I stumbled into the furniture that I had forgotten lay in my way. The floor seemed to move precariously beneath me.

With much more concentration and effort than I had expected, I made it to the window and drew aside the heavy curtains. I squinted as I looked out into the brightly lit night; there was a full moon out tonight. *Strange*, I thought to myself as I noted that not a single leaf of the tree, nor a single twig of the many shrubs that were rooted just outside my window, fluttered in the breeze. If it were possible, the wind blew only against my study window; raising a near deafening racket as the shutters continued to pound against the house.

I'm still dreaming, I thought blankly. I could hardly walk straight, chances were good that none of this was even happening at all. But then, a stray idea occurred to me, preying upon my ruined emotional state to solidify and form. Perhaps it was one of the children outside my window, battering the shutters, asking that I let them in.

As quickly as I could manage, I threw open my study door, feeling the shock of air that was fresh in comparison to the stagnation that existed inside of my office. Using a hand to support myself as I leaned against the wall, I turned away from my study and made my way sloppily toward the front door. I had some difficulty with the locks. I cursed them as I fumbled hurriedly to get them open.

I threw open the massive door and for the first time in two weeks, stepped outside into the dark night. The air was clean and but cloying, smelling thickly of the lilies ran the entire length of the long porch. I gagged. In my current state the scent was nauseating.

I stepped onto the large covered porch, my eyes darting wildly to each of the ornate pillars that spanned the front of the house. The children had loved to hide behind them. There was no sign of them on the porch, so I broadened my gaze, seeking them. I moved to where my office window looked out over the long drive and the massive magnolia that shaded the patio. The shutters had stopped banging entirely.

My momentarily heightened spirits immediately sank.

"Where are you?" I whispered despondently into the still night.

The pain of my longing was beginning to override the numbness. It seared me once again, refusing to ever allow me to heal. I turned away and made my way disjointedly back to the front door. I gave the rocking chairs and furniture that looked suspiciously devious as they sat on the porch a pointedly wide berth. No doubt they were planning to move forward when I least expected, and trip my leaden feet.

I had finally made it back to the entry when a female voice genially said my name, "Daine."

I closed my eyes, enjoying how it seemed to caress my skin affectionately. I turned around haltingly; any movement made too quickly would surely cause me to lose my already shaky footing.

"Maurelle," I said with swagger.

She stood on the ground a few paces away from the front steps. I could hear the wards humming as they prevented her from coming any closer. She was beautiful, her long blond hair gently cascading down her shoulders, her velvet blue eyes soft and inviting.

I wanted to address her face to face.

I swayed as I looked down the steps that led from the porch to the ground. There were only four of them, but they seemed to grow and shrink unpredictably in height as I studied them. I gauged their distance, stepping confidently forward, and ended up stumbling and falling to my hands and knees into the gravel at their base. I stood, leaning slightly as I dusted off my palms, and then resumed a drunken saunter.

Maurelle looked at me, clearly amused. She was undampened, and I didn't care. She looked positively radiant in the moonlight.

I stood in front of her, wobbling a bit, as asked her cordially, "To what do I owe the pleasure?" I gave her a bow, which again sent me reeling in an effort to regain my footing. I place my hand upon her shoulder to steady myself since I could not do so unaided.

Maurelle looked me over, her sweet mouth beginning to turn into a sneer. To my surprise she was repulsed, "You look terrible. And, you smell." She swatted my hand away from where it still rested upon her, stepping rudely away from me. "This is just unacceptable," she added loftily.

"I am sorry my presence so offends thee. . . " I said insulted. Then with a quickness I did not know myself capable of making at that moment, I found myself pressed up against her, her back firmly against the bark of the magnolia's trunk. My hand squeezed her throat mercilessly as I spat, "you did just murder my family." Despite my vision being slightly blurred, I was able to hatefully focus on her intently.

She choked on her laughter, which caused me to clutch her throat tighter. If only I possessed the strength to crush it - I attempted it anyway.

The nature of Maurelle's eyes shifted from amusement to annoyance. With little effort, she reached up to take hold of my wrist, and forced the bones together within her seemingly dainty grasp. I cried out in pain. "You are pathetic," she jeered, looking down her perfect nose at me. She let me go.

I cradled my wrist, my eyes bloodshot as I glared at her viciously.

She circled me, making a tisking sound as she went. Apparently, she did not approve of what she saw. "When was the last time you bathed? Shaved? Changed your clothes?" she scorned.

The answer she received was heard only by myself, *not since I washed my children's blood from my body, and then wore clean clothes with which to bury them in.*

When I didn't respond, Maurelle regarded me with even more contempt. "I came expecting more from you. I am greatly disappointed in having not found it. I could kill you now, without the slightest bit of challenge – but where would the enjoyment be?" She scowled at me, disenchanted.

It was my turn to laugh, I did so bitterly. "You were looking for a fight, were you? Well, I'm afraid all of the fight has been taken out of me. This is what's left," I opened my arms wide and held them out in supplication. "Kill me, please. You will give me great joy in being put out of my misery." I remained prone, hoping that the enticement would induce her to just get it over with.

To my disappointment she did not. She just shook her head, disgust evident on her face, "You did not even have the piece of mind to bring the Sword out with you. You are at best, upsetting. I believed you to be above being so easily defeated. Gather yourself together, Daine. Your children would be ashamed."

"Never speak of them!" I righted myself, squaring my shoulders enraged.

"Ah, now that's more like it," she cooed, her eyelids lowering in desire. "If I had known that all that was needed to invite reaction out of you was to mention your petty children, I would have done so sooner." She smiled fondly, as if recollecting something. "Did you know your sons watched in blubbering terror as their mother transformed before them into the Ban Sidhe? Helpless as Anwyn thoroughly . . . enjoyed them? They were rendered so incapacitated, that they did not even attempt to fight when Ayda flayed them one by one."

"Stop," I said, damaged.

Her mouth quirked as she baited, "If only their father had had his priorities straight, he might have been able to save them. But, alas, he was too concerned with his own *glory* to protect them."

Such and insinuation had me shaking with wrath. I felt my mind being torn apart, as I searched furiously inside of myself for some way to correct her.

"And your daughter - what a beauty she was. I bet it tears at your heart to have chosen yourself, and let her die," Maurelle smiled cruelly.

I advanced toward her. She remained fixed in place, having no reason to fear me without the Sword. When I stood face to face with her, looking down at her from the few inches that separated our heights, her eyebrows hitched, daring me to attempt my worst.

I put my fist against the soft violet of her crimson sashed gown, my sapphire pressed firmly against the fabric that covered the skin of her taut stomach. If the sapphire of my ring was a piece of the Sword, then perhaps it too could do damage to her without the blade – if it was channeled right.

I remained motionless, my eyes heavily lidded, as we continued to regard one another carefully. And then, I did the unthinkable. I called lightning to strike me.

Everything was lost in a blinding white light. I felt my heart stop on contact, my mind lose focus, and the surge of energy as it traveled down to my feet. It then coursed back up and through me, ripping me apart before it shot through my arm, concentrated by the sapphire of my ring, and blasted into Maurelle. The force with which it left me, flung my body through the air as if I were nothing more than a rag doll.

I smashed into the side of my house, passing over the wards that began at the front steps before slamming into the white painted siding. I landed sharply onto the shattered furniture beneath me.

I collapsed immediately.

I raised myself, my ears ringing so loudly that nothing else could be heard above the din. I coughed, wincing at the extreme pressure I felt on my heart and lungs. Everything hurt. My innards and entire body felt singed. I wheezed with the effort to breathe, fighting to regain control of my body as I pushed myself off my chest. I held still as I shook uncontrollably after such a massive jolt.

The ringing that blared in my ears began to subside. I gently raised my head to look around. The night was still full and bright, no breeze stirred the leaves, and no rain fell. All was clear and quiet. I raised my head higher, looking to where Maurelle had stood when I had last seen her. I found her twenty feet from where I expected her to be.

She was lying on her back, struggling to move but seeming to find it difficult to do so, she held a hand tightly against her abdomen.

With effort, I brought myself up to stand. My right leg throbbed, shoots of pain shrieking in protest when I attempted to put any weight on it. Limping, I made my way down the porch stairs, and as swiftly as I could manage went to stand over Maurelle.

Her glittering Fae blood soaked into the ground beneath where she lay. Her abdomen was torn open, the wound terrible. Such an injury would have killed a mortal instantly. But, given time, she would heal.

I did not dwell upon that, instead I basked in the success at having left her so seriously wounded.

"When next we meet," she sputtered, shimmering blood trickling down her face from the corner of her mouth, "I will kill you. Prepared or not." Before my eyes, she sifted away, leaving behind only the wet ground, which shimmered red in the moonlight.

I began to pant; the pain in my leg was agonizing. I looked down to find that a stake from the small table that had landed on had gone entirely through the muscle of my thigh. I was bleeding significantly, but the wood had missed the bone and artery. I peered warily to the back of my leg, and saw the roughly pointed tip sticking a good six inches out of my leg. I cursed, and made my way back to the house.

I shut the front door reassuringly behind me, hobbling my way to the liquor cabinet. Taking an unopened bottle of Bourbon I gimped into my study. I threw open the curtains, hoping the moonlight would be bright enough to see to removing the wood.

I ripped open my pants, feeling dizzy as I saw the wood entering my flesh, and then again as it exited. With determination, I pulled the cork out of the bottle with my teeth, and spit it away. I steeled myself, taking several hearty drinks from the bottle before pouring the liquor on the front of my leg. It burned such that my eyes watered and I grimaced aloud in pain. I took a few quick huffs of air before pouring more of the Bourbon on the exit wound.

I doubted I was strong enough to do what needed to be done next.

In the silence, I heard my blood dripping upon the wood floor. I shook my head in irritation. There was no way around this. I grasped the wood firmly where it extended out of the back of my leg, and began to steadily pull. I grunted loudly, pursing my lips and holding my eyes tight against the water that was seeping through. I continued to pull until the picket withdrew with a sick sounding slurp.

I let the wood drop noisily to the floor, taking the Bourbon in my hand and managing another substantial swallow. I let the bottle down and wiped my mouth with the back of my now bloody hand.

I held my leg stiffly as I maneuvered to the nearby couch. Once sitting, I wrapped a length of my torn pant leg around the wound. Closing my eyes, the words for healing left my mouth as a prayer. Without delay I began to feel the warm tingle as they began to work.

I chuckled to myself, making the mental note to remember to never again be struck by lightning. The fog of exhaustion soon began to encroach upon my mind, and I allowed it to take me. I fell deeply asleep.

My mind opened with a start. I stood once again on the grassy clearing of the hill, with the sounds of the gentle breeze and sea crashing into the cliffs below. It was once more night, though there was neither moon nor a single star in the heavens.

I knew why I was here, and I looked for Máedóc.

I found him at the edge of the clearing, so still that if I had not known what to look for he could have easily been mistaken for stone. He was still cloaked, though instead of being entirely wrapped in it, his arms could be seen, folded over his chest as if in anger.

"You have allowed your grief to consume you," his voice sounded as cannon fire. I covered my ears at the sheer volume of it. "I warned you," he stalked toward me, "and you did not listen."

I had involuntarily cowered down with every word he spoke, the roar of his voice impossible to stand against. "What did you expect me to do?" I shouted at him from where I stooped. I raised myself, directing my fury at him, "They killed my family! My own wife was one of them, and I watched helplessly as she *killed* them!" Now my own anger had risen to match the strength of his voice. My chest rose and fell passionately.

He had closed the distance between us. We now stood at arms length. His face remained hidden beneath the cloak, but my own was seething. "You could have told me. You could have warned me about Ayda," I volleyed at him.

"It would not have saved them," his volume had lowered to the point that it was now tolerable. "If it was not by Ayda's hand, then it would have been by Maurelle's. Believe me, it is better that they died quickly in Ayda's grasp. They would not have been so lucky had it been Maurelle who held them."

I did not know how to respond. I knew that he was right. He was always right. I remained silent, taking solace in my anger. Máedóc noticed.

"Anger is good," he said. "It has the power to focus and motivate. But grief, grief has the opposite effect, causing us to dwindle until we are naught but hollow beasts. Use your anger. Make that your anchor. There is still much work to be done, and only those who are secure will survive."

"I have the Sword," I responded weakly.

"I noticed. I commend you for having found it so quickly after our last meeting. However, now you must use it," he caught my involuntarily wince of pain, "upon the actual Fae," he added for my benefit.

I nodded briefly, "What do you want me to do?"

"What you already know you must."

I continued to nod in acceptance. My mind and heart had both been burnt at having just been asked to remember the only time I had actually used the Sword. The image of Ayda and Bram's bodies impaled by a gleaming flash of silver rampaged through my mind before I could stop it.

Mercifully, Máedóc spoke, interrupting the reverie, "The High King and Queen of the Sidhe are preparing to enter our world. They are anxiously awaiting Maurelle's return where she will present them with the Sword, evidencing that every threat to them has been removed from the earth. If she does not return, they will postpone their visit until a time that they deem it safe . . . considering carefully if that moment will exist for them at all. They will not risk the possibility of any harm befalling themselves; they consider themselves to be too precious." I understood.

It was then that he finally showed me some companionability. His hand came to rest unexpectedly upon my shoulder. We stood face to face, we were the same height. I could just see his face under the shadow of his hood. "It will get easier, Daine," his tone was unexpectedly soft and reflective. "The Curse of the Four Fathers, losing all that you love by the hand of the Sidhe, has always been extremely difficult to bear – even for the most stalwart of men. It was my burden to have the Curse fall to me as well. The loss will always burn, but it will get easier. That I promise you." His hand fell away as he began to retreat, leaving me empty but with the faintest glimmer of hope flickering in my cold heart.

I awoke suddenly, my eyes staring at the corniced ceiling of my study. I still lay upon the couch. I sat upright, prodding at my leg tenderly through the make shift wrapping I had used to bandage it. I felt only the minutest of bruising in the deepest recesses of the muscle. I unwrapped it, inspecting the skin that showed not a single mark.

I stood, and picked up the Sword from my desk's top. I hurried up the stairs, making my way directly into my room where I procured a change of clothing, my daggers, soap, and my shaving razor.

I then left, not sparing a single glance for my memory filled surroundings, nor for each of the empty bedrooms that I passed as I went down the hall. It was the last that I would descend those stairs.

With the Sword in hand I left the house in search of a pond to bathe in. I had been idle long enough and I was angry.

Chapter Twenty-three

I headed for the stables, now cleanly shaven, bathed, and wearing fresh clothes. My daggers were strapped to my waist and the Sword was held in a temporary scabbard across my back. I entered where our horses were kept, and found that every stall was empty. The horses had either kicked out or had jumped out when I had forgotten to feed them. For a majority of the time, I had forgotten to feed myself, so I didn't feel too badly for neglecting the horses.

They wouldn't be far. We had acres of rolling grassy pasture that they would have found irresistible. I picked up a bridle and saddle, and lugged them to the side of the split rail fence that divided the property into fields. I set the saddle on the ground, taking the bridle with me as I slipped through the fence and walked down the rise to where I thought the horses might be.

Only one was there, my quarter horse. Upon seeing me his ears twitched affectionately, and despite having been out to pasture these past two weeks, he allowed me to approach him without darting.

I lay my hand upon his neck and slipped his bridle on. I lay my forehead against his muzzle, feeling relief at having found the only living creature that was left to me. Once saddled, I rode him to the gate. We passed by the stables, and then the silent mansion.

I burned them.

I did not look back or linger sadly as I felt the heat and heard the sounds of wood burning. In town, I set the old house that had been Ayda and I's aflame as well.

Taking one of the long gravel roads that headed away from town, I entered the thick pine forests. I didn't know how exactly I would find it, but I wouldn't stop until I did.

I rummaged around in the heat and the lessening summer light. I knew that when we had stepped through the Silver and into Mississippi, we had been near a temporary timber mill. That left me with a relatively small area in which the Silver could have been hidden. But, it was still like looking for a needle in a haystack.

At length I found it. Feeling entirely different than I had the first time I stood before a Silver. I faced no reservations about stepping through this time. The Silver closed behind me, and I was once again in the vaults. I was not alone.

A Fae guard stood with an upraised sword. A single torch burned on the wall behind him. I moved quickly, refusing to allow him the opportunity to catch me off guard. Drawing my sword, I arced it through the air, my arm smoothly continuing the motion over my other side and up again, creating a figure eight of slashing silver as I moved toward him.

He seemed to growl low in his throat, his sword met mine with a metallic clang. I slid away, opening my mind to the Druid secrets inside. The memories for expert swordsmanship were instantly my own. I met every one of his attacks, my own blade slashing down, up, and inside as I forced him back and against the wall.

I was too fast, feigning one way when I actually moved another. My sword sliced across his sword arm.

His blade clattered loudly to the cobblestone floor. The wound was edged with what appeared to be liquid silver. His glittering blood slid down his arm. His eyes looked into mine, fierce and murderous, looking their last before I cleaved his neck. His head fell with a thunk upon the floor. The body stood a moment on its own, before it fell to its knees and toppled over.

I took the torch from the wall, holding it in my left hand and my sword in my right, as I left the room and bolted down the hallway.

I kept my eyes on a constant lookout for any more Fae who might appear from the seemingly innumerable doorways that ran on either side of me. As well as for my target, the small scrap of the petticoat that Ayda had left upon the floor. When I was beginning to think that I had missed it, and was going to turn around and head back the way I had come, was precisely when I saw it. A small, very dirty scrap of what had once been white lay upon the floor. I strode with purpose into the room.

With great focus I extended my hand toward the wall where I knew the Silver lay. The blood written runes I'd placed the first time I was here were still in place. I opened my mouth and spoke Sidhe. It felt wrong, as though a snake covered in noxious slime was uncoiling itself from inside of my mouth and sliding leisurely across my tongue. I nearly choked. Somehow I said all that was needed to open the Silver.

The Silver revealed itself on the wall, showing a quiet brook running through a wooded hillside. I could hear the birds singing sweetly overhead. I stepped through, feeling relief that I had been able to pass through the vaults so quickly. Nevertheless, I couldn't help but wonder just how much mortal time had passed this time.

I moved as one who knows a place intimately, so well, that they could meet their destination having gone both blind and deaf. I saw and heard all as I moved with haste, not feeling a need to run, but feeling an urging which required a brisk pace.

This place, this prison, never seemed to change. It was as if the trees never grew taller, nor the plants any fuller. For that matter, I did not recognize any new growth. The path, though perhaps having remained unused these past, who knew how many years, was still well worn and remained as it always had been. It was an irrelevant observation, probably a game trail I theorized, as I moved on to crest the knoll and looked out of the trees.

Stretched out before me were the familiar rolling hills of brush and bracken, above all of which the slightest hint of Bram's roof peaked.

I smiled warmly. For everything that I had been through, seen, and lived, I appeared to be thirty-seven but in mortal years was forty-seven … or at least I had been before I had left Mississippi. Still, this place carried the saturating emotion of rightness. I had deceived myself - it was here that was my home, and always had been. It was a balm to my soul.

My purpose in coming here was to study what was left of the Druid texts. I entered Bram's house with every intention of leaving it promptly. However, I found as I walked through the house's corridors, a shadow among shadows, my soul longed to stay. I yearned for it to permit my soul to endure. But, if I somehow survived all this, there would be plenty of time for healing in the future. For now it was best to be brief.

I rummaged through the books in Bram's study, unsure of where exactly to begin. It was then that I noticed a book already lay upon his desk when everything else was put away. I took a seat in the chair that had only ever been his, and opened the book's leather cover. A sheet of paper lay inside, covered with the scrawling slanted hand of Bram.

Daine -

I knew upon leaving here, that it would be my last great
adventure. It is my dying hope that you will read this and learn
from my mistakes – lest the past be repeated. I have always been
proud to call you my son.

- Bramwyll Áedán Roithridh Muireach Macardle

I swallowed heavily, and slowly turned the page to the
first of the book. It was inscribed, "The Journal of Bramwyll A.
R. M. Macardle". Page after page of his journal did little else
than detail his encounters with Maurelle. This was exactly what I
had come here in hopes of finding.

Bram had known more about the Fae than he had ever let
on. He had loved Maurelle, that was undeniable, but he had also
despised her. In loving her he had come to know her every fatal
flaw; and simultaneously as her enemy, her every nuance.
Hopefully, I would be able to use his knowledge as he'd
intended, and end her.

I closed the back leather cover of his journal, and knew
what I needed to do if I was to have any chance at beating her. I
stood up, pushing away from Bram's desk, and went to my room.
I had a knapsack stored away in the armoire, and I doubted Bram
would have done anything with it in my absence. I found the bag
exactly where I had last seen it, sitting on the dresser's floor. I
stooped to retrieve it, and made my way back to Bram's study.

I filled the pack with as many of the Druid texts as I could, concentrating on those that showed the signs of frequent use Bram had left upon their bindings. There was no way that I could take the entire library with me, but I hoped that somehow the books would endure. I picked up the journal from the desk, and used the last bit of available space to wedge the journal inside as well. I buckled my bag shut, and left Bram's library. I shut the door behind me, and quickly crossed the house to the front foyer.

Outside, I replaced the wards, leaving additional runes of my own to reinforce those left behind by Bram. Then, half-heartedly, I left the house behind me, making my way directly for the Silver that lay beside the stream.

My third time through, I did not meet any opposition in the Edinburgh vaults. Though, the body of the Sidhe that I had killed hours before had been removed. I stepped through the Silver and into the woods of Kamarina. I was relieved to find that they still remained. A mill once again occupied the location of one that had been there years before. My pack in place and the Sword in its scabbard upon my back, I crossed through the woods and made my way into town.

Kamarina had changed. I walked down Main Street, unsure of where exactly I should be going. I'm sure it did not matter; Maurelle would most assuredly be coming to me. I entered the pharmacy, a large two story red brick building with windows that faced the town square and courthouse. Just beside the door I found stacks of newspapers. Some were several days old from the larger cities of the east, but the one of most interest was the one printed just this morning. It was then that I learned that today was the morning of November 22, 1915.

I staggered a bit, thrown entirely by the realization that today was twenty-eight years later than what it had been but yesterday. I vaguely recall leaving the store, and making my way to a restaurant as my mind reeled with the lapse of time. The owner of the dinning establishment led me to a seat near the wall. I sat gratefully down in the wooden chair, taking my heavy pack from my shoulders and settling it on the floor beside me. The food was placed on the table before me, and I ate it hungrily, tasting nothing.

I spent the day reluctantly visiting my near, or distant past. Of which, I wasn't sure. I left the last of the golden flowers floating on the pool of water which was filled by a spring that still cascaded the mouth of a stone lion above. They, Bram and my children, had not been disturbed and continued to rest in peace. The thought gave me comfort.

I went to where our large plantation home had stood. Nothing remained. The fertile fields had been divided, and now they were worked by many small farming households. Their meager homes were set up in indication of the ownership of each field. I hoped that the land yielded them better fortune than it had me.

I wandered aimlessly. There was no one with whom I could visit from before, most of my friends had left, either dead or relocated. I stayed on the outskirts of Kamarina, traversing open fields as the workers paused their labors to study me curiously. I still carried the sheathed sword and heavily loaded pack upon my back. If not for my clean cut appearance, I am sure the sight of swords and daggers at my belt would have given them the assumption that I was either a barbarian or murderous hobo. As it was, their ignorance made me a novelty, and they couldn't help but stare as I passed.

I was grateful whenever the opportunity presented itself to make my way into the forests. It was there that their eyes could no longer linger. I could breathe a bit easier, charging and feeling of the earth's strong presence. It was heightened by the lack of man's labors and industrializations to interfere her inherent energy. The day was crisp but invigorating, the cold seeming to lift and strengthen my spirits.

Without knowing how it had happened, I found myself once again near the Silver. The lumber yard was relinquishing the last of its workers for the evening. I stood hidden in the trees, watching as these men, hardened by physical labor, softened to banter with their companions at the prospect of home. It was Monday, and they were all grateful to have the first workday of the new week behind them. I envied them such simple concerns and pleasures.

The sun was now beginning its descent. Despite having eaten so heartily, I felt my stomach rumble in hunger. I ignored it, pushing it aside as I was unable to evade the feeling in my gut that suspected Maurelle would be coming, and soon.

I entered the lumber yard, it was silent and still. With what was left of the waning light, I found a place at the back of the tool shed and began to dig. I needed something to occupy myself with, and welcomed the opportunity to use my body, working a shovel by hand.

Once I had made a hole big and deep enough, I placed the pack and all of its contents inside. I did not want Maurelle or any of her cohorts to get their hands upon our knowledge of them. I regarded it solemnly, not knowing if I would ever return to retrieve them again. I reburied them hurriedly, feeling an unknown haste to hide them. I took care to remove any trace of the soil having been disturbed. Finally, I returned the tools to against the wall where I'd found them. When finished, the tool shed looked as it had when I found it.

I left the shed, carrying the Sword in my hand. Out of caution, I went to each of the other outbuildings, being sure to spend as much time them as I had in the tool shed. I gave off the appearance of inspecting the various implements that each building housed with unmasked interest.

I saved the largest of the buildings for last. It was a massive wooden structure, and unlike the mill that had stood in this place earlier, this one was permanent. It was a single spacious room, sawdust and dirt mingling inseparably upon the packed earthen ground. Inside, it held massive stacks of debranched logs, piled and held in place by enormous chains against the building's walls. Running the length of the center were large saws.

I breathed deeply of the earthy air, running my hands through my dark wavy hair that was brindled by grey. As I exhaled I noticed the vague clouding as my breath condensed in the air. It was quickly growing uncomfortably cold and I had naught but a thin overcoat with me. I instinctively began to wrap the coat a little tighter about my thin shoulders, rubbing my arms in an effort to warm them.

I studied the windowless room for a stove to start a fire in. Seeing none, I reluctantly called fire to me. I startled, as in the dim light that accumulated in my hand a pair of ghostly, but darkly vivid, blue eyes peered at me through the shadows. They stared at me contemptuously. There was no glimmer of affection of amusement in them now. Her lovely face was a terrible front of malice as she glared at me, moving like a stalking cat as she came into the full focus of the light that I made burn all the brighter.

"Daine," she scoffed, "I have looked forward to this moment for a very long time." She wore a long black skirt of flowing silk which was tied at a sash low on her hips. Her midsection was scandalously bare, allowing for only the slightest of coverings with which she hid her breasts. I allowed my gaze to linger on her abdomen. Her skin was slightly mottled with scars, evidence of the gruesome wound I had given her at our last meeting.

My fire grew brighter, highlighting the silver that now mottled my dark hair. "You've aged," she said dryly.

I nodded curtly. I had wanted her to notice. As Bram had surmised, Maurelle routinely underestimated humans because of their physical appearance. To her, one who could not physically age, aging was a sign of weakness. To me, it was a sign of wisdom and strength. Let her underestimate me, it would be the crux of her mistake.

I dropped my fire to the floor, and raised the Sword toward her with both of my hands. Her head gave an almost imperceptible nod, and then she struck.

A blast of energy came from behind, knocking me off my feet and onto my knees. I rolled swiftly aside as she lunged, a nondescript but deadly looking dagger slashing the air where my neck and shoulders had been only milliseconds before. I held the Sword tightly, as I brought it up to match the slice of her dagger again. Her strength was shocking, and I felt the Sword being pushed down as her arm forced the dagger toward me.

I spun away. Perhaps it was I that had underestimated her.

Oh God, I prayed, *let this not all be in vain.*

I moved away sharply, jumping, diving, and lunging in an effort to avoid her blows. I managed to put one of the fixed saws between us, taking a moment's pause.

I watched in wonder as she effortlessly crumpled the steel, bending it impossibly as she stepped beneath the now arched metal frame. I scrambled back, feeling a stack of logs at my back as I lost any further chance of evasion.

She stood inches from me. I was unprepared when she struck out, a fist landing squarely into my stomach. I doubled over, my eyes swimming as blood began to tangle with saliva and hang drippingly from my mouth. I could not breathe, let alone upright myself. She landed another blow, this one upon my jaw. Shoots of color exploded in my vision as I staggered and slumped against the logs. Weakly I spit teeth and blood from my mouth.

They spattered her clothing, and she looked at me cruelly, triumph glittering in her eyes. The dagger shone brightly in the fire that continued to burn where I had left it.

"Poor, poor, Daine. Entirely alone and without a single friend left to aid you. It must be dreadful to have lost everything. Rest assured, your suffering will be over . . . eventually. I intend to have my way with you, insuring you the utmost pain and agony, bringing you to the brink of death over and over again, mangling your body until you are nothing left but living decay. But, hold to the knowledge that eventually, you will have the end that you begged me for last." Maurelle bent close to me, her heady scent causing me to feel the need to retch.

I plunged the iron dagger that had been at my belt up and into her side. A piercing scream echoed throughout the building, the scent of burning flesh filling the air as she removed the dagger and let it fall with metallically to the floor. Her blood literally bubbled and boiled out of the knife wound.

I drew energy from the earth, using its strength to heal the wounds that she had so recently inflicted. I grimaced, feeling my organs and tissues knitting neatly back together. I stood, using one of Ayda's tricks, to launch an inferno of fire up without warning from the floor beneath her feet. The moment I felt the flames beginning to take form upon the earth, I called the wind. The blaze met the wind in an instantaneous combustion, causing the flames to lap at her skin with scorching heat. My hands rose in an effort to shield my eyes and face from the inferno.

I felt my skin prickling behind me. Without knowing how it was that I knew, I turned and met Maurelle's dagger with the Sword. Our battle escalated, she sifting quickly around me, and I instinctively knowing where she would next reappear. I met every one of her tireless attacks.

Her eyes slanted in annoyance as I continued to elude her. I felt a warning as a massive surge of unknown energy approached me. I raised the Sword to deflect it. I was knocked sideways as it bounced off the Sword and shot through the farthest wall, blowing a massive hole in the building. Shards of wood exploded into the air, lodging themselves soundly into the ground and walls around us.

She did not wait, another blast came just as I was finding my feet. The barrage sent me flying through the air, crashing into a stack of logs that was chained against the wall. The chains that held them rattled dangerously as I fell to the floor beneath them, feeling something inside of me crack and break. I was hurt. I knew not how badly, nor did I feel pain. I only knew that I was finding it difficult to move or think clearly.

She again began to stalk, moving unnaturally as she crossed the ground that lay between us. The fire that I had left at a constant burn began to flicker and threaten to go out. It highlighted her movements as she closed the distance. She was livid.

The Sword lay limply in my hand. I could not move my right hand or arm, and my left I knew could hardly move at all. I reached deeper inside of myself, searching whatever was there, whatever was left. Druidry would have no effect on her, neither would the lightning - she would be expecting it. Desperate, I latched onto a set of black runes that pulsed powerfully in my mind and threw them at her.

They glowed red against her black clothing and as they marred her perfect skin. They began to attach themselves. Her steps stumbled. She fell to her knees, her skin beginning to melt away under the affixed runes. Frantically, she futilely fought to peel them away, screaming in pain as their imprints began to blister and ooze with infection.

Still on her knees, she fell forward, her hands catching her before she hit the ground. She seemed to convulse, her eyes looking up to meet my own wide with pain and anger. "You. . ." she growled. Her wounds festered and dripped on the ground. The sores began to spread. The smell was horrendous.

Without warning, she lunged forward. Her dagger landed soundly in my ribs, the knife tip stabbing into the log behind me. I groaned in pain. My lung had been punctured. She laughed horribly, as I writhed. I torturously wriggled the blade's hilt in an effort to dislodge the knife from the wood. I watched, gasping, as the blade finally dislodged. It inched viciously from my body.

I heaved it at her.

She insultingly batted it away as if it were nothing more than a leaf. Having been thus distracted, she was entirely caught off guard when the blade of the Sword sliced cleanly through her wrist, cutting her hand completely away.

The hand fell to the ground, Maurelle's perfect mouth hung agape in abject horror. She clawed recklessly for it, and held it tenderly to her chest. Glittering blood streaked her breast and smeared her face, leaving her pale and gory. A single bloody tear fell from her eye and traced its way down her cheek.

I had collected enough energy from the earth to begin to heal, but was still greatly damaged. It was with great pain that I moved toward her, making it barely to my knees, as I struggled to hold the Sword firmly in my trembling hand.

"Finish me," she snarled through gritted teeth.

Her skin was being eaten away by the runes, revealing the bloody and acid chewed muscles beneath. Her once perfect face now seeped and oozed with sores.

"This does not end with me…" she began to say, but was overcome as the runes began to burn away her face.

I leaned over her, feeling neither gratification nor pity. I grabbed a fist full of her hair and jerked body up from where she had huddled on the floor. I looked into her still frightened eyes as I thrust the Sword into her chest.

She convulsed, her eyes bulging, as she fell against me. She was heavy, so much more than I expected. I fell with her against the stack of logs that were behind us. Her wheezing grew laborious, as her good hand moved slowly away from where it had lain on my chest.

I jerked away as she began to cackle. But, it was too late. She had snapped the heavy chain that secured the logs to the wall. They boomed as they collided, tumbling from their neat stacks to crash upon the floor. We were buried under their immeasurable weight.

I lay there, feeling as life slipped away from my body, broken and bruised beyond repair.

Death was surely almost instantaneous, but those final moments lingered as if they were an eternity. Within the last ounces of my living consciousness, I heard the blaring of trumpets sounding in unlikely harmony with the baying of hounds. The rumble of hooves resonated in the logs above me.

The cold embrace of death slipped over me, and I succumbed at last to the darkness.

To be continued . . .

Dear Reader,

Thank you for reading my book!

Before you give up hope,

Remember that darkness must

Always give way to light.

Believe me when I say there is still much light

to give.

Look for the continuation of Daine's story,

Born of Ash and Iron,

October 2014

In the meantime, follow me:

Twitter: @marie_mckean

www.mariemckean.com

www.mariemckean.blogspot.com

28052812R00225

Made in the USA
Lexington, KY
03 December 2013